P

Palazzo Puro

A Novel about the Hidden Past of the Palazzo

MIRELLA ROSA

© 2025 Mirella Rosa, English first edition
Cover design: Richard Turylo
Photo author: Dana van Leeuwen
Editor: Bianca Nederlof
ISBN: 978 90 832 5664 1
Social media: @renovationpalazzopuro

Sabbia Publishing House

All rights reserved.
No part of this publication may be reproduced or published without the prior permission of the publisher.

For the love of this old house

1

Aron shakes my hand and gives the house a disapproving, sidelong glance.

'I know it,' he says, as we stand in the garden. 'I told my friends it was for sale, but no one liked it. This job is too big, the house is a ruin.'

I try to evaluate what he's saying. He adjusts his glasses, which are too small for his face, and points to the roof.

'Look, everything is completely collapsing and the foundation is in bad shape too. This is going to be an expensive job,' he continues.

'Lorenzo has looked at it and says it's not too bad. For a house that's been empty for twenty-five years, I mean,' I say.

'That's what all Italian contractors say the first time. Until they get the job.'

My eyes glide along the roof and outer walls. The sun has left a golden glow on the bricks. The knee-high grass plays with my skin, tickles, and I stroke my leg. The blistering heat hangs over the wheat field, bouncing off the thick walls of the house. A light sea breeze flaps a broken shutter somewhere.

This Italian house is my new future, in which I am no longer a project manager hired by different companies. No, I'm busy renovating Italian houses, or I'm an interior stylist. Architectural styles, interior trends, structural technicalities, I find everything fascinating. I want to renovate every old house. Restore the original details. Bringing history back to life. I sketch in my notebook with its small, precise grid, a newer, better layout. Yet for years I have been working at companies in temporary positions that do not interest me.

Aron narrows one eye, tilts his head slightly. Like he's observing me. 'Obviously you don't know much about it. I've seen this happening for years now. Foreigners come to Italy looking for a dream, you know, like that book *Under the Tuscan Sun* that came out more than twenty years ago. But then they use their hard-earned savings to buy a ruin that cannot be restored. Discouraged, after a few months they pack up their trailers again and go back home. You know it was a novel, right, that book?'

Further down the property, near the old olive trees, is a dilapidated wooden shed. Part of the roof has collapsed and is dangling down dangerously. That barn isn't pretty, but it could be demolished. How different is the house, or rather the *palazzo*, as Brian, our Anglo-Italian real estate agent, majestically called it when we toured the house last summer? He told us that this house is unique for this coastal region in the south of Le Marche, which is not really much of a tourist area. An old 'palace' built with golden bricks, windows with pale shutters, faded red roof tiles and a real 'Romeo and Juliet' balcony with large circles and arrows decorating the railing. In the middle of a valley of rolling hills full of olive trees, wheat fields and vineyards, along a quiet white gravel road and with the azure blue Adriatic Sea just a five-minute Vespa drive away.

'Don't you see what I mean?' asks Aron.

His pale skin blends seamlessly into his short, blond hair. Apparently, he doesn't go out often, his skin isn't sun-kissed like that of the Italians.

'Do you do renovations like this often?' I ask.

He shakes his head. 'No, I worked in a shoe factory and now I'm a translator.'

Yes, exactly, translator, that's what I thought.

Along the road, which is slightly higher on the hill, a car stops on the roadside. Lorenzo, the Italian contractor who inspected the house before we made an offer last summer, gets out and walks down the hill, waving both arms in the air. His whole body moves with them.

'*Ciao Ragazzi!*'

Hi guys, I smile because of his greeting. Not that my language lessons in the language-learning app have fully prepared me for fast Italian over the past six months, but I do know the basics.

Lorenzo stands next to me, just a little too close – his shirt smells like fresh laundry detergent. Is that a good sign for a contractor, or should his shirt be full of cement residue?

'*Lei è bellissima, vero?*' he asks Aron. His voice is lilting as he reinforces his own words by squeezing his fingertips together, kissing them, and then sending the words toward the house.

Yes, she is beautiful, it screams in me.

Aron looks at Lorenzo as if he can't decide if he's being tricked or not. In Italian he asks doubtfully whether it is not a ruin, whereupon Lorenzo begins to explain in detail about thick walls, a solid foundation and a roof that is still in reasonable condition. The conversation starts like a train that accelerates slowly, but once at full speed it is impossible to keep up. Where does one sentence end and another begin? I nod in understanding every now and then, and when they shake their heads, I shake with them. The conversation stops and Aron stares straight at me.

'The house seems to be in better shape than expected,' he says. It's almost inaudible, as if talking in the hot summer air has dried his throat. Shouldn't one always speak clearly when working as a translator?

'Sorry, what did you say?' I ask. I want to hear it again.

He clears his throat. 'So, it's not that bad, that house of yours.'

Satisfied I nod. Tonight, I will call Roger to discuss whether we need a translator. He is at home with Max. It was the evening before our departure, while we were drinking wine in the garden, when he asked if I could arrange the transfer of the house and get the keys by myself. He was feeling doubtful about our move to Italy, because even though the house was beautiful and life in another country sounded appealing, he wondered if he was ready for it. The renovation costs could be higher than what he had so accurately calculated in his Excel spreadsheet. He didn't want uncertain factors influencing his calculations. His mood changed and he said that he would rather go to the office than on vacation. Max had come to sit with us in the yard, and said he wouldn't leave his friends for an adventure that I wanted, to which Roger added that we couldn't take him out of high school this year. On top of that, Max said, he had an online gaming event he didn't want to miss. 'Big deal, such an old house,' he said. I looked at him with a sigh. 'Your life on the computer with friends who have names like Cheesehead-com and Itzfijk2012 is not the real world,' I replied. He responded with: 'Well, you're always on Instagram. As if that's real.'

Lorenzo has pulled a bunch of keys from his pocket and inserts a long, rusty key into the lock of the wooden front door; the glass is missing from the window above it.

'Okay, the last check of the house before the official handover at the notary tomorrow,' he says.

The door squeaks open. A dove flutters out, skims over Aron's head. This is a good sign, because doves represent peace and love, not the broken windows of an unrecoverable ruin.

'What a mess!' Aron shouts. 'And it stinks. Look at those feces. Gross, there are rats living in here.' He pinches his nose, continues speaking in a voice an octave higher, pointing out all the junk. 'All those empty wine bottles, an alcoholic must have lived here.'

There is a pile of clothes along the wall, and there are many old boxes and an antique wardrobe. A thick layer of dust has gathered around everything, as if it wanted to hold it all together. The wall has chipped stucco. The light falls across the stately red and white of the terrazzo stairs that are desperately trying to reflect the sunlight. I wipe a bit clean with my hand.

'That's unsanitary,' Aron says. 'Not very smart. Do you know that rat poop can make you sick?'

Meanwhile I wonder how he lives himself. It must be a sterile room with white walls, a white leather sofa and a Formica coffee table. There will be fake plants in the windowsill.

'Mirella, look here,' Lorenzo calls from the room next to the hall. He changed my name into Italian, which means I can be a new version of myself here. I don't have to be who I am at home.

The room is dim; light only enters through an elongated window above the wooden stable doors. The three large concrete vats in the corner slowly loom into view as the contrasts sharpen.

'Wine was produced here,' Lorenzo says, pointing to the barrels, each nearly three meters high and at least a meter-and-a-half wide. 'Through that small window next to the door, the grapes were brought in and they were transferred into this tank down a sloping gutter.'

He points to a low concrete box under the window, which has now been closed with a hatch. 'And after the first acidification, the wine was pumped into these large barrels to mature further.'

'I don't think that's quite true,' Aron says, standing behind us.

We walk up the stairs and, halfway up, I stop and stand on tiptoe on the landing to open the shutters of a window. They're stuck.

Lorenzo comes up behind me. 'Look, there's a rusty nail over there, which is keeping the shutters closed.'

He roughly moves the stair railing back and forth. 'I can unscrew, sandblast and paint these. Then it will be like new again.'

The white-gray paint has peeled off the graceful curls and rust has taken over. I rub it gently. Who used to hold this railing?

'There you go again,' says Aron with a sigh. 'It's filthy. It would be better to replace the railing immediately with a new one.'

He's a jammer that keeps breaking the wavelength I feel with this house.

'I think I want to explore more of the house before I replace anything,' I reply, more to myself than to him. 'I want to know who lived here. This house has a past that she wants to tell, I can feel it.'

'Now you sound silly,' Aron says.

In the small corridor on the first floor are two beautiful swinging doors with antique, opal-green glass. I open them and enter a narrow room with a desk full of woodworm holes. There is still a fountain pen and a pile of yellowed writing paper. Curious, I browse through it. Is there anything written on it somewhere? Unfortunately, the sheets are all blank. When I open the high shutters which are installed on the inside of the windows, sunbeams find their way in, bounce off the stucco wall and shoot into the stairwell. A startled gecko flies across the wall and disappears through a crack next to the weathered wood of the window. I open the doors to the balcony. In the distance, beyond the wheat field, the sea sparkles.

'Well, this was a very small kitchen,' Aron shouts in the room next to me. I walk over, look inside.

Lorenzo confirms that it is indeed a *cucina piccola*. I can partly follow his fast Italian, but Aron doesn't wait for him to finish talking and starts translating simultaneously. 'Yes, it's a small kitchen,' he says. 'It may have been a house of rich people who never finished it completely. Weird. Says something about why this house has been empty for so long and no one wants it.'

He added the last part himself, I suspect. In the corner is a small black-and-white speckled terrazzo countertop. I open the kitchen faucet. The lead water pipe thumps a few times as if it is refusing, but then a small stream of brown water flows into the sink. Next to the sink is a white enamel stove. An old, frayed tea towel still hangs from the rod. On the mantlepiece of the fireplace next to it is a vase with dried flowers. Who left it like that? In the room opposite there is an old bed with the mattresses still on it. It smells like urine.

'Let's go outside quickly,' Aron says. 'We have seen how much of a ruin this is.'

As he descends the stairs, Lorenzo and I go up into the attic, which has a roof ridge over five meters high. Both rooms are large and have the same high windows as the rooms below. Here the bricks are not plastered, but left rough. A rustle between old newspapers and boxes.

'Rats,' Lorenzo says.

In the corner of one room is an iron bed frame with faded blue-and-white upholstery, a large trunk and linen cupboard whose mirror is speckled with oxidation. In the other room, a thick wooden branch is hanging from the high ceiling on a steel wire.

'Sausages used to be dried here,' Lorenzo says.

Empty nutshells lie on the floor, probably brought in through the broken window by squirrels.

We go down to the garden, where the oleanders with their white, light pink, and bright pink flowers have grown as tall as the roof of the dilapidated barn. When I was eighteen, I drove through Italy with my then boyfriend in an old VW Beetle Cabriolet, the top down, the music on. I fell in love instantly, not with him – that was long ago – but with the centuries-old houses, the gardens with pine trees and lemon trees in terracotta pots along the edges of the terraces and the profusely blooming oleanders, especially the oleanders. At the end of that vacation, I bought a small one from a nursery and took it home in the back seat. But just as my relationship quickly ended once I got home, so did that oleander, which didn't last a season in our cold climate.

Lorenzo looks at his watch, hands me the keys to the house and tells me he has to leave.

'He's going to drink an aperitivo,' Aron explains as Lorenzo drives off at high speed in his white Alfa Romeo. 'It's almost five o'clock, those Italians all do that.'

We walk to our cars, which are parked along the narrow road. I almost slip on a piece of metal lying in the tall grass. I pick it up and wipe it clean. *Marinolli Pesci e Reti* is written in blue letters on the white background.

'It's a fishmonger and fishnet weaving business,' says Aron. 'It still exists and it's in the city where we have to do the title transfer at the notary's tomorrow.'

The metal is weathered and pieces of the enamel are crumbling; it's been outside for years. When I let go of it, it disappears under the tall grass again. Why is it here in the garden?

'Has the notary sent the purchase contract yet?' I ask Aron.

For the past few weeks, they've been promising that the document would come soon, but the handover of the house is already tomorrow and we still have nothing.

Aron squeezes air between his narrow lips. 'Gee, I don't think so. You better get used to it; everything is chaotic in Italy.'

He removes the silver sunscreen from behind his windshield and folds it neatly to put it back in its plastic wrapper. He takes his phone out of the pocket of his khaki Bermuda shorts.

'Ah, the contract is in my inbox,' he says. 'Yes, and now I still have to translate it. That will be evening work and therefore it immediately falls in the category of an urgent job. For this I charge an additional fee per translated word. By the way, at what time do you expect me at the notary tomorrow?'

'What time do you think the translation will be finished?'

'Well, I'm doing my best. Once it's done, I'll send it by email. Sending it to Roger is sufficient, I assume?'

We won't need a translator anymore after the signing tomorrow, I'll have to discuss that with Roger later. I'm standing on the roadside, the sun sets behind the hill, turning the sky over the field shades of pale blue and pink. The house radiates warmth, as if she wants to call me back. Who left her, with her striking balcony decorated with circles and arrows that protrude above the oleanders, behind?

Lunedì, 5 Giugno 1939

The spring of 1939 started warm, warmer than Sofia remembered from previous years, and made her work in the fishnet weaving factory heavier and dustier. Since five o'clock this morning she had been sitting on the low wooden stool in the dark warehouse. The smell of the hemp she used to weave the fishing nets lingered in her blouse and skirt when she finished late at night and hung her clothes over the chair at home. The other girls sat around her. Their fingers moved at lightning speed, and each time they made a new loop, their wooden netting needles tapped against the stick that had the rope stretched around it. Her mother followed her movements to make sure she wasn't making mistakes. It was warm inside; the sun was burning hard on the flat roof of the warehouse. The girl across from her began to sing. Her voice carried far through the room, high above the sound of the snapping ropes and the tapping of the needles. Other girls sang along with the chorus. The singing and the tapping of the needles was all Sofia needed to start drifting off into a daydream. Her hands moved as fast as they could, forming a fishing net. The song of the weaving girls swelled. She closed her eyes. Her houses. Stucco farms, city palaces and ancient walled houses. Windows, graceful doors. Overgrown walls of bougainvillea and a path to the house where the scent of wild thyme and mint rose as you walked across it. She sketched these houses in her notebook and at night in bed she told her two sisters who shared the bed with her about these drawings. Very quietly, so that their mother, who was sitting on the other side of the curtain by the stove, couldn't hear them. Her sisters completed her stories, imagining the three of them in the houses she drew, making them fall in love with beautiful men, picking flowers in the meadow and tending animals. There in the houses in her dreams, scattered over the olive-treed hills, there was space and light. Nowhere was a dark, small room with one window that had to be shared with her mother and sisters. No narrow alleys in the city where the sun never came. There you could wander in the fields, be who you were or become who you wanted to be.

The ropes fell silent, the singing ceased. She quickly opened her eyes and blinked against the light of the bright factory lamp. The long shadow of Mr. Marinolli fell through the huge warehouse door. He was a figure in black. Black shirt, black pants. They had told her he was one of the *Camicie Nere*, the Blackshirts, who formed a fascist organization. Others said he was a gloomy man who wore the color that suited his character. Cold and hard.

She quickly checked her weaving by pulling the fishing net slightly apart. It seemed good.

'There is a loophole,' her mother hissed, watching from her stool and pointing to an irregular hole. 'A cod can swim through it. Why don't you pay more attention?'

Mr. Marinolli's footsteps echoed heavily on the stone floor. The tall overseer, whom the weavers called skinny Pink, rushed from the storage room, buttoning up his pants. Behind him, a girl fled back to her stool.

'Inspection by Mr. Marinolli,' skinny Pink yelled nervously across the workspace. He made a slight bow. 'Mr. Marinolli sir, the girls have worked hard.'

Mr. Marinolli looked at him contemptuously. 'I can judge that for myself,' he said in a raucous voice.

'Absolutely, my apologies,' said skinny Pink, slowly shuffling backwards, hoping to blend into the background again.

Mr. Marinolli walked past the weavers, inspecting the knotted fishing nets one by one. Sometimes he jotted down something in a green leather notebook. As soon as he passed by, the weaver girl quickly picked up her work and continued weaving. Sofia's mother stood beside her stool while Mr. Marinolli examined her fishing net.

'Good job,' he said after a thorough inspection.

'Stand up,' her mother hissed at her.

Mr. Marinolli came to stand right in front of her. His cologne, with its strong musk undertones, mingled with cigar smoke. He wore his black tie over his black shirt, tucked inside a black waistcoat. His black hair, smoothed with hair oil, everything about him was as black as a dark night. He looked at her and his eyes lingered on her breasts for a long time. Had she closed the top button of her plain white blouse? She rubbed her hands over her long, dark-brown skirt. Everything was fine. The tips of his leather shoes gleamed. He moved her fishing net left, right, up. He dropped the net with a bang. She flinched and blew a strand of hair from her face.

'Sloppy work,' he said. He picked up his book. 'Name,' he said, looking at her breasts again.

'Sofia Bertosi.'

He browsed through the booklet. 'You already have a previous note. That means I'm giving your place to another girl.'

'Please,' her mother said. 'Don't fire her. My daughter has only recently started working here. She can learn it.'

'*Marinolli Pesci e Reti* has a reputation to uphold. I don't accept mistakes.'

'Don't you have another job for her? There are a lot of things she knows how to do.'

'Hmmm,' he said, looking at Sofia again. 'So, your talent lies elsewhere. Turn around.'

He made a circular motion with his index finger. 'Faster please.'

She turned slowly, his eyes burning into her back. Her mother indicated that she should smile. He closed his notebook. 'Come to my office tonight.'

The weaving hours passed, as they passed every day – excruciatingly slowly. Her fingertips were bleeding. The calluses on her skin still weren't thick enough. When hands are too young for this work, her mother had said, the hemp made deep cuts. It should go away as she got older. She washed her tools in the big basin filled with oily water that stank as if three cats had drowned in it.

'Tonight, you get a chance to put this work behind you,' her mother said, standing next to her. 'You always dream of beautiful houses and a free life, don't you? Come, let's redo your hair.'

Her mother dipped her hands into the dirty water and ran them through Sofia's hair.

'Any girl who goes to his office never comes back to the weaving mill,' her mother said, unbuttoning the top button of Sofia's blouse. 'Laugh sweetly and speak softly.'

Sofia looked at the office with its floor-to-ceiling windows that loomed above the warehouse floor. From there, Mr. Marinolli had an overview of the entire space. A long, steel staircase led to the place in this factory where no girl wanted to go.

'I don't trust him,' she said.

'This is your only chance if you want a different life,' her mother said. 'He seeks out girls to be his mistresses. Don't you want that?'

The weaving girls left the room, went home. It got quiet.

'Go on,' her mother said, giving Sofia a light push. 'I will see you at home later.' She turned and walked out.

The steel steps rumbled beneath Sofia's feet. Almost upstairs, the door of the lit den swung open. There was the smell of cigar smoke. Mr. Marinolli stepped aside, motioned for her to come in. A large wooden desk stood in the middle of the room; it was covered with papers. Tall filing cabinets lined the walls. The desk lamp shone brightly. Mr. Marinolli sat down in the brown leather chair, folded his hands over his bloated belly, and loosened his tie. He moistened the corners of his mouth with his tongue, rubbed his small, straight mustache with his thumb and forefinger.

'Let's see what we can do with you,' he said. 'How old are you?'

'Almost eighteen.'

'That is good. Well, pull the bottom of your skirt up a bit.'

A shiver ran down her spine. She closed her eyes, searched for her dreams about houses she lived in; they didn't come. Slowly she pulled her skirt up a little. The door was right behind her, she remembered. At most three steps away.

Higher, yes, higher. Until I see your underwear,' he said.

She opened her eyes and was confronted with the lust in his. She pulled up her skirt a little more, trying to keep her legs from shaking. Smile, her mother had said, smile.

'Great,' he said. 'Now unbutton your blouse and take it off.' He leaned back in his chair.

She dropped the bottom of her skirt. Her fingers trembled.

'Do you want me to do it for you?' he said, irritated. 'Hurry up.'

She fiddled with the little buttons. It seemed as if they no longer fit through the holes. He got up from his desk and came over to her.

'Let me do it, it's taking way too long,' he said excitedly. He tore through the buttons in one go. He quickly grabbed her wrist and, with his other hand on her hip, turned her around so that he was facing her back. He pulled up her skirt with big impatient gestures. She tried to break free.

'Keep calm,' he said. 'It won't take long.'

His grip on her wrist tightened. She stiffened. Blood drained from her face. She had to think, she couldn't. Screaming, no sound came. She tried to turn around, a little further. It didn't work. She turned her head. His flushed face, his heavy cologne, too close. She spat.

'Damn it, you dirty slut,' he said angrily. With the flat of his hand he slapped her hard across the face. Her cheek glowed. He pushed her away, she fell to the ground, on her hands and knees. His hands grabbed her hips and he pulled her toward him. She heard him unbutton his pants.

'What for heavens' sake is going on here?' someone said. At the door stood a young man who was about her age. He was neatly dressed in a dark-grey, three-piece suit.

'Help me,' she screamed.

'This factory maid isn't listening,' said Mr. Marinolli. 'Most won't resist, boy, but this one is a wildcat.'

He laughed, released her and pulled her to her feet.

'Her work in the weaving mill is extremely bad,' he said. 'She had the chance to become my mistress.'

'Never,' she cried angrily.

'You heard her, father,' said the boy. He had striking green eyes. 'Let her go.'

'Come on, we'll share her,' said Mr. Marinolli. 'Learn from me. One woman is never enough. You marry the right woman, someone of our rank, and you use the others.'

'Let go of me,' she said, trying to free her wrist. She wanted to hit him. She raised her other hand, but in midair the boy grabbed her arm.

'I'll take her,' the boy said, taking her wrist from Mr. Marinolli. 'Thank you, father.'

'You're taking the best one from me,' Mr. Marinolli said mockingly. 'Before I could enjoy her myself. I warn you, son, this is a fierce one, you can't just ride her.' He laughed loudly.

The son took her out the door, downstairs, down the dark hall.

'Let go of me,' she shouted. 'Don't touch me.'

He said nothing, but continued to pull her along as she punched at him furiously and he ducked to avoid her blows. He was strong and at least a head taller. She pulled at his gray jacket, a seam tore.

At the large warehouse door he looked at her.

'I'm sorry about what happened to you,' he said, looking down. 'This should never have happened. Go quickly.'

'You're monsters,' she said furiously. She held her blouse closed with one hand. 'Rich men have no decency at all.'

'I'm really sorry. We're not all like that. Wait.' He reached into the inside pocket of his jacket. 'Let me give you money to buy a new blouse.'

'A new blouse?' she said. 'Do you think that will make it right? I needed this job and...'

'If you want to work, go see Marta the fishmonger in the morning. She will keep you safe.' He handed her a banknote. 'Here, please buy a new blouse. I'm really sorry and...'

She knocked the banknote out of his hand, it whirled to the ground. He looked at it in astonishment. She turned, squeezed through the crack of the open door, and ran through the dark, silent harbor. The weavers had gone home and the fishermen were already asleep, so that they could set out early in the morning to the places where they'd left their nets, hoping to find them full of fish. Tears. Why was her life worth nothing? She followed the lit street along the railroad. The houses further up the harbor area were smaller, the streets narrower.

The light in the kitchen of her house was still lit. Her mother and sisters were cleaning up. Weaving fishing nets, cooking, cleaning and then again; every day, for a lifetime. The smell of cooked pasta with roasted tomatoes hit her. Her sisters were playing the riddle game together and smiled at her.

'Now you are no longer a child,' her mother said, as soon as she saw her torn blouse. She pointed to the buttons. 'I'll fix it for you. You better go wash up.'

Sofia shook her head. 'It didn't happen.'

'Not?' said her mother.

'Won't you be a mistress?' asked Sienna, her sister who was a year younger. 'Well, then I will.'

'I don't want to be a weaver girl either,' Angelina said. 'When I turn fourteen, I will work as a maid in one of those villas on the boulevard.'

'You're not good enough for that,' Sienna said. 'You have to be able to talk nicely for that.'

'What should we do now? I don't make enough for the four of us,' Sofia's mother said. She was clearly considering her options.

The hills, the houses. The freedom. It seemed so far away.

'I'll start at the fishmonger's tomorrow,' Sofia said.

She walked over to the bed, dropped on it. No one, no one would ever touch her again as if she were less.

Sienna looked around the corner of the curtain and came over to her. 'Here's your notebook. Are you going to draw tonight?'

Sofia shook her head. 'I'll stop drawing.'

'Why? It's what you always do. The architect believes in you.'

'Mr. Armacci is not an architect, he owns a bookshop, that's all.'

Sofia had been going to his bookstore every Sunday afternoon for years.

The first time, when she was nine years old, she'd stood only in front of his window, looking closely at the books. He had invited her in. He was a little man with little glasses that he looked over when he spoke to her.

'He teaches you how to draw because he believes in you,' Sienna said.

Angelina flopped down on her stomach on the bed. 'He's an architect, nobody knows as much about houses as he does.'

'He knows all about drawing, about symmetry and proportions,' Sofia says. 'That's something else.'

'Well, I think he's smart,' Angelina said.

'Go see him again on Sunday afternoon,' Sienna said. 'He'll be worried if you don't show up.'

If she was sometimes a little later than the agreed time, she would find him nervously waiting at the entrance to his bookshop. Pushing his small glasses up on his face, dabbing his forehead with a handkerchief. He let customers enter the store, but he waited until she was standing next to him. 'You'll scare me if you don't come,' he would say. 'My daughter was eight years old when she was suddenly gone.' Once she had carefully asked about his daughter. He just said that tuberculosis was a dangerous disease. He later hinted that his wife spent days in the dark in their house and that he had traded his job as a mathematics professor at the university for days between the books, where he could escape into another world.

'Leave me alone now,' Sofia told her sisters. She turned and closed her eyes. Why was her life already determined the moment she was born and couldn't she change it herself?

Martedì, 6 Giugno 1939

At the end of the tiled room with long workbenches, and behind them the working girls in aprons that had once been white but were now stained red with fish blood, stood Marta, a short, stout woman. She placed her bloodied hands on her hips and studied Sofia.

'You're skinny. What size are you?' she asked. Not waiting for the answer, she grabbed a white apron from a cupboard along the wall and handed it to her.

'Put it on. Your workplace is there at that table, next to the red one.' She pointed to the other side of the room where a young woman of about eighteen with red hair was working.

'Do you have any experience? The previous girls sent by Mr. Danilo I have fired within a week.'

'Yes, I know how to fillet fish,' Sofia said. She put on the apron and went to the workbench where a shiny, razor-sharp knife lay ready.

'Hello, I'm Sofia,' she said.

'Rafaella, pleased to meet you,' the red-haired girl whispered back.

'Have you been working here long?'

'Four years, but quiet. We'll talk later,' Rafaella said, cleaning a fish.

Marta tossed a large cod in front of Sofia on the workbench and folded her arms. 'Let's see.'

Sofia turned the fish over, took the knife and cut off the head. With a secure cut she opened the back of the fish.

'Good, luckily, you've done this before. When the fish is clean, you can put it in that empty bin.'

The girls behind the workbenches filleted the fish without talking, without singing. Rafaella was lightning-fast cleaning the fish and Sofia couldn't keep up with her pace. Every half hour, Marta picked up a full bin and set down another empty bin. As more fish heads lay on the floor, mingling with bones and fins in a red layer of blood, the salty smell of fish filled the dark room, from which the blue sky could only be seen through a row of narrow windows in the top of the walls.

A loud gong sounded through the room.

'We've got half an hour,' Rafaella said, going over to the sink to rinse her hands.

It was twelve o'clock and they had worked uninterrupted since six o'clock. Sofia squinted at the bright sunlight that hadn't even come close to reaching them over the last few hours. She walked to the quay with Rafaella. Their legs dangled above the azure water where fishing boats bobbed gently. Fishermen wearing caps leaned against the empty crates and smoked cigarettes. Two boys were unraveling fishing nets with their hands and checking for holes that needed to be repaired, so they could be put out again tonight. Sofia took her panino with a thin slice of cheese from her bag. The sandwich smelled like fish. The drinking water in her bottle had become warm. Rafaella ate her plain bread.

'You work fast,' Sofia said to her. 'You cleaned most of our fish.'

Rafaella nodded in satisfaction and took another bite.

'My whole family works in the fish market. And my children will also work here when they are grown up.'

'Do you already have children?'

'Two boys. My grandmother takes care of them. Where did you work before this?'

'In the weaving mill. I was transferred last night.'

'By Mr. Danilo, surely? He often brings girls to us that Mr. Marinolli can't keep away from.'

'Do you know him?'

'Everyone knows him. Not you? Gee, where have you been? His father and uncle set up this weaving mill and a fish trade together. *Marinolli Pesci e Reti* is known throughout the region. Everyone on my street works here.'

Danilo, in the bright light of the factory lamp as he slid open the warehouse door for her. In his rich man's clothes. Clumsy with his words of regret.

'Do your parents have a husband for you yet?' Rafaella asked.

'My father passed away. My mother has pointed out Stefano who lives in the street behind us. He's in love with me, she says, but I'm not going to marry him.'

'Why not?' Rafaella asked, standing up. 'We have to go back.'

'Already? I still wanted to draw.' She'd put her notebook in her bag this morning, knowing otherwise she might miss the chance to get it down on paper if a new house popped up in her head.

They passed a group of boys who whistled at them. Rafaella playfully swiveled her hips and waved at them.

On the edge of the harbor, next to the sheds, warehouses and workshops, stood the large yellow villa with dark red shutters. Three floors and a broad balcony. The Marinolli family home. She had heard that Mr. Marinolli often stood on the top floor with binoculars to keep a close eye on his property.

'What do you think of the Marinolli house?' she asked.

Rafaella looked at it. 'I've never thought about it. It's nice, I think?'

'I think it's a severe house. That row of square, stone masonry on all corners of the house and above the windows, and the balcony railing with its coarse bars. The house would look softer if they painted the stucco in cherry blossom pink or mint green. With white shutters. Like the colors of scooped ice cream.'

They were now standing at the workspace where the smell of fish was unmistakable.

'I want to get even better at filleting the fish,' Rafaella said. 'To be able to take over Marta's work later.'

'Don't you want to do anything else?'

Rafaella shrugged. 'I never thought about that either. Do we have a choice then?'

'I think we should be able to be who we want to be.'

'You talk like a man,' Rafaella said as she took her place behind the work table.

Domenica, 11 Giugno 1939

She had sewn her black bathing suit herself; it had short trouser legs so that the cool seawater immediately caressed the bare skin of her thighs. She swam for a while, parallel to the boulevard and its long row of tall palm trees. Slowly it got busier there, now that the 12 o'clock church service had ended. The people who were walking on this part of the beach, near the seaside villas, were dressed in smart Sunday clothes. Women wore blouses with lace collars and loose dresses made of silk or cotton. Men wore crisp shirts together with a light beige or white jacket. They sat on the shady terraces of the expensive restaurants.

A little further on, a family was sitting under a large white umbrella on the beach. A woman with her two sons. A white-uniformed servant poured water in a crystal drinking glass for the woman on the lounger. The younger son was playing in the sand in his swimming trunks, the older son, dressed in long trousers, a long-sleeved shirt, and leather shoes, sat upright in a chair and read a book. She swam back to the shore and came out of the water. The young man peered over the edge of his book to look at her. It was Danilo. She quickly walked to her pile of clothes on the sand, and pulled her blouse over her wet bathing suit. It clung to her body. Her long, wet hair dripped, making the top of her blouse even wetter. He came towards her, she tugged at the fabric of her blouse, pulling it down on her hips with all her strength. The moment she looked up again, he was just a meter and a half away from her.

'The weaving girl,' he said hesitantly. His green eyes were the color of the sea.

'I don't want your money,' she said.

'I'm sorry I offered it. It doesn't make up for what happened.'

She sat down on her skirt, he stood still. His shadow fell over her.

'Excuse me,' he said when he saw it, stepping aside.

The sun warmed her face. A lock of his dark-brown hair fell across Danilo's eyes. He pushed it back with his hand, but it tumbled back into the exact same position.

'How's work at Marta's?' he asked.

'Better than the weaving mill.'

He nodded and looked away, toward the yellow villa in the harbor.

'My father thinks he owns everyone who works for him,' he said. 'It's wrong.'

'As long as he gets away with it, it could happen to any girl,' Sofia said.

His arms hung limp at his sides, but his fingertips moved nervously up and down the linen fabric of his light beige trousers.

'I've considered going to the police, but he has friends there.' He squinted at the sun a little and tried again to push the hair back from his face.

'Do you live nearby?' he asked. He took a small step closer. 'May I?'

She nodded. He lowered himself onto the sand a meter away from her.

'You don't have to tell me where you live if you don't want to,' he said quickly. He put his hand over his eyes and smiled gently at her. His green eyes.

'A fifteen-minute walk from here, west of town,' she replied, waving above her shoulder in the right direction. She shook out her dark brown hair so it would dry more quickly, and then tossed it back over her shoulders. He looked at it.

'I never really get to that part of town,' he said.

She didn't expect that either. Everyone who worked in the harbor lived in that part of town and everyone who could afford clean, filleted fish lived in the larger houses in the center or in the more distant suburbs.

'We live in that house.' He pointed to the yellow villa with dark red shutters. 'I was born there.'

'You're lucky,' she said. When she and her sisters lay in bed in their small house in the narrow street, her mother on the other side of the curtain lamented the loss of Sofia's father, who had drowned at sea when Sofia was six years old, and the difficult life she now led.

'Not everything is as it seems,' he said. He leaned on his arm, moving slightly closer to her. His perfume smelled like a spring morning after a rainstorm; lime, blossoms, bergamot, and the herbs that grew in the surrounding hills.

'What do you mean?' she asked.

He didn't answer.

Their luxurious city villa where every girl in the harbor wanted to work. Or better yet, where they dreamed of living as the wife of one of Mr. Marinolli's sons. There, behind the first-floor window, must be the dining room overlooking the sea. A happy family at the table. Food in abundance, served by a waiter. His father coming home. After he just summoned a girl into his office. Did he sit down at the dinner table, as if nothing had happened? She looked at Danilo's mother a bit further down the beach. Did she know about that?

'Can you talk to me?' Sofia asked.

He looked at his mother under the umbrella. 'My mother doesn't care about class differences.'

'And you?'

'Me neither.'

'Aren't you warm with your long pants and leather shoes on?'

'Yes.' He brushed some sand from his trouser leg. 'I've already taken off my jacket.'

She listened to his breathing. The sun was high, the sea glittered. He began to roll up the sleeves of his neat, light-blue linen shirt. The sea rippled in the background. A boy with a kite ran past. Tiny dark hair stood out on his tanned arms.

'I'm leaving soon,' he said.

'Where are you going?'

'My father wants me to set up some fisheries in the smaller villages along the coast to the north, as far as the city of Ancona. He has bought land in the valley near the village of Cupra Marittima, and a house is being built there for me and my future family.'

'In the hills?' She looked into the distance, at the sloping olive groves surrounding the city. 'You don't realize how lucky you are.'

'I don't like the fishing industry. Me, I want to plant vines and start a winery of my own.' He gestured grandly with his arms in the air. 'Vineyards, as far as you can see. The salty sea air will give my wine a distinctive, fresh aftertaste. Everyone will recognize it.'

He looked at her enthusiastically. He no longer looked like the timid boy who had clumsily apologized for his father's misbehavior and who dressed as was expected of him as a director's son.

'Excuse me, I let myself go,' he said. 'And you, what do you want to do?'

'What do you mean?' she asked.

'I assume you don't always want to keep cleaning fish?'

His genteel words and clothes, so far from her world, yet so close in the world of thoughts.

'I have my dreams, but my mother says that women of our class only need to do three things: marry the right man, raise children, and work until we die.'

'That's not inspiring,' he concluded.

She shook her head. He looked out over the sea, at his mother and brother, at her.

'I like to draw houses.' She grabbed her shoulder bag and got her notebook out. She opened a page and held it up.

'Did you draw that?' he asked in surprise. He stretched out his hand and took the notebook.

It was a detailed drawing she had been working on as she sat at Mr. Armacci's round wooden table in his bookshop last Sunday afternoon. He was helping customers, but would occasionally look over her shoulder and give her instructions.

Danilo flipped through the notebook. 'You draw beautifully. With so much detail. Are you copying it from a book?'

She felt a tingle run through her body. Never before had she shown her drawings to anyone other than Mr. Armacci and her sisters. What if no one liked her drawings? What if people dismissed them as a child's drawings?

She smiled. 'I come up with the designs myself.'

He looked at her in disbelief and tried to push his hair back into the right position. 'You should become an architect.'

She took the notebook from his hands and put it back in her bag. 'I fillet fish.'

'Yes now, but not always?'

Did he think as she thought? Did he, as she did, feel trapped by the strict rules and the same rhythm every day, determined by church and state? A long chain of vague, interchangeable days in the city, lived with no connection to the rhythms of nature, of the sun and the moon, without wandering through the tall grasses of the fields and imagining all that was possible.

He leaned forward slightly, closer to her. Soft lips, green eyes, the scent of summer blossoms.

'Most of the girls I know just want to embroider, read, or play the piano,' he said. 'You're different. And you need someone to give you space. Who makes your dreams come true.'

He smiled at her. Her cheeks grew warm. Was it the sun or was she blushing? She sucked in his words, took a deep breath, summer blossom, sea-green eyes in which she was slowly drowning.

She stood up, picked up the skirt she had been sitting on from the sand and pulled it on. He got up too, rubbing the sand from his pants. He picked up her bag and brushed it clean.

'Do you come here every Sunday?' he asked.

'Yes, I'll come here before I go to the bookstore downtown in the afternoon.'

He handed her the bag. 'May I see you again next week?'

She slung the bag over her shoulder, raising her hand to shade her eyes so that she could see in the bright sunlight. Was he different from his father? 'That's okay.'

'Thank you.' He turned, walked back to his mother, and gave her a short wave as he settled into his chair. Then he rolled his shirt sleeves back down and buttoned his cuffs.

The following Sunday, Danilo was already standing on the beach next to her clothes, waiting for her to get out of the water. He had brought a silver tray with tea and cake. She sat in her bathing suit, drying in the warm sun, her hair loose over her shoulder. He sat next to her, a little closer. He had rolled up his linen trousers above his calves, and tucked his toes in the sand.

They talked about vineyards full of ripe grapes that would be fermented into the best wine in the region and about houses that clearly bore her signature. He moved a little closer on the sand, the scent of summer blossom. Green eyes like the sea. For a moment it seemed as if their lives ran parallel every day, and not just this Sunday.

'You are so beautiful,' he said.

She smiled. He moved his hand to stroke her cheek, she flinched.

Quickly he lowered his hand again. 'My apologies.'

Together they sat on the sand, looking at the sea. Like in a postcard.

She longed for these Sundays that were so different from the rest of the week. Warmer, casual. Full of possibilities and sweet words whispered to her. The sleeves of his linen shirt rolled up, the top buttons unbuttoned. His long trousers exchanged for shorter ones. The week after with a swimsuit. In the sea, they sometimes accidentally touched each other's hands while swimming underwater. A tingling ran through her body that she still felt for days afterwards whenever she thought of him.

While drying in the sun, he gently kissed a drop of water off her shoulder. His perfume took her into the fantasy world that her sisters invented when they were all in bed at night, as she described a house she had drawn and her sisters colored the picture with seductive romance and intrigue. Carefully he placed both hands on her face, caressing it tenderly. His soft palms glowed on her skin. That tingling again. His breathing close to hers.

'May I?' he asked softly, his mouth almost up to her lips.

She nodded slowly.

His lips on hers, soft and warm.

Long and intense.

The hot summer turned lusty.

2

'Yoohoo, darling!' Margot shouts. Her voice echoes through the baggage claim area of Ancona's small airport, and her blond updo rises above everyone else's heads.

'Here I am! Yoohoo,' she shouts enthusiastically and gives me a big hug. 'Oh, it's so good that I'm here, isn't it, since Roger and Max didn't come along.'

She is wearing her light blue flight attendant's uniform.

'I'm so curious about that little palace of yours,' she says as she lets go of me.

'It's still a ruin now,' I answer. Especially if I were to believe Aron's words from yesterday.

Margot takes my arm. 'We're going to have a great time together; I already know it. Come on.'

She pulls her suitcase with its flashy Chanel logo behind her. Her heels click on the marble floor. The skirt of her uniform is so tight around her legs that she has to take small steps.

'You're not a flight attendant anymore, are you?' I ask.

'No, darling, not anymore. Remember that affair I had last year? Yes, you remember that, don't you? Well, after that little incident I had to leave the airline and he was allowed to stay. Yeah, totally unfair, I know, but they said I shouldn't have entered the cockpit during the flight to make up for our argument. But you know how much I like make-up sex.'

I nod. She winks at a man as she walks past him. He winks back. His wife angrily pulls his sleeve.

'Well, darling, anyway, this suit looks like my old uniform, doesn't it? I had it made by my own tailor. Yeah, I can't quite let go of flying yet. I did it for so many years, you know.'

We drive south on the regional road that runs along the coast of the Adriatic Sea. Margot jumps from one story to the next, naming everything she sees in the meantime. It goes from how her friend caught her daughter with weed at school to 'Oh look, what a cute little church over there on that mountaintop.' And from how that other friend went to a swinger's club with her temporary flirt to 'Ah yeah, I see the sea, look, there on the left.' An hour later we park at the seaside mobile home I've rented.

Margot clasps her hands together in delight. 'Oh, a real chalet! What a lovely place.'

She pulls her suitcase across the grass, then up the two steps of the wooden decking in front of our mobile home. Meanwhile, she waves to the family in the mobile home opposite us and yells, '*Ciao, bellas.*'

Then she turns to me. 'Well, what more could you ask for?' she chirps. 'Our own terrace, right on the beach. This is fantastic! Where is my bikini?'

The sea breeze plays with my hair and at the waterline I kick off my slippers, pull my dress over my head and walk into the cool water. Margot runs past me and plunges further into the sea. I swim towards the long line of boulders that run parallel to the shoreline and form breakwaters. From there – almost at one with the sea and far away from everyone else – I take in the view of the green hills and the old village center of Cupra Marittima, basking in the sun on the hilltop; it's breathtakingly beautiful.

My hair is still wet and salty when the navigator sends me into San Benedetto del Tronto's harbor with its thousands of palm trees. Most of the old sheds in the harbor area are empty or used for boat storage, and a small strip along the railroad has been converted into trendy restaurants and a few offices. High-roofed buildings where boats are repaired alternate with lower, square ones where there are fish markets. Once again, I practice the Italian phrase: *Sì, capisco bene l'italiano, ma parlare è ancora difficile per me.* Google Translate has spoken it to me many times and I have repeated it: Yes, I understand Italian well, but speaking is still difficult for me.

After I park the car in front of an old building, I twist my dark blond hair into a bun. My make-up is minimal and my white summer dress a conscious choice; neat, but modest. A message comes in from Margot. *Good luck darling, I'm proud of you.* After the dive in the sea, she decided to rent a lounger under the blue umbrellas on the beach, next to a couple of young Italian men. 'Oh, they're young, but it doesn't matter,' she said, placing magazines, sunscreen, a bottle of water, a glass, and a bag of raw nuts on the table under the umbrella. Her bikini is tiny. She waved goodbye to me, turned to the men and said, '*Ciao, guys.*' One of the men got up and knelt beside her in the sand.

As soon as I enter the reception room, Brian stands up and walks over to me. He lifts his Ray-Ban sunglasses and casually pushes them into his hair. 'Where's Aron?'

In the small room with its gray tiled floor stands a row of black chairs against white plastered walls. This used to be a storage area or workspace for the fishing industry. A large ficus plant sits in a pot. A faded poster of the harbor hangs with the top corner loose. Why so practical? Why has the atmosphere of the beautiful landscape outside not been translated into a beautiful interior? I rearrange the space; I paint the walls ocher yellow, put a group of palms and ferns in different planters, grouped together in the middle, and some chairs with botanical prints facing each other with a nice coffee table in between. A large entryway at the front instead of this simple door, allowing light to flood into the room.

'Where's Aron?' Brian asks again. He wears a light-blue shirt that is wrinkle free and has a small red and black tartan band along the collar, as if to subtly indicate that he is half English, half Italian.

'Aron isn't coming,' I say.

'You need him, he is a certified translator. If the notary discovers that you don't speak Italian, she may not hand over the house to you. Then it will not be sufficient that you only have me as your purchasing agent.'

A bald man and two older women enter. The man greets me as if he knows me and Brian quickly reminds me that he is the real estate agent I met last summer while touring the house. The two women smile. Their green eyes stand out against their long, silver-grey hair that is beautifully pinned up as if they had just come from the hairdresser. Soft faces with small wrinkles. They wear almost the same satin dresses; one dark green and the other red, the cut of each one distinctive. Elegant, so different from my simple summer dress. I understand that these are the two elderly sisters from whom we're buying the house and I shake their hands, explaining that I understand them well, but that speaking Italian is still difficult. Brian nods in agreement.

At the reception desk I write my name on six forms and sign them. I have no idea what they're for, but Brian indicates it's okay. He apologizes for not being there yesterday to inspect the house one last time before the handover, and asks if Lorenzo was okay and why Aron isn't coming.

They call us into a small office with high, narrow windows through which the daylight hardly penetrates, because it is blocked by the walls of the towering warehouse immediately next to it. The notary sits at the head of a long table. Her black hair falls in a slight curl at the bottom. Her light pink blouse reassures me; she won't be strict.

'*Benvenuto, parli italiano?*' she asks immediately.

I can answer this. '*Sì, capisco bene l'italiano, ma parlare è ancora difficile per me.*'

Brian nods again in agreement, but I suspect he has noticed that I'm repeating the exact same sentence. We sit down next to eachother, the two sisters and their real estate agent sit opposite us. I smile at the sisters and am once again captivated by their green eyes. Is that common in Italy, green eyes? The screen on the wall flickers and the Italian deed of purchase appears. The notary begins to read, and soon I lose track. I grab my phone for the Dutch version of the deed of sale that Aron has sent, but I can't find it quickly.

'*Signora, hai capito e sei d'accordo?*' asks the notary.

What should I understand and what should I agree to? Brian puts the earpiece of his sunglasses in his mouth as a distraction and leans in my direction.

'Yes,' he whispers.

'*Sì*,' I say to the notary, who then shakes her head slightly. She reads on. She says something to the sisters, and they nod. I nod along with them.

I keep trying to recognize words. The language app taught me how to order coffee, book a table, and greet someone but not that a house in Italy is not always connected to the sewage system and that is why a septic tank is dug into the ground. The notary asks me sternly whether I am aware of this. I nod yes. After an hour, halfway through the deed of sale, she gets up, comes to me and hands over the floor plans of the house. Brain explains that I have to put my signature on both maps.

'Go ahead, they are correct,' he advises.

When I have signed my name, the notary takes the drawings back, sits down and starts a phone call on the landline. The two sisters now smile broadly and congratulate me. Brian turns to me and tells me that the notary is transferring our money to the sisters' bank account. They each receive half of the purchase price. When I ask him whether we shouldn't first go through the rest of the deed of sale, he replies that he suspects that the notary realizes that I hardly speak Italian and therefore wants to finish it quickly. She hangs up the phone.

'Who has the keys to the house?' she asks, looking around the group as if expecting someone to raise their hand.

The sisters both point to me, and Brian explains to the notary that I already received the keys yesterday to inspect the house one more time before purchasing. She nods in satisfaction.

'This means that everything is settled,' she says, closing her folder.

Brian congratulates me. I bend down and take two cookie tins with traditional Dutch blue motifs filled with *stroopwafels* and two bags with tulip bulbs from my tote. It seemed like a nice idea to present these gifts at the moment the sale was finalized, but now it feels strange when I give them to the sisters. They smile kindly, look at the tins and the bags with tulip bulbs, and thank me warmly.

One of the sisters opens her handbag and takes out a folded sheet of paper. She gives it to me.

'*È la chiave di un grande segreto,*' says the sister in the dark green dress.

The other sister nods eagerly. '*Che nessuno sa.*'

'It's the key to a big secret that no one knows,' Brian says. 'It's usually that way with secrets, that nobody knows them, I mean. Well, you can take it, you can always throw it away later.'

I take the sheet of paper and unfold it. It is a detailed drawing of the house, colored with pink walls, light blue windows and a mint green roof. As if it had been drawn for children. With colorful flowers on the windowsills and on the balcony. Two girls hang out of a window. In the garden a woman is sitting on a chair with embroidery in her hands and another woman is standing further away, waving to the girls. The sky is light pink, the sun light yellow and the olive trees light green.

'Beautiful,' I say to the sisters. I point to the girls and the women in the drawing. 'Who are these people?'

The sister in the red dress explains something, I don't follow her. 'This drawing was in the will,' Brian translates. 'They don't know why they inherited the house and hope you will find the answer. You have to turn the drawing around, she says.'

On the back there is a text with graceful curly letters written with black fountain pen and marked with a few drops of water. A message from the past, without salutation and without signature. In simple Italian that I almost understand.

Settembre 1996
The longing for what it could have been has always haunted me. I'm sorry about everything. You are special girls, never forget that.

Brian translates it and raises his eyebrows. The sisters say they have no idea what it means and hope I'll call them as soon as I discover something in the house that they couldn't find.

Domenica, 2 Luglio 1939

They stood on the edge of the road, side by side. From the road, the hill continued down for six meters to end on the flat land of the valley of wheat fields. In the distance reeds grew along the banks of the river, and on the other side of the river the valley merged into the sloping slopes of olive trees and fruit trees.

'It's beautiful here,' Sofia said to Danilo. 'Nature is unimaginably delightful.'

Without realizing it, she clapped her hands softly as if giving nature a round of applause for her beauty. He laughed, gently putting his arm around her shoulders. The sun had lifted his dark brown hair. The grasshoppers chirped; the summer breeze played through the leaves of a young fig tree.

'I'm going to dig away a part of the hill here to create a level area where the house can be built,' he said.

'What's the house going to look like?' she asked. A winery would fit into this place. With grey-green shutters and an elegant balcony with white, wrought-iron railings overlooking the sea, which was just ten minutes away by bike.

He raised his shoulders. 'My father had it designed by an architect,' he said. 'It won't be anything special, you could have done better. All of the building materials have been ordered and my father has hired all of the construction workers from this area so that it will be built very quickly.'

A little further down the property there was a wooden shed. 'You can live there now,' she said with a laugh.

'That's an old pig shed,' he said in surprise. 'Nobody can live in that.'

'It's bigger than our house, and I suspect even warmer in the winter.'

In their house in the winter frost crystals spread into flowery shapes on the windows. Her mother covered their bed with woolen blankets that she knitted herself, under which Sofia and her sisters huddled together to keep warm.

'*Buongiorno*,' a farmer shouted over the rumble of his tractor engine. He stopped in the middle of the road next to them and turned off his engine.

'It's already sold,' he hissed through the single front tooth that he still had. His cap was crooked on his head and his blue coveralls were stained. 'I have still to remove the for-sale sign. My brother and I have sold this land to rich people from the city.' With an outstretched arm, he marked the whole area. 'But they never come here. Probably too hot, too far in the valley. Rich people live by the sea or hide within the walls of the cities on the hills beyond.' He waved back, somewhere in the air, to the rolling hills.

Sofia blew a lock of dark brown hair from her face and tucked it back under her dark green headscarf, which was actually too loosely knotted to fit really neatly.

'This is good land,' the farmer continued, saliva forming around his one front tooth. 'In my vegetable garden, the tomatoes are the size of a man's fist. No one knows we are sitting on a spring here.'

Sofia looked at Danilo. 'A spring on the property. Then you can plant fruit trees and oleanders, and start a vegetable garden.'

Danilo smiled, tucking the loose strand of hair that kept escaping, back under her headscarf.

'Who are you?' asked the farmer. 'Are you their son? You drive an expensive car, I see.'

He pointed to the red Fiat 1500 convertible with black linen top in which Danilo had picked her up this morning from the fishmongers in the harbor. He'd put the top down and held the door open for her. Her hands had slid over the soft leather upholstery as she admired the gauges on the dashboard. With her hair flowing under the green headscarf, which he had brought for her, it had been her first car ride. They had driven out of town, along the long coastal road, and past the villages of Grottammare and Cupra Marittima. People looked at them, waved. She waved back shyly.

'Danilo Marinolli, nice to meet you,' Danilo said. 'I'm from San Benedetto del Tronto. My house will be built here soon.'

He walked to his car and from behind the front seats picked up the white enamel sign with *Marinolli Pesci e Reti* in blue letters, and held it up. 'This sign will be posted along the road. The house will also have a new office for our fish trading company and weaving mill.'

'Hmm,' said the farmer. He looked at Sofia. 'It's not going to be your house, that's for sure,' he said. 'Are you his mistress?'

'We're together,' Sofia said.

He slapped his thighs and laughed as if he'd just heard a good joke.

'Impossible,' he replied. 'You're not from his class.'

Drops of saliva flew past his tooth, lingering in the air between them. Sofia ran her hand over her skirt, as if she could smooth out the wrinkles that way. She fumbled at a seam she hadn't finished properly. Her skirt was a little shorter than usual, she didn't like rules about skirt length. Danilo, he would explain everything to the farmer.

'Do you live in this area?' Danilo asked.

Hadn't he heard the farmer? Hadn't he noticed his insult? She was about to say something when the farmer pointed to a neglected-looking house about three hundred yards down the road.

'Yes, my brother and I live there,' said the farmer. 'See that vegetable garden? It's ours. And after that comes the cornfield, and there,' he pointed into the distance, 'just before the river more corn, ours too. Corn on the cob the size of a man's forearm. Did I mention we're sitting on a spring here?'

He started his engine, tapped his cap in greeting, and drove off, roaring, leaving them in a cloud of dry sand that clung to their skin.

'I'm sorry about his insult,' Danilo said.

Before she could say anything, he kissed her. Long and intimate. They were in love.

At night in bed she told her sisters about the ride in the car, the beautiful valley and the passionate kiss.

'Do you let him feel you too?' Sienna asked curiously.

'You're too young to know that,' Sofia said.

'That's not true,' Angelina said. 'I'm thirteen and I'm going to kiss a boy soon.'

'Please, tell us,' said Sienna.

'Okay, ears shut,' Sofia said with a laugh. The sisters put their hands over their ears, their fingers spread apart so they didn't miss a thing.

'He touches me gently under my skirt. He strokes my leg; his hand slides up…'

The sisters giggled.

'I want to do that with a boy,' Sienna said loudly.

'Shhh, or Mother will hear us,' Angelina said.

'We can't do the rest until we're married,' Sofia said quickly, then nothing more.

Once her sisters and mother were asleep, Sofia snuck into the kitchen, which still smelled of onions and garlic, and pulled open the drawer of the cabinet, which squeaked. She picked up a large sheet of paper and the colored pencils that she was only allowed to use on Sundays. The light from the streetlamp flooded in on the table by the window. The street was empty, the houses dark. Working class people went to bed early to get up before dawn. By the light of the street lamp, she designed the winery that she had envisioned that afternoon as she stood on the roadside. Square and symmetrical, with high windows on all sides, like the stately town houses. That suited Danilo; slightly different from the other farms in the valley, but with the allure of a winery. On the ground floor, she drew a large stable door on either side for working the grapes from his vineyard. In the middle came the stairwell, high and stately. She walked up the stairs there in an elegant dress of soft, shiny fabric. At the top of the stairs, she entered a narrow room, where the light bounced off the walls and made its way through the corridors, out to a graceful wrought iron balcony that she tinted a light blue. She paid extra attention to the details of the house. The corners were made of travertine, above the windows were arches of the same travertine. She noted measurements so that the rooms were just the right size. After an hour of sketching, she held up the sheet, tilted her head, narrowed her eyes. The streetlamp made shadows move across the drawing. Yes, everything seemed to be right.

Lunedì, 3 Luglio 1939

'Did you really draw one on a large sheet of paper last night?' Angelina asked. While she was combing her long black hair, she looked over Sofia's shoulder at the drawing of the house.

'Don't show Mom you used a drawing sheet on Monday,' Sienna said, her mouth full of bread. Crumbs fell on the table.

'Actually, it was still Sunday when I started it.' Sofia rolled up the drawing and put a rubber band around it. She put it in her bag by the lunchbox with her bread.

The sun was just rising behind the hills, giving the harbor a soft glow. Everywhere women walked with their lunch boxes. Now they were clean, in a few hours everyone would be smelling of fish or hemp. Monday mornings were the worst mornings. After having her Sunday off, Marta had recovered from the previous week and stamped through the tiled room all morning, roaring that the work had to be done faster or the fish weren't clean enough.

'What have you brought?' Rafaella asked during the lunch break, washing her hands.

Sofia took the roll of paper from her bag. 'I've drawn a house for Danilo.'

'Why?' Rafaella pulled her red hair back into a bun.

'Because I saw this house when I thought about the place. Those rolling hills, that wheat field.' She unrolled the drawing and held it up.

'It's very beautiful, I must admit,' Rafaella said. 'I dream with you. Shortly. Okay, ready. And now you must forget, because what you want is never going to happen.'

'You don't know,' Sofia said.

'Those kinds of men are not for us. We don't have the elegance that women in their class have.'

'We are elegant, all we lack are the expensive skirts and gold jewelry.'

'Okay, you can be elegant, but only in bed without your clothes on,' Rafaella said. 'Be a good mistress and he will take care of you. He might even buy you a room here in town, if you're lucky.'

'He took me to the valley. A man only does that when he is serious and wants more.'

'Showing off, just to impress you and get you in his bed.'

Sofia rolled the drawing back up and put it in her bag.

'Yes, I'll be honest with you,' Rafaella said. 'As a friend, I'm supposed to do that. Marry the boy next door, Stefano, or become one of Danilo's mistresses. You have no other choice.'

While Sofia cleaned the fish, in her mind, she lived in the house. Soon she would no longer be a fishmonger girl.

The summer evening was balmy and it was already dusk when she left because Marta had made her work longer to scrub the tiles. She walked to the corner of a building where Danilo had been waiting for her every evening for the past few days. They would talk, kiss or walk hand in hand on the empty beach. His hand in hers, familiar and safe. Away from the world of fish and net weaving, into a world full of twinkling stars that told her they belonged together.

Danilo wasn't there. She waited, perhaps he was still at work or held up in his father's office. The harbor became quieter, most of the girls had gone home. After waiting fifteen minutes she walked towards the warehouse where they wove the fishing nets. She pushed open the heavy warehouse door a bit, looked into the dark hall. The office was still lit. She was shocked. Mr. Marinolli was standing behind a girl who was bent over the desk. The girl moved wildly, as if she were trying to wrestle her way out. Quickly Sofia pushed the door open further, ran to the light switch and flipped it up. The lights on the factory's high ceiling flickered briefly and then blazed on. As she ran back out, Mr. Marinolli was standing at the office window with his hands on his belt. The girl ran out the door of his office.

Hastily Sofia left the empty harbor area and ran towards the illuminated main road. Her footsteps echoed in the quiet streets. Once at the main road, she walked more slowly. Ahead, a man and woman were standing close to each other under the light of a street lamp. The woman was wearing high heels and her hair was up in a neat bun. Elegant, Rafaella would call it. The man was standing with his back to Sofia; he was wearing an expensive suit.

The smell of his perfume, like a spring morning after a rain shower. He must have smelled her too, because he turned and took a step back, away from the woman.

'Sofia?' Danilo asked.

'Do you know her?' said the young woman with red lipstick. She raised her eyebrows astonished, looked askance at Sofia's skirt. The woman had gold studs in her ears, and they were about the same age.

'Danilo?' Sofia said. 'I waited for you and saw your father in his office...'

'I thought you weren't coming. You were late and...'

'Do you work here?' the woman asked Sofia.

'Yes, she works at the fish market,' Danilo said. 'We met in my father's office. Before she worked in the weaving mill.'

'Ah, one of your father's factory girls.' Her look of disapproval slid across Sofia's body.

'This is Stella,' Danilo said to introduce her.

'Stella Sabbatini, from *Sabbatini Pianti*, the largest plant and flower nursery in the region,' she said.

Sofia was Mr. Marinolli's factory maid, and Stella was anything but that. Stella was what Sofia wanted to be.

She held out her hand. Stella hesitated, shook Sofia's hand briefly, then wiped her hand on her coat.

'I made a drawing of your house,' Sofia said, handing Danilo the roll of paper.

'Why are you drawing his house?' Stella asked suspiciously.

'This design fits well on the plot in the valley. It's a winery,' Sofia said hopefully to Danilo.

He wasn't looking at her drawing, he was looking at Stella's red lipstick. A long lock of hair curled on either side of the gold studs in her ears, freed from her elegant updo. Her clean white blouse was embellished with small pleated seams and a lace collar.

She ran away. Not home, but towards the center of the city. She would have preferred to run out of town, into the hills. Far from everything that held her here.

3

'The house is a-ma-zing, darling,' Margot says, standing in the garden. 'And look at that little balcony, how romantic.' Her face is already tanned from her afternoon on the beach lounger. 'Oh, I can see the sea from here. Come, take a peek.'

I open the front door, it's cool inside. I put a box filled with empty wine bottles alongside another box with a piece of fabric sticking out. I pull it and unfold it. It's a mint green dress with small white dots.

'Fantastic, what a stairwell,' Margot says as she enters. 'Ah yeah, let's sort through all the treasures that are still there. Look, I brought this one for you.'

She hands over a package containing two yellow plastic kitchen gloves, which she takes from her handbag. 'Would you like a dust mask too?'

She squeezes her hands into the gloves. When I told her I was going to clean and tidy the house this week, she offered to help. She takes a roll of garbage bags from her handbag.

'How did you get all that in your handbag on the plane?' I ask.

'Ah darling, just smile sweet and everything is possible.'

'That's not true.'

'Where do you want to start?'

I shrug. 'The bedroom on the first floor? There are dirty mattresses there.'

The damp stains on the walls create circles in the light orange stucco of the high-ceilinged, square bedroom. There's an old bed, an antique linen closet that matches the dresser, and in the corner is a rat-eaten armchair that was once upholstered with a floral print. The floor is full of newspapers and magazines. Beside the bed are a few empty wine bottles.

'So, someone lived here who liked a drink,' says Margot. 'What smells so bad in here? Is that rat piss?'

I point to the pile of old newspapers drenched in moisture. 'I'm sure they'll leave when we're done here.' With a swipe I open a garbage bag and grab some newspapers. In the top corner one of them is dated 1946. Why did someone keep newspapers from that year?

Margot pulls open a dresser drawer. 'Ah, a nest. Look, darling, they've all gathered bits of cloth to make a warm nest for their babies.'

'You know they were baby *rats*?'

She grabs the scraps of fabric and tosses them in a garbage bag. 'Well, it's still cute.'

In the linen closet, everything is in a huge heap on the floor. Torn skirts, a pair of sandals, a cardigan barely hanging together by a few woolen threads. Who wore this? And why was it kept? There are books at the bottom of the heap. *Nella vita del mio tempo*. In the life of my time. I put it aside to keep it.

There are dirty mattresses on the bed against a back wall beautifully painted with lovely bunches of grapes. Who sat here on the bed and read the book?

'Woohoo, darling, lunch is ready,' Margot calls from the yard less than two hours later.

I walk down the stairs, squinting in the bright sunlight.

Margot stands under the old olive tree and waves. 'Over here, come, look how good it all is.'

She has dragged out two old chairs and a coffee table and placed them in the tall grass. On the table is a silver wine cooler with a bottle of white wine and a linen napkin over it, two antique glasses, a wooden tray with Italian cheeses and prosciutto, a salad with mozzarella and olives and freshly sliced baguette.

'How did you do this so fast?' I ask her as I sit down. 'I didn't even notice you were gone.'

She pours the wine. 'Ah, you know, I pretty much grew up in my father's restaurant, right? He had a Michelin star, you remember darling? Look, I found the glasses and plates in the kitchen cupboard here. How nice! And I got the wine cooler and ice cubes from Silvan and Frederico. Oh, you're so close to the sea here, it's only a four-minute drive.'

'Silvan and Frederico?'

'Yes, the owners of that club on the beach, diagonally opposite our chalet, near that harbor. Sweet couple, those guys. Funny, one has long hair and plays in a rock band, while the other is polished, you know, the kind of guy who knows exactly how to dress.'

She takes an olive from the salad and holds it up. The olive oil drips off, her fingers gleam. 'Well, I bought the rest at the supermarket in the village. You know, that's just more of a caterer than a supermarket, really, our supermarkets could learn something from that. You have to taste these little black olives.'

I take the olive.

'How delicious they are!'

We toast, talk and laugh, sitting there in the grass, next to the tall house and the wheat field. Slightly tipsy, I tell her that this place feels predestined.

There's a rumble at the back of the house and I walk around it as Margot clears the table and brings in the crockery. A huge cloud of dust hangs in the garden above the tall grass. A harvester swings at great speed between our old olive trees, the driver gestures for me to move aside.

'I'm harvesting the barley,' the man in his seventies says when he stops in front of me a few minutes later and turns off the engine. 'I'll come to harvest the barley in the front yard tomorrow. I don't know exactly what time yet, because I'm retired.'

Barley, so it's not grass that was in bloom.

'I live next door,' he explains. His cap is half crooked. He points into the distance. 'In the old house next to the road over there, that belonged to my great-uncles. The land you overlook with the grain and corn is mine. Until the river. Would you like to see my vegetable garden? The tomatoes are the size of a man's fist.'

'I'd love to come by sometime,' I say. 'Did you know the former owners of this house? There are still a lot of belongings inside.'

He nods and shrugs. '*Così è la vita, non è sempre dolce.*'

Such is life, it is not always sweet.

'What do you mean?' I ask.

He smiles, starts the engine and drives off.

At the end of the afternoon the cupboards are empty, as are the dresser drawers. The hallway is filled with garbage bags.

'Yuck' Aron says from the hallway.

No, not again.

'Hello Aron,' I say.

'Do you know you can get sick from the rubbish here?'

Just when I want to say something, Margot beats me to it. 'You must be Aron. Darling, this is not dirt, this is a journey of discovery.'

For a moment he seems taken aback.

'This is Margot, my friend. She's helping to clean up the house.'

He observes her as if she were a strange creature.

'I've come to bring my invoice for the translation,' he says to me.

'Really? You could have sent it by e-mail, that would have saved you the drive.'

Margot moves closer to him. 'I think our Aron likes you and that's why he likes to come by.'

Aron's cheeks turn a light red that contrasts sharply with his short blond hair. 'Certainly not, that isn't true. I'm a translator, so I'm professional. No, it certainly isn't true. However, I want to hand over my invoice so that I receive the payment on time. Sometimes you have those people who buy a house and then end up in trouble and...'

Margot pushes him back toward the door with soft pats on the back and takes the envelope.

'Your payment will be fine, I'm sure,' she says.

He looks past her at me. 'Um, well, the payment term is below the invoice.'

Margot watches him go down the stairs. 'Ah, he's pretty adorable, isn't he, darling? With those spiky hairs and those glasses. Just too sweet.'

'You talk about him like you're talking about a puppy.'

'Well, I think he's cute.' She shrugs, turns to the closet, and starts pulling on the armchair. Together we push it into the hallway and down the stairs. We drag it outside and put it in the shed for disposal. The phone in my pocket vibrates. A message from Brian. *Your land is worth more now. There are two natural springs under your property and they are officially registered.'*

Soon we will be showering every day with crystal-clear spring water. The oleanders recover after a hot day as the water seeps from the sprinklers, finds its way along the roots, back into the ground to be purified again in the spring.

Roger calls. He has received the same message and asks if I can search for the springs on our land. It could be a nice windfall to offset the costs, he thinks. He tells me that it's raining at home and Max is doing fine. He has progressed to the next league in the game and has decided to become a professional gamer.

After carefully looking over the property, I find both of the springs in stone wells. One in the tall grass under an oleander, the other in the middle of the wheat field. I slide open the rusty lid covering the round pit, look over the edge and shrink back. I can't see the bottom. My fear of heights, which kicks in at just two meters, prevents me from checking whether there is water in the well. I pick up a pebble from the ground, throw it over the edge with a slight arc, and wait. No splash. Another attempt, and again nothing.

I take my phone out of my pocket and hold it over the well with my arm outstretched. I send the photo to Roger, slide the lid back on and walk back to the house.

Early in the evening Margot and I drive from the valley, which is bisected by the small river, back to the coastal strip with its hotels, beach restaurants, and colorful umbrellas. Some farmers still work the land or at least the vegetable gardens that every house here seems to have. Small nurseries sell oleanders and palms in all sizes. The roadsides are full of wild flowers and on the slopes olive trees that are hundreds of years old continue to produce fruit. In the valley behind me, the striking balcony rises above the treetops. She is so pure as she stands there. Palazzo Puro.

First we take a swim in the sea to rinse off the dust, then we put on our summer dresses and flipflops before strolling up to the restaurant called *Uccelli del Mare*, birds of the sea. We sit at a table covered with white linen, looking out over the yellow and red striped umbrellas. There is a wooden bar with modern, stainless-steel lamps hanging above it.

'Oh darling, what a beautiful beach club of Silvan and Frederico, isn't it?' says Margot. 'I love these kinds of places.'

My phone pings and I read *That spring is quite dry* in the message. Roger has seen the picture of the well. *We should have Lorenzo check on that.*

'Have you seen that menu yet? All such tasty dishes,' says Margot. 'Look, *polpo* is fresh octopus, but then sliced very thinly and marinated in something acidic. How delicious is that!'

She tosses ice cubes into my glass and pours sparkling water. The restaurant is still empty, early in the season there are few tourists. A man is at the bar refilling the ice. 'Silvan,' Margot calls out. 'Now, this is Mirella, from that house in the valley I told you about.'

Her index finger wiggles back and forth in front of my face, as if it might be unclear who she's talking about. Silvan approaches. He has his long hair tied up in a ponytail, which he will probably let down tonight when he is on stage with his band, as Margot said.

'Welcome,' Silvan says, and shakes my hand. 'Frederico and I have already said to each other that we admire you in advance. That you are going to restore such an old house and emigrate to our country with your family.'

'Thank you,' I say. 'You have a nice restaurant.'

He nods happily as he looks around. On the terrace a man is looking at his phone.

'Oh, he's cute, isn't he?' Margot says when Silvan is gone. 'This beach club has been in the family for generations, ever since that little harbor was here, he told me this afternoon. His grandfather used to be the bartender here and the fishermen came in the morning to drink their espresso and share tough sailor stories.'

'Nice. Shall we order now?' I ask. 'I'd like to eat something after a day of lugging.'

Margot looks at the menu. 'I don't understand what it says here, do you?' She reads it aloud, stumbling over the Italian words. 'No, I really don't understand.'

'I'll look it up on my phone for you,' I say.

She waves her menu. 'Frederico, *tesoro, qui, qui!*'

The man on the other side of the terrace looks up from his phone.

'Yes, he needs to come over,' Margot says. '*Tesoro* means darling, and *qui* is here. Oh, nice language it is, that Italian, and I pick it up so quickly. He's beautiful, isn't he? And he knows that himself, I think. Look at him wiggling his hips.'

Frederico still has his phone in his hand when he comes up to us, as if he would have preferred to continue with what he was doing.

'I just read that it's better to wear your pants just above the ankle, sweetheart,' he says, running his finger over the screen of his phone.

'Fashion is so important. It's all about your appearance, how you present yourself.'

He runs his eyes over my dress, leaning over to get a better look at my shoes.

'Margot, sweetheart, you're all in style, but your friend we have to make her more fashionable,' he says, pointing to my dress. 'You're too plain, sweetie pie. Everything on you is bland, there is no striking color or good cut in your outfit.'

'Yes, I tell her that so often too,' Margot says. 'Yes, darling, that's true, isn't it? But she doesn't dare to wear anything that is too tight or outstanding.'

'Shame on you, shame on your beautiful body, sweetheart,' he says to me.

'What are you doing here in the restaurant?' Margot asks. 'You belong somewhere where the streets are catwalks.'

'That's what I always say to Silvan, sweetie. Seriously. A restaurant is not for me, all that fiddling to prepare food. But he doesn't believe me, no no, really, I keep saying let's go to Milan. But he won't do it, and now I'm sitting here with pants that are too long.'

'Yes, terrible for you,' I say.

'Exactly, sweetheart. But what do you do about it, huh? Well, shall I get you a nice bottle of *vino*?'

'Well, Frederico, I thought you'd never ask,' Margot laughs. 'We'd like that nice wine, uh, what's it called again? The one that I drank here with you yesterday afternoon when she was in town. Yeah, she likes that too. Oh yes, pecorino. Yes, that is such a nice grape. They grow them locally here, darling, that's what they make their wines from, so flavorful. Actually, we should import it, because you can't buy it at home, you know.'

'Sweethearts, it's coming *subito*.' He drifts away.

'He's so cute,' Margot says. 'Silvan is nice too, but much more serious. He must have got that from his grandfather. He told me that his grandfather in the early days carried a girl out of the sea here. There must have been something wrong, you know, with that child, otherwise you wouldn't walk into the water. In the winter.'

Lunedì, 17 Luglio 1939

She chopped off the cod's head, harder than necessary, and began to fillet it hastily.

'Are you all right?' Rafaella asked. 'You never act this way.'

'I'm fine,' Sofia said. The sharp blade slid through the fish and within minutes she tossed some of the cleaned fish into the box Marta would retrieve. She tried to hide her unstable feelings deep below the surface; it was oppressive and painful.

'You're heartbroken,' Rafaella said.

'No, I'm over it,' she said. 'It was a flirtation and didn't mean anything.'

She'd been avoiding Danilo for the past two weeks. She longed for his fragrance, his eyes, his smile, his voice and their conversations. The woman with red lipstick overshadowed everything. After Sofia had run away that night, she hadn't gone home. She wandered the city for hours. Past illuminated shop windows displaying skirts in bright colors that were so different from the brown skirt she wore every day, the color of which was slowly fading. The toes of her leather shoes were worn bare. Her own reflection in the shop window made clear what her mother and Rafaella kept saying; she would always come second, not good enough for a boy beyond her means. She had gone to the police station to report Mr. Marinolli. The policeman who heard her story said he couldn't do anything without evidence and had sent her away. With a strong whipping motion she threw the rest of the filleted cod into the box and roughly pulled the next fish across the workbench with her fingers in its eye sockets. Angry, she chopped off its head.

'Listen, everyone,' Marta yelled loudly across the tiled room. The girls stopped working. 'We're going to have a visitor in twenty minutes. Hurry up, mop the floor, empty the trash cans of fish heads, bones and fins, scrub the work tables. Rafaella, the small windows at the top can be opened, to let in some fresh air. When everything is clean, you come and get a fresh apron, put a new fish at your workplace and make one neat cut.'

Everyone ran from their places to do what Marta asked.

'I think Mr. Marinolli is coming to inspect,' Rafaella said quickly. 'Then Marta always panics, even though it's a fishmonger's shop. It will always smell like fish here.'

Sofia was shocked. Two weeks had passed since she turned on the lights in the warehouse. Had he recognized her? Perhaps the police had told him about her report?

Right on time, all the girls were ready behind their workbenches, waiting for the inspection. Nothing happened for ten minutes, the room was quiet. Secretly everyone enjoyed the tranquil moment. The double swinging door opened, Marta came in and next to her was Danilo in a light-gray, three-piece suit and carrying a briefcase under his arm. A sigh of relief filled the workspace. Quickly Sofia smoothed her hair.

'Inspection by Mr. Danilo Marinolli,' Marta said loudly. 'Filet the fish and show that you can do it fast and well.'

The girls immediately grabbed their knives. Sofia's hand trembled. She tried to cut, but she hit the bone. The scent of summer blossoms next to her.

'Sofia,' he said softly. The sound of the knives on the metal benches in the room was silenced. Slowly she took her eyes off the fish and looked at him.

'It wasn't what you think,' he whispered.

'She's not our best girl,' Marta said, standing next to them. 'I kept her because she was sent to me by you. To be honest, I'm just as happy to let her go.'

'I want to talk to you,' Danilo said to Sofia. 'Will you step outside with me?'

Marta stared at them uncomprehendingly as Sofia took off her apron and walked around her table without looking at him.

'I'll write it down as her break time, Mr. Danilo sir,' said Marta. 'No problem.'

Outside they walked into the narrow alley next to the low building, out of sight of passersby.

'Sofia, I'm not like my father,' Danilo said. He stood slightly crooked. 'You have to believe me.'

He wanted to stroke her cheek, but pulled his hand back. Again, he held out his hand hesitantly, she turned her head away.

'Everyone warned me about you,' she said disappointedly, when she finally dared to look at him. 'But I believed in us.'

She looked away, so did he. They seemed to drift apart. He sighed deeply.

'I'm building your house,' he said.

She glanced up, her eyes wide with surprise. 'What do you mean?'

'Your drawing was perfect, almost as good as an architect's. I have had the construction plans adjusted accordingly.'

She didn't understand him.

'Did Stella like the drawing and does she want to live in a house I drew?' she asked.

'I want to be with you,' he replied.

Her breath caught in her throat. The blood drained from her face and her ears were ringing lightly.

Be with her? Did he want to be with her?

'Don't you want that?' he asked. 'I miss us, together on the beach. With you I can talk about things I can't talk about with anyone else. My winery, your designs. About a future in which both of us can choose what we want to do, without every day being predictable. You see me like no one else sees me.'

She loved him. How could she not love him?

'I don't think I can be with you,' she said.

'Why not?'

'There are many reasons, but the main one is your relationship with another woman.'

'I'm not in a relationship with Stella.'

Should she believe him? He smiled gently at her, but waited patiently while she thought.

'I don't come from a rich family, I'm not a good housewife. And then there's your father…'

'My father will leave you alone. He will respect you as soon as he knows I chose you.'

He chose her. His sweet words took her back into the dream she didn't want to wake from. Not now, not in this moment.

Domenica, 19 Novembre 1939

The warm summer months had turned into autumn with heavy storms and rain showers. In the pouring rain, Sofia and Danilo ran to the entrance of the house. Large puddles formed in the grass, where the construction vehicles with their heavy loads had created deep potholes. Muddy water splashed up on her skirt. Danilo pulled her behind him by her hand. She stopped him, right in front of the entrance. Rain poured down on her face as she looked up.

'The balcony is wrong,' she said. 'The pattern is different. It looks too harsh on this house.'

The cast concrete balcony with its railing decorated with circles and arrows looked nothing like the graceful wrought-iron balcony she had drawn.

'My father wants to express his support for Mussolini,' Danilo said. 'He has been a member of the Blackshirts for years.'

'What does that mean?'

'He believes in the fascist movement. That we must be a nation with a strong leader who decides everything for the people. The shapes of the balcony resemble their symbols. I don't believe in it myself, but I had no voice in this.'

'It's not pretty, though,' Sofia said.

They ran into the hall with its high ceiling and she wrung the water out her ponytail. He picked up his cap, shook it off. Drops flew from it. She gave him a playful push; he wrapped his arms around her waist and kissed her neck.

'What do you think?' he asked. 'You have designed your first house!'

The red-and-white marble staircase with a graceful wrought-iron railing had turned out well.

'Very special,' she said. 'And yet the house already existed in my dreams. I saw us living here and knew what it felt like.'

In the space to the right of the hall, the grapes would soon be brought in through the small hatch next to the stable doors. They would fall into a marble gutter behind it and rolled over to a large vat to ferment.

They walked up the stairs to the kitchen with a fireplace on the first floor. There was a white enamel stove along the wall on one side, and a small stone countertop on the other, next to the two tall windows. The sea was visible in the distance through the window, which had no glass in it yet. The sun breaking through the gray clouds fell on the wall, forming a soft pattern in the still half-wet stucco.

'So just the windows and the floors are left to do?' Sofia asked.

'Yes, everything will be ready in two weeks. What color shall I have the walls painted?'

The lighting was special, and the colors came naturally to her.

'Light blue, the way the sky colors at sunset. Or a gray-green shade like the color of olive trees.'

He nodded. 'I believe I understand you. And what kind of tiles shall I have on the floors?'

'Hand-painted tiles,' she said firmly. 'It will be beautiful.'

'Yet it will always pale in comparison to your beauty,' he said, and gave her a kiss. He walked away to another room and returned with a present wrapped in expensive paper.

'Do you want…' he said.

He seemed to be searching for the right words and looked away. The moment he looked back at her, his eyes seemed greener than ever before as they caught the wonderful light beaming through the window.

'Would you… No, why don't you open my present first?' he said.

He handed it to her.

What did he want to ask her?

She untied the bow.

'It's fragile,' he warned her.

She unwrapped it. Inside the box was a hand-blown vase. Graceful and shiny blue. Way too expensive for her to have bought for herself. Did he want her to come live here, to marry her? Is that what he was trying to say with this vase?

'It's really beautiful,' she said, kissing him. She put the vase on the mantelpiece, distanced herself. Yes, it was beautiful.

'Do you want to…' he asked.

Yes, she wanted. Fresh flowers every week, for a lifetime. With him. His father, she never wanted to see him again, but he was clearly different. He had not inherited his father's character. She wanted to be with him, not with Stefano, the sweet, safe boy next door her mother had chosen. She moved a little closer to him.

He smiled at her. 'Do you want to have dinner with me here, every

Sunday?'

The wall behind Danilo moved. The sun disappeared behind a cloud; the room went dark. Have dinner? Rain pattered through the open window onto the floor. Drops on the floor. Dinner on Sunday? And what about the other days? He seemed so close, but yet so far away.

'Do you like that idea? I'll have the furniture sent next week. A dining table, chairs, a bed. Then we'll meet here on Sunday, instead of somewhere in the city on the street…'

He wanted to keep her out of town, not to be seen with her. He wanted her as a mistress.

'I'll buy you a motorcycle, a new one, would you like that? Then you can come here on Sunday whenever you want and start cooking. You like independence, I know.'

Cramps in her stomach, a wave of sickness.

'As soon as I can get away from my family on Sunday, I'll come over here to have dinner with you. Maybe we can even stay the night?'

She ran out of the house, into the rain. He wanted her as his mistress.

'I love you,' he called after her.

Domenica, 17 Dicembre 1939

The winter brought a heavy storm, which meant that it might start snowing. Sofia said goodbye to her mother and sisters who were playing cards.

'Are you going outside in this bad weather?' her mother asked. She looked at her in disbelief. When high waves formed in the bay and a cold air swept through the streets, the city fell silent and no one walked out on the streets unless it was really necessary.

'You know your father drowned in this kind of weather,' her mother warned.

'Mother, why don't you let her go?' Sienna said, winking at Sofia.

Sienna and Angelina wanted to be woken up by her tonight and hear all about her romance with Danilo, the man she still believed in, even though he almost broke her.

'It's your turn to play a card, Mother,' Angelina said, motioning for Sofia to leave quickly.

The wind howled around her head as she pulled the key to the small storage room from her coat pocket. She rode down the long coastal road on the brand-new red motorcycle Danilo had bought for her. At work Rafaella had called her naive. She was not. She was merely eighteen and in love for the first time.

It was raining and an earthy smell wafted up, drifting in through the first-floor kitchen window. The grain field below was empty and brown; the harvest was in; the land was plowed. The different-colored oleanders, which she had shown Danilo at the end of the summer at the nursery further down the valley and which he had planted by a gardener, swayed in the storm. Once they had grown several feet high, their sweet scent would drift through all the windows and spread throughout the house. The bleak wind came in, pushing the wooden interior shutters further open. She closed the window.

The kitchen timer rang and she opened the oven, shoved in the baking tray with the fresh tomatoes from the vegetable garden. She sprinkled the tomatoes with dried rosemary, basil, and salt, and drizzled them with extra virgin olive oil. Soon she would cook the homemade pasta and make the fresh pesto.

She lit the candle on the dining table and pulled her thick shawl tighter around her shoulders. Although the fire crackled in the fireplace and gave a warm glow, it was never completely reliable. That's why, just in case, she extinguished it at night when she crawled under the colorfully stitched woolen blankets with Danilo to sleep for a few hours before driving back to the city at first light.

As soon as she heard his footsteps on the stairs, she lowered the pasta into the boiling water. The kitchen door swung open, he smiled at her.

'The roads out of town are dangerous with all of this rain,' he said. 'What a storm. Was it not difficult for you on the motorcycle this morning?'

He took off his scarf, wrapped his arms around her waist and kissed her softly. She ran her hands through his hair, softly swept aside the errant lock that was always falling across his forehead, and stroked his neck.

They drank wine. The flame of the candle danced between them, casting shadows on the white lace tablecloth.

'The house is quiet during the day without you,' she said. 'And I don't like to cook.'

'I wish everything was different,' he replied.

Did he really want that? She was never sure after a day alone in his house.

'You know I love you,' he said.

Was that so? They were more without each other than with each other. But when they were together, the rest of the world wasn't there. When they lay in the bed in the bedroom next to the kitchen, under the covers, gently caressing each other's warm skin. When they kissed passionately as if every kiss could be the last.

'Something happened that I need to tell you,' he said gravely.

It started to rain harder. Other than that, it was quiet.

Terribly quiet.

Too quiet.

She listened to his breathing. Too fast. His lips moved. No, don't say it. No.

'I'm engaged,' he said softly.

First the flame of the candle moved slowly to the rhythm of his words, then quickly to the rhythm of her increasingly frenetic breathing. The walls parted. The kitchen receded into the background. Further and further away. Her head was spinning, a wave of sickness set in. She grabbed the edge of the table with both hands. Her hands trembled.

'Sofia!'

His voice, so far away. The kitchen timer rang, the smell of roasted tomatoes. The water in the pasta pot boiled over. A chair slid across the floor.

'Sophia, please.'

His hand on her shoulders, his mouth by her cheek. She pushed him away. He grabbed her shoulders again, pulling her toward him.

After their nights together, had he driven back to town to get into bed with Stella? How could she be so stupid. There had been so many signals, yet she let it happen. His father, he did what his father did.

'My parents chose her. Stella can't help it.'

The ceiling was spinning, faster and faster. Stella. The elegant Stella. She fell off her chair, hitting the concrete floor, which had yet to be tiled, hard. She was gently pulled up, lifted, carried. Placed on the bed in the bedroom next to the kitchen. The smell of burnt tomatoes.

'If I don't marry her, my father will disinherit me,' Danilo said. 'Our love is forbidden, a secret, it may not exist.'

Her throat swelled. Engaged? They were in love, and now he was engaged to someone else? Arrows of fire shot through her brain, hitting the sides of her head and shattering and crackling before she was able to make sense of it. Talking was no longer possible. She lay on the bed crying. He stroked her hair, her cheek, and wiped her tears with his handkerchief.

'I loved you,' she said, sobbing.

'I still love you,' he said. 'And I'll never be able to forget you. Never.'

It was cold, she was shivering. He put a woolen blanket over her. She kept shivering, he crawled under the blanket with her. Close together, as one, their bodies against each other. She didn't want to let him go. He kissed her, she kissed back. Long and intense. Their hands moved over each other's bodies, searching for that moment in their own world, far from reality. She was young, just eighteen, and perhaps brash. Very brash, because they did what the church forbade them to do, which no one should ever know about.

4

It's only seven o'clock in the morning and the small boulevard is still quiet when I drink my coffee on the veranda of our mobile home. The palm trees sway gently in the wind, the umbrellas on the beach are folded and the sea is as smooth as glass. A man cycles past in tight cycling shorts, but has no intention of coordinating his outfit. An old woman walks a little dog with a pink bow on its head. Empty wine bottles from last night have gathered on the corner of our patio.

I walk in when my coffee is finished. It's quiet in Margot's bedroom. Her rhinestone-studded, black eye mask is across her face, her blond hair is tangled on the pillow. I gently close her door, walk down our wooden deck and across the dew-drenched lawn to the boulevard.

At the end of the boulevard, just past the white 1930s hotel, the sandy beach turns into pebbles. There in the small harbor of the village, men pull their fishing boats onto dry land. Their faces are charred by the sun, they wear high boots. A black cat meows, begging for fish from behind a pile of buoys. Under the awning, a man is unraveling the wet fishing nets and checking for holes. He stops and asks me to come with him.

'*Guarda qui,*' he says, holding open a faded green beaded curtain of a mini-shed. In the small square space of less than two by two meters is a display case where fish in polystyrene foam trays are placed on blocks of ice. Another customer comes in, standing behind me and suddenly I'm in line. The fisherman looks at me expectantly and I point to a mini-fish. He takes a piece of paper and puts four fish on it.

'*È solo per te?*' he asks.

No, it's not just for me, also for my friend who still sleeps in the mobile home. He adds four more fish. I do not like fish. I pay with a smile.

In the harbor parking lot, my car is parked next to a few others, but the size of the lot promises that it will get busy here in a few weeks when the high season has started and the Italians start making their way from the mountains to the coast for a beach holiday. The heat of the previous day escapes from the car when I put the fish in the trunk.

My phone rings. I answer quickly so as not to disturb the silence of the small campsite with the eight mobile homes, six of which are still empty.

'Good morning, Brian,' I say. 'You start work early.'

'Italians work in the morning before it gets too hot, but I don't call for that.'

I slip behind the steering wheel, ready to tidy up the house for a few hours. When I open her shutters now, fresh air blows through.

'I found the springs yesterday,' I say and start the engine.

'I'm not calling for that. There's something else I just...'

'Something went wrong with the transfer? Did the notary realize that my Italian is not good enough?'

'Relax, there's nothing wrong. I found an old drawing of your house in an archive folder of another house in my office. Apparently it was stored incorrectly. Not the floor plan you signed at the notary, but it is a drawing of the front view. And what is striking is that...'

The door opens and Margot plops down in the seat next to me. She is wearing a bright yellow mini dress. Her legs are tanned by the sun.

'Darling, I've been looking for you. You're not leaving without me, are you?' she says.

'Oh, how nice, Brian,' I say quickly. 'I'm already in the car, give me fifteen minutes, I'll be there in no time.'

'Really, darling, that freight train last night,' Margot points to the railroad just behind the mobile homes, 'I thought it was coming into our chalet. I was shaking in bed. That railroad is so close by. This only can happen to us, I thought. Did you feel this too?' She lowers the passenger-side sun visor and checks her make-up. 'Or were you out, because of the wine? Yeah, you must have been, you can't handle that at all.'

'Some people have to get used to it, someone said to me recently, because that's what you get here in Italy,' I say. 'The railroad track runs from northern to southern Italy, along the Adriatic Sea. It must be a beautiful ride; I want to do that one day.'

'Are we going to the house to tidy up?'

'Brian asked me to visit his real estate agency in Ripatransone.'

We drive through the valley where Palazzo Puro is. We don't stop, we drive further up into the hills. The road winds, the valley deepens, and there's no barrier anywhere. I clamp my hands around the steering wheel.

'Ripatransone is medieval, has a large square and a church,' says Margot. She looks at her phone. 'There are sights. Oh darling, we have to visit them.'

The narrow roads lead up to the highest mountain peak in this area and I'm relieved when I finally park the car under the city wall. My dress clings to my back when I get out, but the landscape of rolling hills full of olive trees, grain, and vineyards is breathtaking. In the distance is the sea.

The old, yellow bricks of the buildings give the city the same warm glow as the house in the valley. The cobbled streets are quiet and the only shop is closed. Every time we turn a corner, we enter another charming alley. A kitchen door is open, a cheerful conversation between two women rises above the clatter of pans. Waving laundry on a balcony spreads the scent of spring. The town houses are tall and stately, and Palazzo Puro would not look out of place here. Everywhere, neat flower baskets hang on the balconies and on the walls.

'Yes, you should do this too,' Margot says. 'These geraniums on the balcony of Palazzo Puro. Just too cute.'

She leads the way and keeps saying out loud whether we should turn left or right. She repeats what Google Maps dictates on her phone. She's searched for Ripatransone's top-ten tourist sights – but nowhere has a list gone beyond a 'top two' – and now we're on our way to the number one sight; the narrowest street in Italy.

'Oh, how sweet, look at this. This must be it,' she coos as she stops at a narrow alleyway between two tall houses. 'Would you like to take a picture of me?' She hands me her phone.

The alley, less than half a meter wide, slopes down to the alley below, and halfway up there are two small steps and a street lamp.

Margot steps into it. From below, an overweight man with a camera resting on his stomach walks into the alley. He wants to pass Margot. How could he have imagined that he would fit?

'*Signore*,' Margot tells him, waving her hand. 'You've got to step back, you know, and wait there. Yes, a little further. Just go around the corner, yes, that's ok.'

'I can still see his belly in the picture,' I say.

'Woohoo, *Herr*! I think he's German, don't you think so? *Herr*, darling, *ein bisschen weiter*, further. Yes*, das is gut, ja.*'

'This isn't the alley,' I say, checking her phone screen to take the photo. 'There's another narrower alley.' I point to the sign on the wall behind her indicating that the narrowest alley in Italy is to the right.

'Well, you better take this picture anyway. I don't know if I'll fit in that other one. Wait, let me hold my dress up a little. Do you see my cellulite like this? No, you don't, huh?'

We walk to the next alley, which is indeed even narrower. The sign says it is only forty-three centimeters wide.

'Well, I don't like this one. This one is missing that cute street lamp,' Margot concludes.

Ten minutes later we are in front of tourist sight number two from the top-two list; a church. The murals are indeed impressive. We light a candle.

'There are posters of deceased people here,' I say when we're standing outside again. 'Look, with their photo along with the text.'

Margot reads out the names and ages, and concludes that everyone here is getting old. She notes that the average age is just above ninety years.

A man comes and stands next to me.

'Could he have lost someone?' Margot whispers, trying to look around me to get a better look.

I shrug, put my index finger on my lips and say shhhh.

'Maybe we should give him our condolences. How do you say that in Italian?' she whispers.

The church bell rings.

'Let's go see Brian,' I say. 'He's waiting for us.'

Brian's real estate agency is located in an old building on the square. The old-fashioned doorbell rings as we enter. There is a wooden desk and two brown leather armchairs that gleam from everyone who must have sat here before us.

'I don't think he's here, darling,' Margot says.

'We have an appointment,' I say.

A few old drawings of houses are hanging on the wall. The details are fascinating. A balcony with a pattern of openwork bricks, ornaments above symmetrical windows.

'This front door looks like the front door of Palazzo Puro.' I point to an old drawing of an elongated farmhouse.

'A lot of houses in this area look alike,' Margot says. 'I noticed that right away when we drove up here.'

A door at the end of a narrow hallway opens and Brain looks at us in surprise.

'Sorry, we're a little late,' I say.

'You didn't have to drive by. I was going to say that, but you had hung up already,' he says. 'I could have brought the drawing to your trailer park at the end of the day. I'll be in the area for a home tour with potential buyers.'

'It's okay,' Margot says, moving closer to him and pushing her breasts forward a little further. 'It's good that we meet, because she's already told so much about you.'

I hadn't said anything besides mentioning that he is an Italian-English real estate agent.

'I'll get the drawing.' He walks back to the room behind the shop.

'You should have told me he's such a beautiful man,' Margot hisses quickly.

Brian returns and unfolds the drawing on the wooden desk. He puts a stapler and paperweight in the corners, smoothing out the creases.

'The drawing came from the folder of the house I'm going to visit this afternoon. It was apparently misfiled.'

'Never mind, darling, everyone makes mistakes,' Margot says, sliding closer to him.

'It was filed by the previous owner of this real estate agency. Look, the sketch was not drawn by an architect, because there is no stamp or name on it. However, it is accurate and even the correct measurements are already included here.'

The drawing is of the front of the house. The windows, the ornaments, the front door, everything is built exactly like that.

'The balcony!' I shout in surprise. 'It's different now with those circles and arrows. Here it has a graceful wrought-iron railing.'

'I noticed that right away,' Brian says. 'I'm surprised that everything has been included in the construction drawings that must have been there, except that balcony.'

'Maybe you should get a local smith to do a railing like that,' Margot says, tapping the hand-drawn railing. 'You can hang those geraniums on it.'

Brian folds the drawing back up, hands it to me and puts on his sunglasses. He opens the door for us.

'I have a business lunch,' he says. 'If I may give you a suggestion, here under the city walls are the vineyards of Adamo. He makes the best pecorino wine in the region and exports it to expensive restaurants in Europe. Perhaps worth a visit?'

Margot claps her hands and bounces up and down. 'I love tasting wine,' she says enthusiastically.

Brian lets us out.

We walk past the arcade near the old theater on the Settembre XX square where the hiss of an espresso machine can be heard through the open door of the cafe. We take a seat at one of the white marble cafe tables under ancient arches and order an espresso and a panino with mozzarella and tomatoes.

After the long lunch we come back to our car, which is parked in the full sun.

'What smells so bad?' Margot asks.

'Those are the fish in the trunk.'

'Fresh fish, delicious. I'm going to prepare it in our chalet tonight with rosemary and lemon.' She pops into the passenger seat.

'I don't like fish,' I say.

'It's going to be so good, darling.' She looks in the mirror on the sun visor and takes her eye pencil from her purse. 'If you taste them the way I bake them, you won't want anything else.'

Margot checks Google Maps and nothing it says is correct. The winery should be a fifteen-minute drive from Ripatransone, but we have been driving on narrow roads for almost an hour and are hopelessly lost. A woman standing with her daughter at an old house along the road points to an exit further on when we ask her where the winery is. We drive there and on a small white sign with gold letters it says *Adamo Winery, Le Marche*. In the distance, where the road heads towards the high top of another hill, it is difficult to estimate what comes after the sharp turn.

'Just do it,' Margot says. 'There are only vineyards here, it's small slopes, nothing can happen.'

I drive on slowly. The front of the car is tilted at such a sharp angle that the road ahead is barely visible. A tractor turns onto the road and comes driving in our direction. Excruciating slowly I steer the car onto the shoulder, one wheel sinks into the dry ground and I give a small scream. The tractor honks, the man raises his hand. I clamp my hands around the steering wheel, Margot waves back. When we are on the next hilltop, a rock wall looms up. The rolling hills seem to come to an abrupt end in a deep valley ahead. My heartbeat quickens, my palms sweat.

'This is not good,' I say.

I clamp my hands even tighter around the steering wheel, take my foot off the accelerator and shift the car into reverse. A delivery van appears in the rear-view mirror and drives right up behind us. He honks.

'Oh no, we can't go backwards,' I say anxiously.

'Just drive on. You don't even come close to that cliff; they really wouldn't build a road near it.'

'No, I can't. I'm going off the road. Oh, it's steep here. Can that car pass behind us?' I check the rear-view mirror nervously. 'No, that won't work. Let me have a look on Google Maps, how far is it? Does the road go along that cliff?'

'You have to stop now, darling. You are giving yourself a panic attack. As a flight attendant, I've seen that happen so many times. Come on, I'd better get you out of the driver's seat and drive myself. Yes, I think that's the best plan.'

'That scares me even more!'

I remember vividly the times I've sat next to Margot in the car as she flew through intersections, tore through a yellow traffic light, or whipped through a roundabout at high speed.

The driver of the van knocks on my window, but I don't dare take my hands off the steering wheel to open it. He asks loudly through the closed window if we have *un problema*. I shake my head and slowly press the accelerator again.

'Oh,' Margot sighs. 'All these men here are equally beautiful. Did you see those muscles under that T-shirt? Okay, darling, so follow the road here and at the end, uh… just before that cliff, turn right.'

We follow a gravel path down to a white stucco winery with olive green shutters.

'What a perfect picture that house,' Margot says, clapping her hands in delight. 'You can do that too, plaster your whole house. And those vines, oh, and beyond that you can see the sea. I love tasting wine so much, yes, it's good that we're doing this.'

There is a large, white-gravel parking lot with only one other car. A tall man in a white linen shirt approaches as we get out. My dress clings to my body again and I quickly wipe my hands on my skirt.

'*Benvenuto*,' the owner says, shaking our hands. His brown curls are everywhere, as if they themselves have decided that this is the ultimate haircut for him. He leads us to the wine tasting room.

'He's beautiful, isn't he,' whispers Margot, as we follow him. 'He's also high for an Italian.'

'Tall, not high,' I say. 'You think every man is beautiful.'

'Yes, most of them are.'

We step into the cool room with a vaulted ceiling. Along the wall is a cupboard with old wine boxes and bottles, and next to it is a huge fireplace. The owner invites us to take a seat at a long wooden table where the wine glasses for a tasting are already waiting. He walks away to prepare something at a bar further at the other end of the room.

'What a place, darling,' Margot swoons. She gets up and walks over to the owner.

'Oh, this ham, how delicious,' she exclaims. 'Must be so tasty!'

Further in the garden is a swimming pool where a woman our age is swimming laps. Margot and the owner walk back together laughing. He pours wine into the large crystal glasses.

'Adamo is going to tell us everything about these fine wines,' explains Margot. 'He makes them himself, you know, darling. And all organic.'

She subtly pulls her dress down to reveal her cleavage a little further. We taste the wines; first three types of white, then a rosé and we end with two different red wines. If I don't finish what's in my glass because I still have to drive, Margot pours it into her glass. Adamo says that his vineyard was built on the hills where the Romans used to cultivate wine. Can we taste the salty influences of the sea in his wine?

'You really like red, I see,' he says to Margot. 'Come along, I've got something you're sure to enjoy.'

We descend to the wine cellar and he takes Margot's hand to help her down the narrow stairs.

'So charming,' she says to me over her shoulder.

The space is carved into the rock and it is at least ten degrees colder than in the wine tasting room where we were just sitting. Small wall lamps illuminate the rough walls and large wooden casks are lying on their sides.

'The red wine is maturing in oak,' says Adamo. He pours a bit from the tap of one of the barrels and lets us taste it.

'Heavenly,' says Margot. 'It fits perfectly with the dish I'm going to cook tonight in our chalet. Yes, please, I would like to buy a bottle if possible?'

'Red doesn't go with the fish, does it?' I say.

She looks at me like I shouldn't say anything right now. Then she looks back at Adamo. And he at her.

'This wine has yet to mature, but I have a beautiful wine from a previous vintage,' he says. 'It's not here, it's in my warehouse. Shall I bring it by tonight?'

The woman in the pool. I'll have to tell Margot about that later.

As we descend the hill to the sea, we drive to the mobile home instead of the house, too tired from the wine to clean up the house today.

The street lamps on the small boulevard along the beach turn on. The beach and the sea are slowly disappearing from view. Margot has turned on a lounge playlist and is swaying to the music while she is preparing the fish in the kitchen. I sit at the round, green plastic table on the terrace, bent over the floor plan I'm making for the new layout of the house. I want to keep her as close to the original as possible, because she's already beautiful and we can reuse her layout.

'My God,' I say. 'There's Aron!'

As he comes a little closer, I see that he has a briefcase under his arm. Margot immediately pokes her head around the corner of the kitchen door.

'Hide,' I hiss.

'Ah, how dull,' she says and starts to wave. 'Woohoo, Aron!'

Aron looks our way.

'Are you renting this?' he asks, bewildered as he looks at our mobile home.

'Yes, isn't it just amazing? We're sitting here in the front row with a sea view!' chirps Margot.

'Do you live around here?' I ask.

'I had an appointment with Brian and his new clients. They've bought a ruin and don't know what to do. They need a translator because before you know it...'

'Would you like some wine?' Margot asks.

No, please don't, say no.

Aron says he would like that, steps onto our terrace and sits down opposite me. Margot pours him a glass. He smiles at her.

'What I was going to say,' he says, 'so those people are also buying a ruin, but you'll see, their marriage is crumbling faster than they can rebuild the house. And before you know it...'

Margot turns from the kitchen. 'Better not to talk like that, darling.'

He looks at her in surprise.

'You have to empathize more with other people,' she says. 'Some people think it's an adventure this way, they really do, you know.'

Aron looks away. I close my graph-paper notebook, get up and place the notebook on the table in the small living room with its lilac sofa and lilac curtains on the window behind the sofa.

'Ah, Brian is done with the customers too, there he is,' Aron says.

'How nice! Brian is such a pleasure,' Margot says, delighted, and grabs an extra wine glass from the cupboard.

Brian doesn't hesitate when Margot invites him for a glass of wine, he pulls out a plastic chair and sits down, tucking his sunglasses into his hair.

We eat the fish; Margot, Aron, Brian, Adamo – who arrived with six bottles of his own wine – and I. It's an odd group.

Aron is full of praise for Margot's cooking and I discover that he knows how to use positive words. Adamo tells us how the Romans used to grow grapes on his hill and Brian says that the housing market is picking up again.

'Darling, show Brian your drawings for the house,' Margot says to me after we're done eating. 'Brian, she's making wonderful plans in her graph paper book, you really have to see that.'

I pile up the empty plates and walk to the kitchen. Margot comes and stands next to me with the empty dishes.

'Please, get your notebook,' she says. 'Brokers like to see things like that.'

'My plans are not ready; they could be better.'

'Nonsense, you're way too modest,' she says, pushing me toward the living room.

Adamo enters the kitchen with the salt and pepper grinder and begins to help Margot. He puts his hands on her hips. Aron looks at them, Brian takes another sip of wine.

Brian carefully studies my floor plans and listens to my ideas for the new layout, looking at where I have drawn a living room on the ground floor in the space where the large vats now stand. The empty space on the other side of the stairwell becomes the kitchen, and the existing small kitchen on the first floor turns into a bedroom with adjoining bathroom. The narrow room near the balcony remains the same and next to it comes the bedroom for Max. And there are bedrooms for our guests in the attic with its high, sloped ceilings.

'I want to realize this while preserving the original layout and details as much as possible,' I say finally. 'I don't want the atmosphere to be lost.'

'Well, that atmosphere stinks otherwise,' says Aron and he laughs. 'Rat piss is everywhere.'

It's not funny. Adamo disappears into the bathroom, Brian takes another sip of wine. Margot gives Aron a punitive tap on the arm. She hangs over his shoulders and points at me.

'Look, my girlfriend, don't be mistaken about her,' she says. 'You know, she designed her own house where she lives now, too. She just drew it on graph paper. And then she arranged the entire construction with those beautiful construction workers herself. Yes, this surprises you, doesn't it, but she really can do that, you know. Show him your house on Instagram, darling.'

I open Instagram and hand my phone to Brian. He looks at the images of our house, far away from here, in the far north where it always rains.

Margot walks away. Aron tries to see the images of our house on my phone, but Brian is holding it a little bit too far away for him. Adamo fills his wine glass again and walks over to Margot.

'We can work together if you like,' Brian says to me. 'I'm looking for someone who helps foreigners who want to buy a house here, but have no idea where to start or how to turn a ruin into a holiday home.'

'Does this mean we're going to be colleagues?' Aron asks Brian, moving his index finger back and forth between himself and me.

'Your work is nothing alike,' Brian says.

'I now also know a lot about houses and renovations,' Aron answers confidently.

'That's definitely not true,' Brian says.

Meanwhile, Adamo and Margot have walked off the terrace. Aron watches them open-mouthed, as if he wants to say something, but can't think of what.

'You have talent, don't waste it,' Brian says to me. 'Your skills are exactly what we need here.' He empties his glass.

Aron stares into the distance. It is now so dark that the beach and sea are no longer visible, but the white of Margot's smile carries a long way. Brian stands up, thanks me for the hospitality and asks me to think about a collaboration. He leaves and Aron and I look at each other. I really have no idea what to say to him.

The silence becomes painful.

'What are your hobbies?' I ask.

Is this really the best I could come up with?

'I don't have any hobbies.'

Silence.

Also on the beach.

'And yours?' he asks.

'I like to renovate houses.'

'Oh yes, I already knew that.'

I wonder where Margot and Adamo are.

'Have you always wanted to be a translator?' I ask.

He shakes his head. 'We wanted to start a campsite here.'

'We?' I ask in surprise.

'Yes, and for my ex-wife and the carpenter it was a successful project. They have that big campsite by the sea, you've probably seen it, just outside Cupra Marittima.'

Just when I want to ask more about it, Margot and Adamo walk up again, laughing. Margot carries her flipflops in her hand, there is a loose strand of blond hair hanging from her bun. She holds Adamo's arm tightly. She drops her flipflops on the terrace.

'How's it going here, darlings?' she says, straightening the bottom of her dress. 'Oh, we had such a nice moment, back there at Silvan and Frederico's shower cubicles.'

Aron stands up, takes his briefcase and gives Margot a long look. 'A girl once walked into the sea in the winter. That place doesn't bode well, I can tell you.'

He walks away.

'Now he's bringing it up again about that girl in the sea,' Margot says. 'Why, I guess, that was a long time ago, right? And where has Brian gone?'

'Some men are not good at suppressing their jealousy,' Adamo says, kissing her neck. 'He's just making something up.'

It's almost midnight by the time I get into bed. I'm editing a few more photos of Ripatransone and posting them to my new Palazzo Puro Instagram account. Immediately a few likes appear. Max is the first to write a comment below the post. It says the city looks old-fashioned. I say that here you find that the narrowest alley in Italy, and a church. He doesn't find that interesting. Just as I'm about to fall asleep, a freight train rumbles by and shakes my bed.

Domenica, 24 Dicembre 1939

Sofia mia was gracefully written at the top on the writing paper with expensive family crest.

I choose you, Danilo wrote. *You see me as I am. I want to take care of you and support you in who you are. So strong, independent and talented. You are beautiful.*

He chose her, just as she had chosen him this summer. A week ago, he pushed the letter into her hands after she had finished her work.

This Christmas Eve, everything would change. Tonight, he would tell his father that he chose her. They would be infinitely happy together. Soon, he would be packing his suitcase to come to the house.

Her mother was pleased. Although her daughter hadn't gotten married, she had a good life as a mistress. She gave Sofia unsolicited advice: she shouldn't just keep her husband happy between the sheets; it was important that she cooked well for him, grew her own herbs, vegetables and flowers in the garden, designed her own family monogram and embroidered it on all his handkerchiefs.

A layer of fresh snow had fallen. She left the city center on the motorcycle with a heavy bag on one side of the handlebars; it held her two skirts, three blouses, and her underwear. On the other side was a paper bag with the ingredients for the *frustengo*, a sweet cake traditionally eaten at Christmas, which her mother thought she should bake for her man this year. It had been quite an expense for her mother, as she had brought walnuts, dried figs, oranges, raisins, cinnamon, white wine, and cocoa. The espresso that should be added to it should be made by Sofia in the house, her mother had explained.

It was dusk. Was Danilo now sitting down with his parents to tell them he was leaving them?

She drove through the village of Cupra Marittima where the street lamps were just turning on. Near the square, the men's choir was performing *hallelujah*, and she slowed down to listen. The beautiful tenor voices carried far on the square, bouncing off the tall houses around it. She sang along softly, as she had done this evening with her sisters in the church near the harbor. The Christmas lights over the square were mesmerizing.

The church bell chimed six times. She would be too late if she still wanted to bake the frustengo. She pulled the knitted woolen hat over her ears, and buttoned up her thick coat. She felt a sharp cramp in her stomach. She pressed her hand over it; it must just be nerves.

She quickly started her motorcycle and drove off. It was dark when she left the village and followed the coastal road.

After a few minutes, at the edge of the village, the valley loomed. The outline of the olive trees was blurred. It got colder. She turned to cross over to the narrow road through the valley. A large house stood at the intersection, and a family was sitting at the dining table in the brightly-lit dining room. They laughed with each other, the father slapped the boy on the shoulder. A car honked at her; she was driving in the middle of the road. She veered sharply and quickly turned her motorcycle back into the right lane. Her shopping bag with the ingredients scraped against an olive tree, a handle broke. Gripping for the bag with one hand, she again lurched precariously forward. Fresh snow whirled up as another car drove by. With a bang, the bag fell to the ground and the ingredients for the Christmas cake were scattered across the road. Oranges rolled in every direction. The paper bag of raisins burst open. She looked around, there was no traffic. After parking the motorcycle on the side of the road, she gathered the groceries together in the light of the house. Her mother had spent too much money to leave it out here on the street.

Swirling snowflakes covered everything in a thin layer of white. She pushed the snow aside and picked up the cocoa. And the walnuts. Beyond the road lay the dried figs. Just as she was looking for the oranges, a loud horn sounded. Startled, she looked up, headlights shining in her face. The driver was approaching her at high speed, the tires made a screeching noise as he hit the brakes. The passenger door flew open, a red satin skirt was being sucked out. It was close to her. She ducked sideways. The car door hit her thigh with a loud thwack. She fell backwards onto the shoulder of the road, pushed herself further to the side, away from the car. Where was it? In the middle of the road the car had slipped on the snow and spun on its axis. It skidded left across the road, hit an olive tree, bounced off it, and shot back across the road toward the wall surrounding the yard of the house. She heard the scraping of metal, screams, a loud bang.

The night became quiet again.

One headlight blinked, the other was off. A small flame came out of the hood.

Burning pain in her leg, cold snow on her face.

The door of the house flew open, a man ran past her.

'Oh, *Dio mio*,' he shouted.

Another man came running up and yelled too. He shone a flashlight on the red car. Sofia got up and pain shot through the knee of her sore leg. Her pain didn't count, she dragged her leg, she had to get there. The flashlight shone on the driver who hung hunched over the steering wheel.

'On the other side is a woman on the ground,' a man called out.

Someone pulled the driver into an upright position. 'He's stuck,' he shouted.

'I think she's dead,' replied the man who was bent down on the ground beside the woman.

Burning pain in her leg. She was close by and hardly dared to look. One of the woman's legs was still in the car, trapped under the front seat, her body was on the ground. Her head was turned at a strange angle, as if it no longer belonged to the rest of her body. Red satin, spread across the snow. She made a gurgling sound.

Red lipstick.

Stella.

The flames grew higher, spreading from the hood to the linen roof of the car. More people gathered around.

'His face is covered in blood,' the man yelled.

No.

She ran around the car as fast as she could.

No, don't let it be.

Someone pulled on the limp driver like he was a doll. High flames. A red Fiat 1500. The man's injured body, his face; the blood running across his closed eyes, his lips. He opened his eyes and looked at her, his lips trembling.

'Sofia,' Danilo muttered. He was breathing heavily. Snowflakes on his face, melting instantly in the warm blood.

'He's trying to say something,' the man shouted. 'What did he say? His wife's name?'

Sofia grabbed his face, shaking. Tears clouded her eyes.

'Danilo,' she whispered. Her voice was too soft and disappeared into the noise around her.

'Don't touch him,' yelled a man at her. 'He's seriously injured.'

This would have been their night, the beginning of everything. They looked at each other. Everything went silent.

'The woman lying here doesn't seem to be breathing,' she heard a man say in the distance.

Sofia ran to the house, shooting pains in her leg.

'An ambulance!' she yelled to the woman standing in the doorway, hands clasped over her mouth. 'Please call an ambulance.'

'Isn't it too late for them?' asked the woman.

'Please call.'

The woman pointed to the phone.

'The number,' Sofia asked. She grabbed the receiver off the hook. 'What's the phone number?' The woman dialed it.

After the short phone call, Sofia ran back to the car where the flames had now completely engulfed the car. Danilo. He looked at her. Her whole body was shaking.

'I'm so sorry,' she said. 'I am so sorry.'

'Stella?' he said, coughing up blood.

Stella with her red skirt in the snow. Everything was red. In a black night. He was with Stella and not with her.

More and more people came running from the surrounding houses, forming a circle around the burning car. A long chain of people passed buckets of water to extinguish the fire. The ambulance signal lights flashed in the distance. A police car came from the other side driving up with loud sirens, behind it the fire brigade.

Danilo was on the stretcher under a blanket and Sofia placed her hand on his. The officer asked her if she had seen anything about the accident. She looked confusedly at the officer and nodded.

'Don't move,' the nurse said to Danilo.

Danilo turned his head with effort and shook it almost imperceptibly. His dark brown hair was wet with blood. Her lips trembled; she rubbed her eyes to hold back the tears. 'No,' she said to the officer. 'I didn't see anything.'

The stretcher was carried away and pushed into the back of the ambulance. The officer warned her to avert her eyes.

'A woman was thrown from the car and it doesn't look pretty,' the officer said. He pointed to Danilo. 'And he won't make it either. What a loss, two young people on Christmas Eve.' He shook his head.

The ambulance drove away. She closed her eyes. The police officer gently shook her shoulder and told her to go home. She grabbed her stomach. Stitches in her side. Nauseous, she picked up her motorcycle and brushed the snow off the seat. The black sky held no new swirling snowflakes. The oranges on the road were crushed. It would never be possible for her to bake a frustengo with that.

Stiff with fear, Sofia was still sitting up in bed hours later in the large house in the valley. Her face was wet and her eyes swollen. Every now and then she dozed off to sleep and then woke up again.

The first faint rays of sunlight fell through the high bedroom window. The farmer's rooster crowed. She pulled on her skirt and drove through the valley back to the coastal road, to the intersection. Danilo's burnt-out car was still there. Around it the snow was colored red with blood. The shutters of the large house along the road were still closed.

The beach was quiet, except in the small harbor where fishermen were busy with their catch. She asked them what they had heard about the accident, but no one had an answer. Further along was a small harbor cafe, *Uccelli del Mare*. The bell rang as the door opened and the man behind the bar looked up in surprise as she entered. She sank onto the bar stool.

'What's the matter with you?' he asked, looking at her kindly. His black mustache danced when he spoke. He walked over to the coffee machine, turned a few knobs and the machine hissed. He placed an espresso on the bar in front of her. 'I think you could use this.'

Sofia took a sip. 'There was an accident last night,' she said.

The bartender nodded. 'Just so, I heard it from the farmer who brings fresh milk and eggs here every morning,' he said. 'An unknown man from the city shattered all the bones in his body from the force with which he slammed his car into a wall. He only said the name of his fiancée who was thrown from the car.' He made the sign of the cross. '*Dio mio.*'

Stella in Danilo's car. On the night he would have come to her to be together in the house forever, free from everything and dreaming about his winery and the possibilities of her house designs.

'The car door flew open,' she said desperately. It was her fault; she had caused everything by stopping in the road in the dark.

'Did you see the accident happen?' the bartender asked.

'Her car door flew...'

'Yes, that sometimes happens when someone accidentally touches the door handle. With last night's snow they didn't stand a chance. They didn't survive, I understand. The ambulance came too late.'

He crossed himself again.

Sofia pushed back her barstool, slid off. Lightheaded as if everything around her didn't exist, pain in her leg. She walked out the door without saying a word. On the beach. She didn't stop there. The cold seawater slowly lifted the bottom of her skirt. Danilo with his green eyes looked at her, across the sea, from afar. She heard his voice, far away. She held her skirt together with her hands as she walked further out into the sea. She'd been on the road; he'd been trying to avoid her. It was her fault.

Someone called to her. She looked over her shoulder. The bartender waved frantically from the beach. Again, the pain stabbing in her stomach, she folded her hands around it and cringed. Stella in red satin next to him in the car. Her skirt slid into the water. Cold. Emptiness. She had killed them both. Slowly she lowered herself, closed her eyes, the cold water streaming down her face. The depth of the ocean. She would go from the dark to the light, to the twinkling water reflections that formed her stars in the afterlife.

5

We drink an espresso on the terrace at Silvan and Frederico's. The sun rises over the sea, giving the sand a soft copper glow.

'Was it late last night with Adamo?' I ask.

Margot shakes her head. Her make-up from the previous evening is still visible. 'No, not so late. We did already have our moment at the beach, you know. When he slid his hands under my dress, oh, you don't want to know. He's got pretty strong hands, I guess from grape picking.'

'He's married.'

'Oh, I don't know, darling. We didn't get that far and...'

'I saw his wife in the pool.'

'Maybe that's why I haven't heard from him yet. For a moment I thought it was the sex. Well, it doesn't really matter.'

'That does matter. You don't want another man who's already taken, do you?'

'Well, try to find a good man who isn't in a relationship.' She looks away.

'How long has it been since Tom?'

'Almost ten years. But I can never forget it.'

'That would be better though.'

'Tom has done so much damage to me. Otherwise I would have been happy by now.'

'You don't know. Maybe it's a good thing you found out he was cheating on you all the time, so now you can start over with a man who will give you the love you deserve.'

'I don't think I can ever trust a man again. And maybe I don't want to either.' She looks past me to the inside of the restaurant. 'Silvan, can we have another espresso?' He waves from behind the bar that he's understood.

We drink our coffee in silence. Margot is willing to talk about her brief affairs and sex, but not about Tom who lied to her for almost eight years. Or about the fact that she was pregnant with his child and that her world was shattered by a miscarriage that he waved off as if it were nothing, while she was destroyed by it. After that, in the evenings she would sit next to me crying, until she finally made the decision to leave him.

'The contractor will come by the house later on,' I say finally. 'We're making plans for the renovation. Are you coming with me?'

Margot takes the last sip of her coffee and picks up our empty cups. 'Well, I'll see,' she says as she walks to the bar. 'Silvan, is there anything I can help you with?'

Back at the mobile home I grab my floorplans and the laptop. First, I want to call Roger, so that I can go over the plans with him which I want to discuss with Lorenzo. In the distance, I see Margot walking through the restaurant carrying plates and napkins.

When we arrive two hours later, Lorenzo is waiting in front of the house with a folder under his arm. Margot introduces herself and smells his shirt.

'Delicious,' she says.

He smiles at her, puts his hand on her back. '*Ciao, bella.*'

Margot clasps her hands in delight. 'Oh, another charmer!'

Shaking my head, I open the front door. Lorenzo looks at the dark room with the tall wine vats on the right side of the hallway. I flip through my notebook with the floorplan I have drawn and say I want to turn this into a living room. He writes something down in his notepad.

'That means we have to level the floor here with the floor in the hallway,' he says. 'It is not only too low, but it is also slanted. And we need to provide the space with windows.'

I nod. I had thought of this myself.

'What do you want to do with those rotten barn doors?' he asks. The tip of his pen is already on his notepad.

'I want to replace it with two French doors with glass.'

He scribbles something. 'And you see that the window frames have a curve at the top? That will be expensive.' After inspecting the other room on the left side of the corridor where the new kitchen will be, we walk to the first floor. We go to the balcony. Margot is in the garden picking flowers. Lorenzo picks at a section of the railing with his screwdriver, exposing a rusty steel bar.

'Concrete rot,' he says. 'You'd better not stand here.'

Because the railing is covered with moss and an old grape vine is growing over it, the balcony seemed as if it were made of natural stone.

'The balcony has to come off,' he says, pausing briefly between each word, as if he'd rather deliver the bad news slowly.

'It's dangerous,' he explains. 'You can choose: either you have the balcony copied in concrete – that is expensive, because a mold of this design has to be specially made – or you install a wrought iron balcony, you see a lot of them here in the region.'

I take a picture and send it to Roger. He'll probably immediately add a line to his overview for these extra costs, and this is probably exactly what he's afraid of. When I tell Lorenzo that we want to enlarge the bathrooms, he notes that we not only have to break through walls, but also put in extra support beams. Furthermore, all of the window frames are rotten and the single-glazed windows all need to be refurbished. He calculates on his notepad that there are approximately eight windows per floor, so twenty-four windows in total. That's not cheap, he warns me.

In the attic there is water damage to the wooden beams and the cross beams installed between the thicker beams are too thin.

'The wood rot is due to those plants growing out of the roof,' he says. 'Water has been seeping in here for twenty-five years.'

The ridge is more than five meters high and it is difficult to see exactly what water damage he means. The terracotta roof tiles have all turned white. Lorenzo explains that they will need to tear down the roof from the outside, tile by tile, and then replace all the wooden beams – which are expensive – and then apply a layer of insulation, after which the old tiles can be put back, because they are, in themselves, still good.

I take a picture and send it to Roger. *The roof tiles are still good*, I write below. Well, that's something.

Lorenzo isn't done yet. He says that something strange is going on with the walls in the attic. These are thinner than the walls downstairs and cannot withstand any earthquakes. There are special guidelines from the government that the construction must comply with and the only solution is rebuilding all interior walls or stretching elastic netting over the walls that can move during an earthquake and hold the stones together. Afterwards, stucco can be plastered over it.

There is also the repair of the shutters and the doors that are full of woodworm. The replacement of the wiring and plumbing. The damp spots on the walls inside means that the mortar between the bricks outside has become porous. It has to be tapped out and replaced. The old septic tank for collecting the drain and sewer water from our pipes needs to be dug up and replaced with a new one.

'And did you want to have the railing of the stairs sandblasted or not?' he finally asks.

Margot calls from the kitchen that she has found an old vase, in which the wildflowers from the garden look so nice.

'You've mentioned issues you didn't mention on the first inspection before we bought the house,' I say to Lorenzo. 'You told Aron she's beautiful.'

'She's beautiful, but a ruin.'

He explains that he based the first estimate on a quick tour of the house, and that it was not an actual budget for the renovation. The costs are often higher.

Margot enters the attic room with the old vase of flowers.

'Beautiful, isn't it?' she says. She looks around at all the stuff everywhere. 'So, we've got to deal with the treasures here too, darling.'

When we say goodbye to Lorenzo, Margot stands on tiptoe and turns her cheek towards him. He gives her a small kiss. I'm trying to figure out whether he cheated us in the pre-purchase inspection.

'Oh, how cute he is,' Margot swoons. 'Do you know if he's married? Yes, he would be, huh? Well, that doesn't really matter.'

'Yes it does matter,' I say fiercely.

Do all Italian contractors work like this? First a low estimate to complete the sale and then give a higher estimate?

Margot walks over to some boxes in the corner of the attic and looks inside.

'Sorry,' I say. 'That was way too rude. It's because of Lorenzo, who has come up with new problems he didn't mention last time.'

'It's all right,' she says without looking back.

I walk over to her and put my hand on her arm. 'Sorry, I mean it.'

She smiles again and hugs me. 'Go on, I know you want to call Roger.'

My feet dangle over the edge of the big old trunk I'm sitting on when I call Roger. As I tell him what Lorenzo just said when making the renovation plans, he types on his computer.

'This house will suck us dry,' he finally says with a deep sigh. 'I knew it. We're not ready for such a large project yet.'

'Would it be useful if you and Max come over here so we can talk together with Lorenzo?'

'That makes little sense. If he sends me his cost overview, I will first calculate everything myself and see how we end up with our savings.'

I hang up.

Margot, who is still busy with the boxes in the corner, looks around. 'It will be all right, darling. Just trust your own feeling with this house. That is very strong, I know it.'

We examine the chairs that have been eaten by woodworm, the wooden planks that are sitting everywhere, and old tables. Then there are the rusted mesh bed frames, broken antique chairs, empty wine bottles, mattresses, a light blue wooden wall rack, clothes, and more newspapers. Old doors and hordes of mosquito netting line the wall. Everything we want to keep – like the old, metal-mesh bed frame that will soon find a new home in the garden under an olive tree where it will make a wonderful daybed with a pile of cushions on top – we put in one corner of the enormous space, the rest, which has to be thrown away, goes in the other corner.

With my dirty hand I wipe a strand of hair that has stuck to my cheek and open the next box. Old magazines. In bright red letters it says in the top left corner: *Il Tempo*. The time. The first cover shows a woman in a mini dress with graphic prints. August 1968. Underneath is one with a beautiful model in a striped blue and white bathing suit. July 1967. Followed by a woman with a cocktail and cigarette. June 1966.

'You have to frame those covers,' Margot says. 'They are just too good to throw away.'

We let ourselves be transported to the Italy of the sixties; the island of Capri, a couple in love on a Vespa, an advertisement for red lipstick and a kitchen in the trendy color mint green. As the stack gets smaller, the covers change. The color disappears, the photos become black and white. A cover with a photo of an Italian man with small straight moustache and uniform. A soldier shows his rifle. A battlefield. Poverty. Raw images. 1948. 1947.

1946. I'm getting cold.

'They can go, far too gloomy,' says Margot.

'You know of what I have to think?' I say. 'The balcony with the circles and arrows. That is fascist architecture, now I understand.'

'Was that a building style? That seems strange to me.'

'It was a movement that emerged in the years before World War II when Mussolini came to power. Perhaps they replaced the graceful balcony with this one because they supported Mussolini?'

'I would just throw those magazines away anyway.'

I browse through the rest of the pile. How far do they go back in time? Suddenly shreds of paper fall out. A few words are written in elegant handwriting with large curls. I pick up one, the corner of which has visibly been nibbled by rats.

engagement
talk to you, know

The sentence doesn't go any further and I turn to look at the next snippet. They are parts of sentences, nothing more.

..car door hit
wall. I am so sorry.

urs, Danilo

The sender is Danilo. And a little further away I found a piece with the date.

Dicembre 193

There is no full year. I flip over the last two pieces.

Stella saw you and said that
    straight anymore, we spun and

      Sofia,
Please don't give up

Curious, I search for more pieces between the magazines, there is nothing else. I shake out a few in the hope that more fragments will whirl out.

    Margot comes to stand next to me. 'Did you find something?'

    I start to slide the pieces in position. 'Yes, a letter.'

    Large holes are left in the letter on the floor if the pieces are in the proper order.

    Dicembre 193

Sofia,
Please don't give up

                                      engagement
                                      talk to you, know

Stella saw you and said that   *car door hit*
    Straight anymore, we spun and   *wall. I am so sorry.*

urs, Danilo

'It sounds dramatic,' I say. 'The letter is from Danilo, but is it addressed to Sofia? He also mentions Stella. It's not a love letter, I think, it's more like a goodbye note.'

'It's a pity we don't have everything,' Margot says, turning over a few more magazines and shaking them.

'Maybe this has to do with the secret of that fantasy drawing?' I say.

'Well, I'm just thinking; two women's names in one letter, that's trouble in paradise. And I should know, darling.'

Mercoledì, 27 Dicembre 1939

The snow had melted and the road was no longer slippery. She rode her motorcycle from the valley along the coastal road to the city. Her heavy skirt was blowing in the wind, her tights didn't seem thick enough to withstand the cold. Her headscarf had blown off, fluttering around her neck. It was busy on the street. Her hands were sweating, she was startled by every car that drove by. Her body cold inside, as cold as the morning she lay in the sea. In that one moment when the seawater washed over her. The rustle of the depth. Danilo motioning for her to turn. She had walked deeper, until the bartender lifted her and carried her out the sea. Numb, she had sat in the corner of the bar with a blanket wrapped around her while he poured her rum. She hadn't warmed up since then.

Christmas had passed in the house in the valley without her noticing. No carols, no Christmas dinner as she normally had every year with her mother and sisters. Only emptiness and silence. She hadn't been out of bed; she'd stared at the ceiling at night and at the gray winter skies by day.

Her leg had changed color from red to dark blue. Every time that her stomach started to sting viciously, she had become nauseous. She broke out in a sweat. Danilo's bloodied face, his shattered body. Stella with her cracked neck. It was her fault.

She drove into the harbor, past the tall palm trees on the boulevard. Men were loading the ships and they pulled up large wooden crates with a pulley. The wind cut. On land, fishermen in caps, thick woolen scarves and gloves were unloading the catch. This place didn't seem to want to let her go. Just when she'd thought she could escape into the valley, she was thrown back into the life that seemed to have been mapped out from birth to death. Fishermen and net weavers; they proudly passed on their craft to each new generation.

She walked into the tiled hall where Rafaella was already standing behind the workbench, waiting for the fish.

'What are you doing here?' Rafaella asked in surprise.

'Something terrible has happened,' Sofia said quickly.

'I know, everyone knows,' Rafaella said. 'Of Danilo.'

Marta slammed a fish onto the counter. 'You here? If you come to work, you are late. I'm taking a note.' She squeezed her chubby body between two workbenches and continued on.

'It was my fault,' Sofia whispered. 'I was on the road and the door flew open. The car hit...'

'Where's your apron?' Marta yelled at her.

'Luckily, an ambulance arrived quickly, otherwise he would never have survived,' Rafaella said softly.

'What do you mean?' Sofia asked. Her muscles tightened, she held her breath.

'Close your mouths. Rafaella, a note for you too,' Marta snapped. She came back to their workbench. A new girl asked her something and pointed to her fish. Marta shook her head and showed her how to cut the fish.

'Danilo is in such bad shape they don't know if he'll ever get out of the hospital,' Rafaella said.

'Hospital?' Without waiting for an answer, she ran off. He was still alive, she had to see him, embrace him, say she was sorry she was on the road. That everything was her fault.

'Where do you think you're going?' Marta bellowed after her. 'Don't even think about coming back!'

Nurses walked through the hospital corridors that converged in the high marble-floored and pillared reception area. Behind the counter sat a nurse with small round glasses and gray hair topped with a white cap.

'I'm here for Mr. Danilo Marinolli,' Sofia said.

Without answering, the nurse ran her finger along the names in a large notebook.

'Christmas Eve is not a good night to die,' she finally said. 'He had an angel to watch over him. He's in room 203. Visiting time starts at nine. You can wait there on the wooden benches.'

Sofia ran to the stairwell, while the nurse yelled at her not to go upstairs. Once in the hall, she had to catch her breath. He was still alive. She ran on. Her footsteps echoed in the marble-tiled hall.

She looked carefully through the small, round window of room 203. In the middle was a bed surrounded by devices. She didn't recognize him. His head was wrapped in white bandages, and both his arms were in plaster. An iron splint hung from the ceiling with a heavy structure holding up his left leg. She opened the door softly and walked over to his bed. He didn't look up.

'Danilo,' she whispered.

Slowly he turned his neck. His eyes were dark blue all around, almost black, and stood out sharply against the white bandage.

'Sofia,' he said in a fragile voice.

'I thought you were dead,' she said, kissing his lips gently.

His breathing was abrasive. There was a bandage on his chest.

'I'm so sorry,' she said.

'It was... not your fault,' he said laboriously.

The door swung open and a nurse entered with a tray. She smiled kindly, asked him to open his mouth, put medicine in it, then he swallowed and she gave him a sip of water.

'Your parents are coming soon, Mr. Danilo sir,' the nurse said, and walked away.

'I'm leaving quickly before your father arrives,' Sofia said. 'I'll be back tomorrow.'

Danilo slowly moved his head.

'Please, wait,' he said, placing his fingers on her hand, which was on the edge of the bed. His fingers were cold.

'In the car, Stella did...' he began.

She pulled her hand out from under his fingers. Stella's name again. He spoke softly, but she heard it loud and clear now. He hadn't been on his way to her, probably never intended to be. For months she'd waited for him, while he had been with Stella.

'Sofia, please listen. Our relationship, my mother did say…'
Sofia turned decisively.
'Sofia,' he begged.

She stormed out of the room. He was exactly like his father. Fierce stitches in her stomach, nausea. Why had she always believed in their love? In the hall she sank onto the wooden bench along the wall. Her body shook, a tear made its way down her cheek to her neck. A man and woman walked by; the man handed her an ironed cotton handkerchief. The abdominal pain lasted longer than usual, but when the nausea finally subsided, she went to the room the couple had entered. She waved the handkerchief in front of the round window. A silver thread monogram was embroidered in one corner. The man saw her and opened the door.

'Keep it,' he said. 'It's dirty now anyway.'

The mother sat next to the bed and stroked a girl's forehead and her long dark hair, which was fanned out in a perfect wreath on the pillow. There was just a glimpse of a soft blue nightgown, a small edging of white lace was just visible.

'She seems so far away, our girl,' the woman said in a broken voice.

'You better go,' the man said to Sofia. 'Our daughter is always asleep. Her neck and back are broken. I've always said those Fiat doors are dangerous…'

'My dear, don't start again,' the woman said. 'Stella needs us.'

Stella.

'That Fiat's hinges are on the wrong side,' Stella's father said. 'It seems that no one understands that. The front doors hinge towards the rear of the car. If you are speeding and the door is accidentally opened, the wind grabs the door and pulls the car completely off balance. Then…'

'My dear, please,' Stella's mother said. 'You're not helping anyone with your reasoning. How is this supportive for my girl?'

'I'm terribly sorry for you,' Sofia said to Stella's mother, just before her father closed the door.

Her footsteps echoed in the long hallway as she sped away. Danilo's parents walked by.

'Hey, that's the factory girl,' Danilo's father said.

Domenica, 31 Dicembre 1939

She awoke to the bang of the front door against the wall in the entryway and sat up. Voices coming down the hall. She threw aside the knitted woolen blankets, jumped out of bed, took a skirt from the closet and put it on over her nightgown. Footsteps on the stairs. A woman's voice explained that they hadn't been here often. A man spoke to another man. Naturally she put her hand in front of her breasts. She quickly put on her cardigan and slipped her feet into the slippers that were waiting by the bed. She ran a hand through her long dark brown hair, which was now full of tangles. Mr. Marinolli walked into the kitchen across from her bedroom, talking busily with the two women and another man. One of the women turned and let out a cry. The rest turned also around.

'What are you doing here?' Danilo's father asked. He turned to his wife and the other couple. Stella's parents. 'This is a girl from my factory.'

'I remember you,' Stella's father said. 'I gave you my handkerchief at the hospital.'

'My poor girl,' her mother said. 'She doesn't even know it's December 31st today. She's missing everything.'

'I don't understand,' Stella's father said, looking at Mr. Marinolli. 'Why is she here?'

'What the hell are you doing in our son's house?' he asked her.

Danilo's mother said nothing, looked around. As if she was trying to understand what was going on here. She and Sofia looked at each other for a moment. Did she recognize Sofia from the beach where she spent a summer with Danilo? His mother looked at the unmade bed and went to the shutters.

'It's already noon,' she simply said, opening the indoor shutters. The winter sun poured in through the high window and caressed her face. She opened a window and let in fresh air. Sofia dared to breathe again.

'I don't know if my girl wants to live here,' Stella's mother said, walking around the kitchen.

'I'm taking you to the police,' Mr. Marinolli said, taking a step in Sofia's direction.

'I think my girl should stay in town with us,' Stella's mother said. 'The engagement between your son and our daughter is cursed.'

'This girl has polluted everything,' her husband said. 'She's like a savage. Look, that dirty hair is full of tangles and lice. Can she even talk?'

Sofia looked at the coat she'd tossed on the chair in the corner when she got back from the hospital. An empty water glass sat on her bedside table next to the brown core of the previous evening's apple. Next to it was an unopened envelope from Danilo, written in the hospital and sent to the house in the valley. She didn't want to read the letter, but she couldn't throw it away either.

'We'll allow the wedding go forward,' Danilo's father said. 'And we'll take care of Stella.'

He grabbed Sofia's wrist and pulled her roughly toward him. Stella's parents took a step back. He yanked her down the stairs, so fast she nearly lost her balance. That grip again, just like the night he had grabbed her in his office. She wanted to say something, couldn't find the words. He dragged her down the hall, threw her outside. It was cold.

'Get lost!' he shouted. 'I never want to see you here or in the harbor again.'

A farmer drove by on his tractor, waved and shouted, 'Good morning, neighbor.'

'Wait,' said Danilo's mother, who was standing in the doorway, along with Stella's parents.

In her hand she discreetly held Danilo's letter. Had she opened it and read it? It was hard to see. Nothing went unpunished. Not the love between her and Danilo, not that winter night when she sinned against everything the church stood for, and not the reason for the horrible accident.

'Let her go,' his mother said. 'You go in, I'll take care of this.'

As the others walked back in, she came over to her and held out the letter. Sofia wanted to take it, but Danilo's mother held on to it. She gave Sofia a piercing look.

'My son has a cast on both arms and can barely move his fingers,' she said. 'Yet he wrote you a letter. Then you must be important to him.'

The envelope. Danilo's normally graceful handwriting was messy and there were ink stains where he left the pen on the paper for too long.

A window opened upstairs. Danilo's father reached out and dropped her handbag. He closed the window with a bang.

The bike ride was cold, long, and above all hopeless. It brought her back to the place she had left for a life that was not meant to be.

Her sisters embraced Sofia in the small kitchen. Her mother dropped her embroidery on the table and stood up.

'We thought you were dead,' her mother said. 'Why didn't we hear from you over Christmas? Your sisters were worried too.'

Sofia looked at her uncomprehendingly. 'Why did you think I was dead? I was in the house in the valley.'

'Mr. Danilo Marinolli and a woman were involved in a car accident. At the hospital they wouldn't confirm if you were that woman.'

'I wasn't in the car; his fiancée was with him.'

'Then I don't understand why you're only coming home now.' She picked up her embroidery again and was silent.

Sofia went to the bed behind the curtain in the room and took the letter from her bag. Sienna came up behind her. 'Will you come to live here again?'

'What kind of letter do you have?' Angelina asked curiously. She dropped onto the bed and started to take the envelope from Sofia's hands. 'A love letter?'

'No, a goodbye note,' Sofia replied. 'I don't want to read it.'

Angelina leaned over to examine the back of the envelope. 'It has a heart drawn on the back, so it's a love letter.'

'How long have you had it?' Sienna asked. She had sat down next to Angelina on the edge of the bed.

'A couple of days.'

Sofia turned the envelope, looked again at Danilo's name and the large heart he'd drawn as a seal.

'Please open it,' Angelina whined.

'Okay, but I'll read it myself first,' Sofia said. Turning her back to her sisters, she carefully tore open the envelope and took out the sheet of paper.

Mercoledì, 27 Dicembre 1939 16:00

Dear Sofia,

Please don't give up, believe in us. I want to explain everything to you, so you know I love you. Before I came to you, I broke off my engagement to Stella. She was upset. She got in the car and wanted to talk to you, to get to know who you were. In the car she told me that she wanted to offer you money to make you leave the city. You were sitting on the road in the dark and I was braking hard, trying to avoid you.
Stella saw you and said you were unimportant. The car door hit you, I couldn't keep the car straight anymore, we spun and slammed into the wall. I am so sorry.
Sofia dear, don't leave me. Wait for me at our house, I promise you I'll be back there. I only love you.

Forever yours, Danilo

Outside, the fireworks exploded, illuminating the water over the harbor. It was 1940.

6

The umbrella flaps in the wind, along with the dozens of other umbrellas neatly aligned on the beach. The back of my lounger is upright and I'm hunched over my laptop where the budget Roger sent is open. He added dozens of extra lines with costs based on an email he received from Lorenzo. At the bottom is a bold red number totaling all of the calculated costs. The amount for the renovation is four times higher than we had calculated in advance, which makes it impossible to restore the house with our savings.

'Lovely, such a morning dive,' Margot says when she comes back from the sea. She stands next to my laptop, soaking wet in her crochet mini-bikini, looking at the screen. 'Has Roger calculated it?'

A drop of water falls between the A key and S key.

'It's too expensive to rebuild everything,' I say. 'We can never do it speedily. And how are we supposed to live here if we will be on a construction site for years to come? Roger no longer sees how we can do it.'

'He didn't see it before anyway, did he?' She dries her hair, her breasts almost falling out of her bikini top.

'You have to straighten your top,' I say.

She pulls the triangles into place. 'I mean to say it's always been more your adventure than Roger's. You always say that he is so precise and never wants to change.'

'No, I always say he likes to be in control of a situation. And I take care of that as best I can, so that he doesn't get stressed in unfamiliar situations.'

'Exactly, and that's the opposite of an adventure.'

'In the end he and Max will love it here, once I've arranged everything. He just doesn't see that yet.'

I always convince Roger with my plans. He hangs on until the end, giving me space to carry it out. Once everything is under control, he will feel calm again. He settles down, and I look for a new adventure.

'Well, darling, don't make a big deal out of that, I mean, the house is beautiful already,' Margot says. 'You just fix up room by room while you live there. That's what those people do on that TV show *Living abroad* too, you know what I mean, right? Yes, that often goes wrong, that's true, but it doesn't have to be that way with you, does it?'

'I can't do that to a teenager, can I? Max doesn't feel like going on this adventure at all.'

'Ah, he will soon be very popular with the Italian girls here with his blond curls.'

I open a new document on my laptop. I need clear planning and a good approach, otherwise Roger would rather put a for-sale sign in the garden. Timelines with tight deadlines and clearly visible results at every milestone; I can do this. That's what I usually do in my job as a project manager. I send an email back to Roger and tell him I'll take care of it.

'Or you just start such a nice bed and breakfast?' says Margot, when I have just noted down the first activity – *looking for another contractor*. 'The house is too big for you alone anyway. And with the money you earn with those overnight stays, well, you can renovate another room.'

I shake my head. 'I'm not a caring type. I think I even like houses more than people.'

'Yes, I think so too. Anyway, I can prepare the breakfasts for the guests.' She lies on her lounger with her eyes closed. 'Really, my dad had a restaurant, remember? Yes, I'll stay here. Yeah, we should do that, darling, yes, that seems like the best plan to me.'

I send a message to Max to ask how school is going. He answers with *fine*. Then a longer message comes in: *I understand from Dad that we bought a ruin after all?* I say it's not that bad, he says Dad says it is. I reply that I am cleaning up the house and that I have found fragments of a letter. He asks why that is interesting and I explain that something happened here in the past that no one understands, and that the two sisters have asked me to sort this out. I type in the second activity: *making a list of jobs we can do ourselves*.

'Do you like that?' Margot asks, opening her eyes again and looking at me enthusiastically.

'What?' I ask.

'And I've already come up with the name: *M&M B&B*.'

'I'm not following you anymore.'

'*Mirella & Margot's Bed and Breakfast*, that wasn't that hard, was it?'

'Nice, but I don't want that.'

After an hour of searching on the internet I found two other contractors with whom I make an appointment for tomorrow to visit the house.

I call Lorenzo and tell him I'd like to come by to discuss the cost overview and determine what we can do ourselves and what he could possibly do at better prices. He explains that he doesn't have time because he is visiting the owners of another house that he is currently renovating. If I don't settle for it, he says he'll be back at his workshop in San Benedetto del Tronto by the end of the afternoon. I confirm to him that I will be there then, because I want to send Roger a first draft of an action plan tonight. Margot overhears and gestures that she will come along.

The heat of the past few days has lingered in the mobile home. I sit on the lilac leatherette corner sofa and start a video call with Roger to tell him what I'm up to. Margot says from the kitchen she'll walk over to Silvan and Frederico's.

'Darling, you know I want you to be happy,' he says as soon as he appears on screen. 'And you do have that urge to do things like this, but this time it seems like a nonstarter.'

'No, no, it's going to be all right, trust me,' I say.

'I always wonder why I went with this. I don't even know if I'll find a good job there.' His lips are tight and his cheeks are slowly turning red. He keeps pulling on his left earlobe. 'And we have to think about Max, and we've got...'

'Really, it's going to be okay,' I say again. 'It worked with our own house, didn't it? And we didn't just have to build that, I had to design it first.'

'I think there's someone behind you.'

I don't understand him.

He points past me to the small window with lilac curtains behind the sofa. I turn around.

'Woohoo, darling, look what I've got for us!' Margot yells through the small window. She's wearing a mint green moped helmet with two black stripes on it that is too small. Her blond hair sticks out loosely and the helmet strap is tucked under her chin. Her cheeks appear plumper than usual. She taps the window and holds up a bunch of keys. I wave her off and pull the lilac curtain closed.

'Sorry,' I say to Roger. 'Where was I?'

Just as I try to reassure him again, Margot sneaks in through the open doors on tiptoe. She waves a gray helmet and points at me.

'I didn't realize you were still busy when I looked through the window, so funny,' she whispers too loudly.

'That's not funny, Margot,' Roger says. 'Not everything in life is a joke.'

Margot puts her hand over her mouth and I tell Roger I'll send him a plan tonight. We end our conversation with an 'I love you'. When the computer screen is black again, I sigh deeply.

Margot hands me the gray helmet. 'Well, put it on.'

I pull the helmet over my head. 'It's way too big.' I grab the lower edge with both hands and move it back and forth to show her that it's the wrong size.

'No, that's fine,' she concludes. 'Silvan and Frederico don't need their scooter today. It's a real Vespa, you know, darling. A mint green one, just too cute. Those men have taste.'

The wind blows. I cling tightly to the rack on the back of the scooter. A truck passes us, the suction pulls the scooter towards it and Margot swerves, the smell of the tires on the asphalt. He honks, it sounds loud and dangerously close. Margot waves to the driver.

'Keep your hands on the wheel!' I say loudly.

She looks back and yells that she doesn't understand me.

The provincial road along the coast is busy. It's two single lanes, but the Italians around us make it into four. We leave Cupra Marittima and drive through the village of Grottammare towards the town of San Benedetto del Tronto.

I sit as straight as I can to look over Margot's shoulder at the traffic, her loose blond hair constantly whipping into my face. Every time a car noses out onto the road from a side street, I get a shock. Margot drives around it at full speed.

She looks back at me. 'We're doing great, aren't we?'

Finally, she makes a turn signal with her hand as if she were on a bicycle and turns left into the city. We drive through the small railway tunnel and arrive at the harbor area where we pass countless fishmongers and large sheds. The metal sign I found in the yard, does it come from here? Just when I want to ask Margot to drive around and see if *Marinolli Pesci e Reti* still exists, she accelerates into the almost empty parking lot by the sea and throws her legs in the air. She whoops.

Large and small fishing boats lie in the water. Buckets with nets are on the quay, the buoys and flags are drying. Some boats have large metal racks up front. Margot lets off the gas pedal slightly and points at it. 'That's for shellfish, they catch them with those boats. Nice huh?'

I answer that this also counts as fish which I don't like.

She answers with a questioning noise, and points across the water to a terrace with a striped awning in the marina.

'We can have an *aperitivo* there after your conversation with Lorenzo.'

Pleasure yachts bob up and down, sailors walk the gangways in sporty T-shirts.

I point out that we have to turn right at the end of the harbor area, where it changes into an industrial area. Margot turns left towards a long pier that juts far out to sea and encloses the harbor.

'This is the number one sight in the city,' she yells. 'There are big stone sculptures somewhere on this pier.'

Margot drives past the closed barrier.

I quickly tap her shoulder. 'This is not allowed!'

'What? You really need to speak louder, darling.'

'This is a pedestrian-only area!'

'No, I don't understand you. But all ok, I'll take you to those statues. They must be beautiful, Google never lies.'

We drive at high speed down the wide boulevard, which is covered with unattractive asphalt and enclosed by blocks of travertine to protect the harbor against the waves that break against it. The blocks are worked by sculptors. The sun is high, it's scalding under my moped helmet.

Halfway down the pier is a copper artwork in the shape of a large round circle with seagulls. An elderly couple is resting on one of the benches and signals that you are not allowed to drive here. Margot waves back enthusiastically. We swing around a fisherman who is walking along with a fishing rod and a bucket on the handlebars of his bicycle. He yells something, presumably that you are not allowed to drive here.

'There's the statues, darling.'

She presses harder on the accelerator, and I squeeze the iron rack behind me harder. When we get close to the statues, she brakes hard. I shoot forward against her.

'What a nice trip it was, huh? Please, help me, darling.' She bends her head towards me and I pull hard on the mint green helmet. There is hardly any movement.

'Oh, wait a minute,' she says.

I let go of her and she stands straight with a red face. 'I hadn't released the chinstrap yet.'

When she takes off the helmet, there is a mark on her chin and the tight helmet has left an imprint in her hair.

Via two steps we climb up to a small concrete platform of one square meter, where we stand between the life-sized stone statues. A man carved from white stone sits on the back of a dolphin, a woman in a long robe looks out over the sea, and another man sits thoughtfully on a rock. The coastline of the city, with the harbor on one side and the beach with all the colored umbrellas on the other, lies in the distance, just before the green hills that roll down to the beach.

'Will you take a picture of me?' Margot asks, trying to pat her hair into submission. She hands me her phone. 'I thought, of course it's nice when I'm sitting on the lap of that stone statue of that man by the sea.'

'I think we're supposed to stay on this small concrete platform. Look, there are all kinds of deep cracks between those boulders. That seems awkward to walk on with your high heels.'

'Darling, you don't want to know where I've been walking in my heels. They are high, but they are platform shoes, you know, really sturdy.'

She steps off the concrete platform and stands on a square boulder. From there it slopes downwards, towards the sea. She wiggles, steps up and climbs onto the lap of the statue which is on the last boulder.

'What does this look like? Me and my husband looking out to sea, just too funny. Do I look good on it?'

It looks strange on the phone screen. I step aside to get a better view. It doesn't help much.

She points to one of the boulders next to her. 'You have to stand there.'

In my flip-flops, I step over the crevices and stand on the designated block. Margot sits up and sticks out her breasts.

'Or shall I sit on his lap the other way around? Ha-ha, yes, that's a funny pose, hold on, darling, give me a moment.'

She slides off his lap and climbs back up the other way, so that she is now looking at his face. 'Wait, my skirt has blown up.'

'It can't,' I say. 'It's way too tight and too short for that.'

She pulls at the bottom of her green jersey skirt; her black lace panties stick out from underneath. She shouts, 'Never mind,' shakes her hair, throws her head back, and laughs. I take the picture.

'Yes, done.'

'Let's see what you got, darling.'

I step across a few blocks in her direction and hand her phone back. She looks at it. She moves her fingers across the screen to enlarge the photo.

'It looks like I'm having sex with him!' she says loudly.

That's probably an exaggeration. She holds the screen towards me and I lean forward. The sun is shining on it.

'Please, hand it to me, I can't see anything,' I say.

I stretch out my hand, she hands the phone towards me. She almost loses her balance. She grabs onto the statue's shoulders, struggles up on his lap, pulls her skirt back down.

'You see, darling, like I'm doing it with a stone statue, isn't it?'

'Give me the phone then.'

It takes two seconds and then Margot screams, 'Oh no, darling!' and I yell, 'You let go of it!'

She quickly scrambles off the statue and I step forward. We're looking for the phone on the blocks, it's not there. We crawl on our hands and knees, and peer between the cracks of the boulders. The fisherman with the bicycle and fishing rod passes by and shouts: '*I complimenti.*'

'Yes, I see it, darling. Here in this crack. Luckily, it's waterproof.' She sticks her arm down between the big boulders.

'Maybe we should ask that fisherman with the bike for a fishing net,' I say.

I walk back to the concrete platform, step onto the asphalt path, and yell, '*Signore, scusime.*'

The fisherman looks at the phone in the crack, shakes his head and says in as many words that the phone is lost. And that we are not allowed to drive the scooter here.

We walk down the pier pushing the scooter.

'Darling, it's a good thing I saved everything in the cloud, otherwise I can't even post a photo on Instagram. But I don't remember what number two and three on the list of sights are,' says Margot. 'Something with a square tower and a special garden. Shall I find out on your phone?'

'I have the appointment with Lorenzo and no time for sightseeing.'

Once we get off the pier, we drive back through the harbor to the restaurant we passed on the way out. Margot selects a table in the sun with a good view of the pleasure yachts. She waves to a man in a blue and white striped T-shirt who has just come out of the cabin of his sailboat. I study the route through the harbor to the small industrial area one more time and hand her my phone.

'Good luck with Lorenzo,' she says. 'Keep the conversation a bit short, because when you come back, I will surprise you with a nice experience that I will plan now. What is your phone password?'

As I drive through the harbor area, I come to a small-scale industrial zone. A weathered sign with the name of the contractor *Lorenzo Marchogioni, società appaltatrice*, hangs on the black-painted brick wall of a warehouse.

The high space is dark and dusty, and full of building materials. Long shelving units with screws, insulation material and paint. A tall stack of wood. All kinds of tools, of which I only recognize the drills and saws immediately. A man in blue overalls comes around the corner of the shelving unit and asks if he can help me. When I ask for Lorenzo, he points to the office in the corner of the room, which is brightly lit and where I see Lorenzo bent over a desk in his neat shirt.

'Sorry I'm late,' I say as I step inside. 'Margot's phone fell between those rocks by the statues on the pier.'

He looks at me uncomprehendingly. I sit across from him at the table, take my notepad from my handbag and draw a table on a blank sheet; with on the left a column *do ourselves* and on the right a column *outsource*. I want to work it out with at least eight to ten jobs in both columns before I can give Roger a good rationale for the plan.

'Okay, I'm now writing down *Demolition of the shed plus extension* and

Demolishing two bathroom walls on the right,' I say.

'What do you want to do with that list?' he asks.

'We want to do this ourselves.' I point to the left column, then the right column. 'And this is what a contractor has to do. Look, I write on that column, for example, *Replacing the beams in the roof.*'

He looks at it, shaking his head and sighing deeply. 'There are building regulations,' he says. 'Such as insulation values, bearing capacity, foundation principles that you have to adhere to. You can't do it yourself.'

Then he turns the screen of his computer towards me and starts scrolling through pictures of houses he is renovating. The finish on the outside and inside is of a high quality, he explains. Steel beams reinforce the old ceilings, new window frames with double-glazed panes, concrete floors with underfloor heating, modern kitchens with the latest equipment. Pools poured 'into the work', as he calls it, with piles to support them that extend to impressive depths. The houses are all perfect, almost as if they were newly built. Palazzo Puro without the interior shutters with peeling paint and with new double-glazed windows, does that suit her? Isn't she asking for something else, something more authentic?

'That's not possible for us, given our budget,' I say.

'So, what were you thinking when you bought the house?'

He clicks on to another file on his computer and opens a map. He has made a building plan for our house.

'Everything is ready. If Roger agrees to my cost overview, we will put up the job-site fencing around the house next week, so that no one can enter during the renovation. It will be ready in nine months and you can move in.'

Nine months is just as long as a pregnancy, that was also a long wait.

'Can't we go into the house during this time?'

'Yes, of course you can. Under supervision and with a hardhat on. Those are the rules for your own safety.'

Palazzo Puro would be far away. She would be changing without us, without us knowing what she'll look like.

Lorenzo points out the rooms on the floor plan that he wants to create in the attic. It's not the way I designed it. The bathrooms are too narrow, you can't stand comfortably behind the sinks. A door is in the wrong place, giving one of the bedrooms a strange corner that you couldn't do anything with. A window has been bricked up, and a new window has been drawn in another place. These are things that were different on my drawings.

'I'll print these drawings so you can sign them for approval,' Lorenzo says.

'The drawings don't match my drawings,' I say, pointing to the narrow bathroom.

'Your drawings didn't make sense, hence my elaboration of doing it this way. Of course, I can still change things if you want? However, I have to submit the plan to the municipality soon in order to obtain a permit, because it will take three to six months before we can start. Until then, nothing can be done in the house.'

Once outside the sun falls on my face and I close my eyes as I stand by the scooter. Renovations always require a lot of patience, flexibility and money, only here everything seems more difficult than usual.

When I return to the restaurant, Aron is sitting at the table with Margot. He's wearing Bermuda shorts in an indeterminate shade of green. There is a wet plastic bag on the table.

'Darling, it's good to have you back. How did things go with Lorenzo?' Margot asks.

I sit down. 'Good afternoon, Aron.'

'You won't believe it, darling. This sweetheart brought my phone! It's now inside, behind the bar, drying in a tub of salt.'

She pulls Aron towards her and kisses him on the cheek. He blushes.

'After her message, I searched those crevices on the pier,' he says.

'Did you text him with my phone?' I ask Margot.

'It was pretty deep,' Aron says. 'But I got it out.'

'With a fishing net, I assume?' I say.

He nods proudly.

That was my idea.

Aron takes a sip of his water. He loudly sucks the water out from under the ice cubes and swallows it.

'I understood from Margot that you have no money for the renovation?' he asks. 'Exactly what I predicted on the first day. I recognize the pattern by now.'

'We'll work it out,' I answer. 'We can do a lot of it ourselves; we have done that before.'

'You're not considering doing the work yourself, are you? That is not professional and before you know it you are not following the building regulations that apply here in Italy.'

'Shall we go back to the mobile home?' I ask Margot. 'I want to develop my plan further.'

'That's all right, darling, but can we stop at the museum in the harbor for a while? That was a tip from Aron.'

'Why don't you go together? He can bring you back.'

Aron nods eagerly.

'No, of course not. I'd like to do that with you.' She gets up and walks to the bar to pay and get her phone.

Old black-and-white photos of the harbor area hang in the museum. Fishermen pose in front of their boats; women wait on the beach as the boats are pulled onto them. Knotting ship ropes, weaving large fishing nets. A photo shows a warehouse with a *Marinolli Pesci e Reti* sign above the large doors. Exactly the same sign that is in the tall grass in the garden. Under the sign a man poses presumably with his son and a whole group of women in the background. *The largest fish trade in the Le Marche region, today still a family business in San Benedetto del Tronto* is written below it on a card.

Domenica, Febbraio 1940

Sofia was standing on the road by the house in the valley. The shutters of the kitchen were open, the rest was still closed. Was he behind the kitchen window there? If Danilo was home, he was here. The words from his letter echoed in her head. He had asked her to wait for him and it could only be here. News had quickly circulated in the harbor that he had been released from the hospital. For the past few weeks in their tiny house in the harbor, her sisters had been asking her whether she would return to him if she still could. When the three of them lay in the bed behind the curtain at night, they would ask her how intense love was, and whether this feeling could be ignored or not. Rafaella, however, thought he was an impostor and her mother wanted to solve the unfortunate situation by inviting Stefano, her boy next door, to dinner and giving him a place at the head of the dinner table. She asked if he had any plans to get married and thought Sofia was a good fit for him. He thought so too.

She knocked on the high wooden front door. It remained silent.

She knocked again.

Footsteps on the stairs, the key turned in the lock and the door swung open. Danilo laughed.

'I saw you standing on the roadside,' he said. 'You're home!'

The bone structure of his face appeared to have been slightly altered by the accident. He opened his arms and hugged her for a long time. His smell was the same. His warm body. They kissed each other.

'I thought of you every day,' he said.

'Me too about you. So much. I was afraid of losing you.'

His green eyes, his playful smile. He closed the door behind her and, holding his cane in his left hand, headed for the stairs. He was dragging his leg.

After transferring the stick to his other hand, he reached for the railing. 'After you,' he said, leading her up the stairs.

Her hand ran over the smooth, white-lacquered railing with its graceful curls. Light flooded in through the high window in the first-floor hallway and danced across the floor. Danilo hopped after her and gently stroked her hip. She looked at him, he laughed. How could she have considered marrying Stefano?

She walked across the narrow room to the balcony, opened the doors and stepped out onto the balcony. The sea.

'Coffee?' Danilo asked from the kitchen.

'Delicious,' she said, walking towards him. In their bedroom the shutters were still half closed and it was dark. She narrowed her eyes. Their bed, the blankets that kept them warm, and where they snuggled and made love two months ago. She stroked her stomach.

There was a moan from the bed. She gasped in shock

Danilo came and stood next to her. 'She does that more often now.'

Sofia took a step into the room. Stella lay in the bed, under her covers. On her back, her eyes closed. Danilo stroked Stella's hair that fanned out around her face.

'The doctors said we shouldn't give up on Stella. It is not clear how much brain damage she sustained from the blow to her head, but luckily, she will recover. Then perhaps movement will return to her whole body, and perhaps her speech as well.'

A woman her own age, no longer able to move or speak. And it was all her fault. Her irresponsible behavior in that one moment, those few minutes of standing in the middle of the road in the dark, had made her what she was now; remorseful and therefore more insecure than ever before.

'Why... is she... I mean, why is she here?' Sofia asked.

'The hospital can no longer care for her.'

Sofia's breathing quickened, her voice raised. 'What about your letter? You wrote that you had broken off the engagement and wanted to be with me.'

He looked at Stella, then at her. 'I'm sorry. I have to take care of her. Our parents...'

'You've never been honest,' she said doubtfully.

He took her hand. 'My heart is with you, not with her.'

Stella moaned again. A long, low sound from deep in her throat. Complaining, as if she wanted to say something.

'She hears everything,' Sofia said.

'She doesn't understand anything anymore. She's breathing, that's all.'

Danilo went to the bedroom window and opened the shutters a little wider, letting in the light. It touched Stella's face, which was white with dark circles under her eyes. Young and vulnerable, lost.

'I don't understand why she's not with her parents so they can take care of her. You broke off the engagement and we...'

Stella let out a long, deep moan.

Danilo came up to her side and put his hand on her shoulder. 'There's one more thing you should know about Stella...'

Sofia grabbed the footboard of the bed. She didn't want to hear it.

He sighed deeply and looked at her. 'The doctors have determined she is pregnant.'

Sofia's breath came faster, high in her throat. She became nauseous. Again, it happened again. The walls set themselves in motion.

Danilo grabbed her. 'Sofia, the child is not mine!'

Stella moaned loudly and blinked furiously. Sofia tried to control her own breathing. Her knees gave way. She sank to the edge of the bed, grabbed the woolen blankets, squeezing them hard. Her head was spinning. Everything had happened again. He always pulled her into his world where they were allowed to be together, and then pushed her out again. Danilo sat down next to her, grabbed her face and gently turned it his way.

'Sofia, look at me, please. The child belongs to another man.'

Stella's moan turned into a loud whimper. Danilo let go of Sofia's face and put a hand on Stella's belly. 'It's all right, calm down,' he soothed her. His hand caressed her belly. 'The baby is coming in August.'

A baby. She folded her arms in front of her own belly. Everything was suddenly clear.

'I don't know what to do,' he said. 'Everyone thinks I'm the father and...'

'You're going to be a father,' she said.

He shook his head. 'You must believe me, Sofia, the child is not mine.'

She took his hand and placed it on her own belly. 'You're going to be a father.'

Stella wailed.

Domenica, Aprile 1940

At the corner of the narrow street by the harbor, Stefano was reading the newspaper at a newsstand. Another man also bought *Il giornale della domenica*, and opened it. The newsboy shouted loudly that there was news from the front. She walked over to Stefano.

He looked at her wildly and the newspaper trembled in his hands. 'They predict that Italy will join the fight on the German side.' He pointed to an article. 'I've been called up.' His voice fell. 'Yesterday the letter came from the army.'

Stefano had just turned eighteen. He looked in the paper, then back at her. 'Sofia, I'm scared.'

She put a hand on his arm. 'I'm sure the war will be over soon,' she said hopefully.

'All my friends and I,' he said. 'We all have to report.' He slammed the paper closed. 'I have to go home. Pack up.' He looked at her one last time, anxious. Then he ran away.

At home, her mother was scrubbing her sisters' skirts in a large washtub.

'All of the boys have to report to the army,' Sofia told her. She went to the stove and put on a kettle of water. Every Sunday morning, when Danilo went to church, she drank tea with her mother and sisters.

Her mother looked at her and nodded. 'Many men in the harbor who support Mussolini have even volunteered. Can you pass me the soap?'

Sofia took the carton of soap powder from the counter and handed it to her.

'You'll have to go see Stefano tonight,' her mother said.

'Why? I just saw him on the street.'

Her mother stopped scrubbing and looked at her gravely. 'Because I see your belly. You are pregnant.'

Sofia quickly pulled her vest over her stomach.

'It'll soon be noticeable,' her mother said. 'You have to make sure Stefano thinks he's the father.'

'That's not possible!'

'It's your only chance not to have an illegitimate child. No one will calculate exactly when the child was conceived later on.'

'I can't cheat on Stefano with someone else's child, can I?'

'In a few weeks, when he's at the front, you'll write him a letter that you're carrying his child. It will help him, then he will have something to hold on to in the war.'

'It's cheating.'

'Do you want to live a life of poverty and shame? That's what you get as an unmarried mother with a child.'

'I don't even love Stefano.'

'He can provide you with a good life. He is a neat and nice man. His parents will welcome you with open arms. Leave the house in the valley and go to Stefano, now you can change your life.'

'I love Danilo and I'm carrying his child. I want to be with him.'

'He has a wife,' her mother said. 'And mistresses should not have children. You will be spoken of evilly.'

She grabbed a dirty blouse and scrubbed hard. 'You've always been so different from your sisters.'

'Where are they?'

'In the bookshop in the center. Mr. Armacci is missing.'

'Missing? How is that possible?'

Her mother shrugged. 'More people are just disappearing.'

She raced on her motorcycle to his shop. Her sisters were looking through the shop window with their hands over their eyes.

'We've knocked on the door a few times and called his name,' Sienna said. 'He's not here.'

'I walked around to the back of the store,' Angelina said. 'The planter was wobbly, but I could just see through the high window. His coffee cup is there.'

Sofia also cupped her hands over her eyes and set them against the window. Everything seemed the same as on other days, except the store was dark. There were some drawings on the wooden desk at the back of the shop.

'I heard he secretly printed partisan pamphlets at night in the space above his shop,' Sienna said.

'I hope not,' Sofia said. 'Maybe he was arrested.'

'Then you also won't be able to take any more drawing lessons from him,' Angelina said disappointedly.

'Come on, there's nothing more we can do here,' Sofia said. 'Let's stop by again next Sunday to see if he's back.'

On the motorcycle, she rode past the fields where the new grain was growing as the valley slowly turned a light green. On either side on the hills, olive trees glistened silver in the sun. The spring wind brought fragrances of thyme and other herbs that grew along the side of the road. Red poppies popped up among the overgrown grass. Her house in the valley. She was home.

Sofia brought tea to Stella in a porcelain cup with pink flowers. The same cup she's been using for Stella's tea every afternoon since she'd moved here. She put it next to the bed in the bedroom where she herself had slept for a long time, but which she had now exchanged for a room in the attic. Everything was so different from what she'd imagined when she drew this house and Danilo had it built for them. Not for Stella.

When she was in her room in the attic, she did her best to forget that

Stella was lying motionless in the bed because of what she'd done, but as soon as she went to the kitchen opposite Stella's bedroom, she could no longer ignore her.

She opened the shutters and Stella followed her with her eyes.

'Good afternoon,' Sofia said. 'You slept a long time.'

In the night Stella could wail for hours. Sofia tried to keep her ears closed by wrapping her pillow around them. Stella's every moan caused her guilt to sink deeper into her.

Stella made a noise like saying hello back. How would she feel about her tea being brought to her by a woman she thought of as unimportant, as Danilo had said to her in the letter he had written from the hospital?

She lifted Stella's head, plumped the pillow and placed an extra pillow under it, making it possible for Stella to sit up slightly. She picked up the teacup, checked it wasn't too hot and held it up to Stella's mouth. Painfully slowly she took a sip.

'Shall I read something?' Sofia asked. She set the cup down and brushed Stella's hair. Stella's days were long and monotonous. She barely moved and sometimes wet the bed. Her stomach was slowly getting bigger, just like Sofia's.

'Ba...' Stella said. Her arms lay motionless beside her body, only her fingers moved slightly up and down. Sofia took Stella's hand and placed it on her belly. Stella seemed pleased.

'Ba...'

Danilo sat in his shirt and trousers at the dining table Sofia had set for lunch. She sat across from him and poured coffee.

'Did Stella say something?' he asked.

'No real words, although I feel like her sounds are changing. Like she's trying to say something.'

'That is good news. Her physical therapist is coming in the morning and I'll pass it on.'

Danilo continued reading the copy of *Il giornale della domenica* that Sofia had brought for him. 'The war in Europe is spreading. Mussolini has to pick a side and it looks like he's choosing Germany.'

'What does that mean for you? For us?'

'We have to wait and see.'

He got up, put his coffee cup on the counter and kissed her hair. He walked into Stella's bedroom.

'Shall I help you get dressed?' he asked her. 'It's Sunday afternoon and our parents are coming soon.'

'Y-y-y...' Stella replied. 'Y-y-yes.'

Lunedì, Giugno 1940

Sofia straightened the white crochet bedspread on the bed in the attic. She had designed these spaces in her original drawing of the house as storage and drying areas for fruit, meat and flowers. The pitched roof was more than five meters high and the walls were not plastered. The bricks gave a warm glow to the otherwise bare space with a concrete floor. There were two simple bed frames next to each other, close to the window, with a view over the fields and sea. Along the long coastline in the distance, Danilo had spent the past few weeks driving from village to village buying up fisheries, so that his father and uncle's family business grew.

She opened the linen closet, took out a simple light-blue skirt she'd bought in town with the money Danilo gave her. She put on a blouse and a creamy white cardigan over it. The wide skirt made her belly less noticeable.

She walked into Stella's room, and found her sitting up in her bed.

'Which book do you want to read today?' she asked.

'Ne...lla vi...ta,' Stella said. Her sounds slowly formed into recognizable words.

Sofia went to the linen closet and picked up the book. *Nella vita del mio tempo*. She pushed her chair closer, opened the book and began reading.

Stella tapped her arm. She pointed to her own belly and then Sofia's.

'Yes, we're both going to have a baby,' Sofia said.

'Ba...by.'

Stella slowly moved her hand to her belly. The pupils of her brown eyes widened as if she was scared. There seemed to be a deep pain inside her. Sofia stroked her hair to reassure her, as Stella's panic normally resulted in long and loud whimpers that lasted for hours.

'It's going to be okay,' she said. 'Women can do this.'

How would this go with Stella? She was able to move her upper body again and her speech was slowly returning, but she was still paralyzed from the waist down.

'Can we talk?' Danilo asked, standing in the doorway.

Sofia closed the book and put it on the bedside table. Stella closed her eyes.

Sophia followed Danilo outside. The oleanders were already forming buds and it wouldn't be long before they started flowering. The olive trees and palm grew fast. Everything seemed perfect, but it wasn't. Definitely not.

'Mussolini has declared war on France and England. Our army has invaded the south of France.'

Sofia was shocked. It had happened. She had expected, or perhaps only hoped, that the war would stay far away.

'As a Blackshirt, my father is very loyal to Mussolini. He's already volunteered to go to the front.'

His father, always dressed in black. She looked at the fascist balcony. It didn't surprise her.

'And you?' she asked.

He brushed the lock from his face, which fell back, then stroked her hair. 'I'll stay with you as long as I can, until they call me up.'

7

When I sit on our terrace, I see them approaching in the distance. I quickly put down my coffee. They're both pulling suitcases with them and look around in amazement. Max has grown again and is only a head shorter than his tall father. Their movements and posture are exactly the same.

'What are you doing here?' I yell, and run up to them and fling my arms around their necks.

'Unexpected, right?' says Max. 'You wouldn't expect that from Dad. But he can't handle it at all, huh, Dad? He was upset at the airport in Ancona.'

Roger has dark circles under his eyes and sighs deeply. 'Darling, I didn't know you were staying in a mobile home.'

'When did you arrive?' I ask. 'Had you warned me last night or this morning, I would have arranged everything for you in advance.'

'Pretty small,' says Max, standing in the living room of the mobile home. 'Oh, hello Margot.'

'Hey darling,' Margot says from her bedroom. 'Sorry, I was still asleep. I didn't know you were coming, oh, how nice. Your mom must be happy to see you, huh? She's been a little stressed about the house.'

Roger looks at the sea and then back at me. 'I didn't want you to solve this alone. Yes, I know you can do it, but we got into it together, so now let's see how we can work it out.'

'Where do we sleep, Mom?' Max asks.

'Dad can stay with me in the bedroom, and you can go on the sofa bed.'

'Did Margot get my bed?' he asks.

'No, darling, it's not like that,' Margot says, rummaging around in her bedroom.

'There's no real good gaming spot,' says Max. He puts his gaming laptop on the dining table and starts installing everything.

'You can walk straight onto the beach from here, and there's an ice cream shop further down the road,' I say.

'I'm not going to sit on the beach without my friends. Do you know how weird that is?'

Roger starts to unpack his suitcase in the bedroom. There is not much room in the narrow lilac Formica closet, and he pushes my dresses aside. Ironed and uncreased, he takes his shirts and polos out of his suitcase.

On the terrace, I open a new page of my notepad and make a chart with the days on the horizontal axis and the times on the vertical axis.

'Roger, darling, would you like a nice coffee?' Margot asks him, poking her head into our bedroom. Before he can answer, she gets to work with the little Italian coffee maker. Soon, hot steam was pressing the boiling water up through the finely ground coffee, creating a delicious espresso.

'Look,' I say to Roger when he comes out. 'I've made a plan.'

I turn the notebook towards him. In the time blocks created in the schedule, I planned all activities: the appointment with the two new contractors this afternoon, an introductory meeting at the town hall, a meeting with Dutch people who have renovated a house in a village more inland in the hills. Every day I end with dinner; at home or in a nearby restaurant. Alternately.

Roger studies the graph.

'Hm, well, I don't know. It doesn't look very complete.'

'In the blocks where there is nothing, we have time to view the surroundings, or, for example, go to the seaside for a swim.'

His index finger slides along the diagram. 'Isn't dinner scheduled very late?'

I close the block. 'We can still change it.'

'Do you like it here, Margot?' Roger asks as she brings the coffee. 'How long will you stay?'

'Darling, as long as you need me. I already told your wife that I would be happy to help with your bed and breakfast.'

Roger looks at me in surprise. 'A bed and breakfast?'

'No, no, I said we're not going to do that. That doesn't suit us.'

'We may have to sell the house,' Roger says. I am startled. This is exactly what I was afraid of.

'Then my plan seems better, darling,' says Margot. 'Really, there are plenty of people who would like to stay at Palazzo Puro. Look, I asked my followers on Instagram.'

She gives us her phone. She took a selfie in a dress with a plunging neckline, with the house faintly visible in the background. The photo has 1,521 likes. *Looks yummy*, is written in a comment below. *I want to meet you, babe*. I scroll further down. *Love your breasts*.

'This doesn't say much about the house. They're all messages from men wanting to meet you,' I say.

'Now, you don't have to be so precise. That is not nice. Women, men, it doesn't matter, darling, as long as you can afford the renovations with it.'

Roger laughs, as he often does when she says something. Her comments are always so far away from his reality that I think he sees her as some sort of stand-up comedian.

'Good joke again, Margot,' he says.

'Mom, where is that ice cream shop?' Max asks. He's put on shorts and a clean T-shirt, and hands me his phone so I can point it out on Google Maps. As he walks across the terrace, a girl with shiny black hair watches him from the beach with interest. He waves gently at her.

'He's got a girlfriend right here,' Margot says. 'He's become such a handsome boy; he's going to be a real womanizer.'

Later in the afternoon we walk into the house and enter the narrow room on the first floor that is now tidy and clean, except for some new feces left by a gecko that has entered through a crack in the window's woodwork. I walk on, open the doors to the balcony.

'Do you still like her?' I ask Roger when he comes and stands next to me on the balcony.

'I like you.' He smiles and looks around the room. 'And the house too. Let's hope the quotes from the other two contractors are better.'

The first contractor is a Slovakian, a broad man with tattoos on his arm, and he has brought along a colleague, two-heads shorter and wearing round glasses, who walks diagonally behind him. As we move from room to room, he speaks in Slovak to the little man behind him who writes everything down on a sheet of paper clipped to a black plastic board.

Max comes over and says there's no Wi-Fi. I tell him to enjoy himself some other way, because we're busy right now. Half an hour later, when we are back in the garden, the Slovak contractor takes his little colleague's writing board and looks at the notes.

'Anything you want is possible and you don't have to worry about the cost,' he says. 'The walls are good; the roof beams are thick and sturdy. Nothing needs to be changed. So, it is at most a matter of breaking down a few walls and rebuilding the larger bathrooms and a kitchen.'

'And what if there is an earthquake?' Roger asks. 'I understood that the house is not strong enough.'

'An earthquake won't shake this house. It has been standing for almost a century and for good reason.'

'When can you start?' I ask. I regain confidence that my original estimate was correct when we bought the house, and that the condition is not so bad.

'My men will arrive from Slovakia in a few days. It's a fresh new crew of masons, carpenters, electricians and plumbers. They can start immediately and their rate is about a quarter of the price that Italian contractors charge.'

Inside I am cheering. They can start right away.

'I can work with your drawings,' he tells me. 'They are detailed enough.'

We say goodbye and I hug Roger.

'You see? It's going to be okay,' I say.

Half an hour later the second contractor arrives. He has worked for many foreigners in this region, he says. He does not do the work himself, but hires other contractors that he manages. It is a big job, he thinks. The house is in an earthquake zone, did we know this? There are all rules regarding construction. As a result, the house is now uninhabitable. The walls and floors have to be reinforced; the whole roof has to be removed. What did we calculate ourselves to renovate this all? We tell him our budget and he starts laughing out loud. He's not even putting in a new shed for that amount, he says, pointing to the dilapidated wooden shed.

All our savings is barely enough for a new shed?

He explains that he charges an eleven percent commission for all work that we want to execute. My drawings are not detailed enough, a *geometra* has to look at that and add more details to it, otherwise we can forget the building permit from the municipality.

'Another contractor is already working on the drawings and permit application,' I tell him.

Lorenzo with his fresh scented shirts. Despite the fact that he was hugely wrong with his first estimate of the renovation costs before the purchase, I now miss his calm explanation and gestures.

The contractor looks at me and closes his notebook. He says we can call him when we really need his help.

'Maybe it wasn't so helpful to tell him that we've already talked to someone else,' Roger says as the second contractor drives off.

'Did you know that there is a furnished baby room upstairs?' Max asks.

'Yes, that will be your room,' I say. 'I'll briefly discuss with your dad what he thought of the contractors, and then we can start cleaning up that baby room together.'

Roger and I are sitting on the grass under the palm tree. The leaves provide much-needed shade as the sun climbs to its highest point. There is no wind, no cooling sea breeze. Roger chews on a blade of grass and says nothing. He stares at a point on the ground. He is probably making calculations in his head and weighing the different scenarios.

'Did you like that Slovak contractor?' I ask after a few minutes.

'A nice man, but something isn't right. His story is too different from that of the other contractors.'

'Maybe they don't make such a prestige project out of a renovation in Slovakia? Those Italian contractors seem to want to renovate it almost too perfectly.'

'I don't know,' he says. 'Maybe they don't do the renovation as well. We'd better save until we can hire a good contractor.'

'If we sell the house where we're living now, we can use the surplus value for the renovation here.'

'And where do you want us to live until the renovation is done?' he asks. 'We can't stay in that mobile home by the sea for a year. That's not affordable.'

'Maybe we should put a big caravan here in the yard?'

He blinks nervously. 'I hate caravans. They are plastic boxes with minimal facilities.'

'A big second-hand tent, or a gypsy wagon? If we put the tent here in front of the house, just next to this palm tree, there is still enough space around the house to be able to renovate.'

'Why do we want to live in a tent here, if we already have a nice house? A house that you even designed yourself.'

'A yurt then?' I ask. 'They're big and high, and have a stove in the middle with that big pipe through the roof.'

'That's a round tent,' Roger says, frowning. 'This project is far too extensive for us.'

'I have an idea. Why don't you take your laptop out of the car and complete your table with costs? Maybe that give us a better overview and peace of mind? I promised Max to clear out the baby room.'

Roger heaves a sigh of relief, gets up and goes to the car.

The pink walls in the baby room are covered in cobwebs and moisture stains. This was once a pretty room; the two white bedsteads are beautiful and matched well with the white shutters. Max starts filling boxes with the half-worn clothes that are scattered on the floor. I grab the dirty children's mattresses and throw them down through the window. Fresh air flows into the room.

'Look at this,' says Max. He has pulled back a piece of cloth in the corner, and a red wooden roof sticks out from between the boxes. He pulls it with both hands. A wooden dollhouse, made of small slats. A little bed has even been made in one of the rooms.

'This is cute,' I say. I look for more furniture among the boxes, but there isn't any.

'It's a girl thing,' says Max.

'It doesn't have to be, dear.'

When I slide the cribs into the hallway, a rag doll with a yellow dress comes out from underneath. It is homemade with neat stitching.

'That one can go too,' says Max.

I put the doll in a box on which I have written *save*.

The low bookcase along the wall is filled with yellowed books with moisture damage. Children's books with colorful drawings and short stories. I can read the simple Italian sentences; it is kindergarten level. I also find an old bible. A book on wine production. A few novels.

In the other corner is a low linen cupboard. Dozens of feathers fly through the air when I open it. I jump back.

'Dead birds,' I shout. The feathers flutter in the sunlight.

'It's down from old pillows.' Max pulls a cover from the closet. Underneath are handmade baby clothes. A sun hat, crocheted cardigans and socks. All valuable enough to keep, yet left behind when they closed the door behind them and left Palazzo Puro.

My phone rings loudly in the increasingly empty baby room. Brian. He asks if I want to come to a viewing of a house by a German couple. They have been looking for months and still haven't been able to decide, he explains.

'If this couple can see what you see in houses, they'll come to a different understanding,' he says. 'Can you come tomorrow afternoon at three o'clock? I'll pick you up.'

'Who was that?' Max asks as soon as I hang up.

'The real estate agent is asking if I want to help him sell a house. Maybe I can make this my job.'

'Yes, probably. You always say that you love houses more than people.'

'You're an exception to that,' I say, putting my arm around his shoulder and pulling him toward me.

We drive back to the sea.

'Mom is going on tour with the real estate agent tomorrow,' Max tells Roger.

'Are you serious?' Roger asks in surprise. 'Why? We just got here. It's not on our schedule either.'

'Brian has asked me to do this in response to my drawings for this house and the photos of our own house. He wants to work together.'

'And this is what you want to do?' Roger asks in disbelief.

'At least I can try it once. And it fits into tomorrow's leisure block on the schedule.'

It is already almost half past seven in the evening when Roger and I are waiting on our terrace for Max who is still taking a shower. It's actually too late for Roger to go out for dinner, but I have made reservations at restaurant *Il Sale* in the old village center of Cupra Marittima on the hill and they don't open earlier.

'I think we should start the renovation ourselves,' I say to Roger. 'Why don't we try to fix up the shed first? If that works out well, we will fix up the rest of the house ourselves.'

Adamo approaches, greets me, introduces himself to Roger and enters

Margot's bedroom. She giggles, and not much later they come out arm in arm. Aron follows behind them. Margot pushes back a chair for Aron; Adamo sits down in it. He's going to disappoint her in everything. Max comes out freshly showered, says hello to Aron and Adamo and the three of us walk away. Max looks back one more time.

'Margot has two husbands,' he says.

'I'll explain it to you later,' I reply.

Margot waves after us, Aron too. Adamo takes a sip of his own wine.

Venerdì, 9 Agosto 1940

A sweet smell spread through the attic room. She reached for the white iron crib with embroidered sheets beside her bed and looked over the edge at her baby. Green eyes and downy black hair. She stroked her gently. There was nothing more beautiful.

Carefully she lifted Valentina and placed her on her lap wrapped in a woolen blanket she'd knitted herself. The name suited her, it meant strength and bravery.

A primal cry from below, it was just the way her screams must have sounded three days earlier. Fast footsteps on the stairs. Danilo's soothing voice. Just like when she gave birth to Valentina. The voice of the doctor and the midwife. Another scream. Danilo would now wipe Stella's sweaty face, as he had done for her. The doctor and midwife were trying to get the baby out from her still motionless lower body. Stella must be scared.

'We must be quiet, Valentina,' Sofia said. She gave her baby a soft kiss on her cheek.

It wasn't until early evening that Danilo came up. He looked at Valentina sleeping in the crib and gave Sofia a kiss. 'It's a girl and she's perfectly healthy. Her name is Rubia.'

Sofia was relieved and happy. And restless. 'Are you going to search for the father of Stella's baby?'

'Stella still can't say his name.'

Why not? Her speech was good enough for it.

Danilo leaned over, kissed her, then Valentina. 'I love you so much.'

The next morning, the first rays of sunlight crept through the slits in wooden shutters, casting long, narrow beams into the attic room. Valentina was awake in the crib next to her bed, making soft sounds.

'Hey, little girl, come with me,' she said. She snuck out of the bedroom as Danilo turned over in bed one more time. The iron bed springs squeaked.

She went down the stairs to Stella's bedroom. It was dawn, the shutters were still closed, and Stella was asleep. She tiptoed over to the crib; it was the same as the one upstairs in her room. Rubia was awake and looked at her wide-eyed. She stroked her hair.

'Hello Rubia,' she whispered. She looked at Valentina who she held in her arms. The same look.

'Baby,' said Stella, who had woken up. She stretched out her arms.

Sofia turned to her. 'This is Valentina, my baby. Congratulations on the birth of Rubia.'

She held Valentina closer to Stella to show her. Stella grabbed Valentina and pulled her. 'Baby. Give.'

'No, this is my baby. Let her go.'

'Give, give her.'

Sofia grabbed Stella's hand and pulled it away. Startled, she took a step back. She pointed to the crib. 'Rubia is in the crib next to you. Shall I give her to you?'

Stella shook her head. 'That baby! Mine.'

She cried with long sobs.

Sofia walked to the armchair by the window where she carefully placed Valentina. She folded her blanket in half at the front so she wouldn't roll off. Morning light poured in through the shutters she opened. She lifted Rubia.

Green eyes.

The same color as Valentina's.

All Italians have brown, or sometimes green eyes. Yes, that's so. She gave Rubia to Stella who immediately stopped crying and hugged her baby.

Sofia sat on the edge of the bed with Valentina.

Stella looked from one girl to another. 'Two babies. Sisters.'

'No, not sisters. They are friends.'

'Two babies of mine. So, sisters.'

'Valentina is my baby.'

'No, not true.'

Sofia walked out with Valentina. She opened the balcony doors in the narrow room and placed her hand on the railing. The cold concrete with its arrows and circles seemed a harbinger of dark days.

Maggio 1941

The car drove down the narrow country road. Nothing betrayed that it was war, and yet Danilo had left for the front. The wheat had been harvested while the vegetable garden was still green. The olive trees would soon begin to produce their small fruits. Danilo had promised to write a letter as soon as he arrived at the army basecamp. His conscription was unexpected. Danilo had been in the hospital when the first call came and his mother had torn the letter up. The second letter she received was menacing. Danilo would be considered a collaborator if he did not report to the army in Milan within two weeks.

Sofia had suggested that he hide until after the war. She did not believe he should take part in a war on the side of Nazi Germany.

Stella said he must do his duty and not be a traitor to his own country. She had opened her arms and said she would be proud of him when he fought for their country. He had kissed her on the forehead.

Sofia looked out over the field. She was living as an unmarried woman with a child from an extramarital relationship in a house that did not belong to her. Together with another woman and with two babies who didn't realize that the world outside was slowly being destroyed.

'I want to go home,' Stella said. She sat in a wheelchair at the dinner table with Rubia on her lap. 'I want to go back to the city and live with my mother.'

Her ability to speak was improving faster and faster. Danilo had called it a miracle; the therapist had indicated that this was to be expected. In a detailed, long-winded explanation, he'd told them that the damage to her neck and back hadn't been permanent and that her functions were slowly recovering as the nerves got stronger and sent better signals from the brain to the limbs. Sofia's deep-seated guilt had not diminished.

'That's a good idea,' Sofia said. It was not a bad plan for Stella to be gone as soon as Danilo returned from the front and she herself would be less confronted with her lame legs. 'Your mother can take care of you.'

'That's not the point, because here I also have a therapist and you as my assistant, but it's better for the education of the girls.'

'For the girls?'

'Yes, it's not safe here in the valley without Danilo's protection.'

'It's safe here. Our house is remote, no one will stop here.'

'My house. And if I leave, you must also leave the house.'

Leave the house? Danilo had built it for her. She opened her mouth, clenched her fists, pressing her fingernails into her palm so hard that it hurt.

'No, I'm not leaving,' she said. 'If you want to go with Rubia, I understand, but I'm waiting here with Valentina for Danilo.'

Stella shook her head. 'I'm taking both babies.'

A slight panic came over her. Had Stella suffered permanent brain damage in the car accident due to the impact? She and Danilo had explained to her several times that Rubia was her daughter, but Stella continued to claim that both children were hers.

'Who is Rubia's father?' Sofia asked. She walked away from the window and began to nervously shuffle the porcelain cups in the china cabinet.

Stella laughed mockingly as if the question was ridiculous to her. 'Danilo.'

'No, that is not true. Danilo is Valentina's father,' Sofia said, turning to her. 'But who is Rubia's father?'

Rubia started to cry. Stella's knuckles turned white; she squeezed Rubia hard. 'Danilo is her father! And after the war we get married.'

Rubia cried louder. Sofia walked over to Stella and tried to take Rubia away.

'Let go of your baby, you're hurting her.'

'You're his whore. That and no more,' Stella said angrily.

Rubia was crying hard, Stella shook her from side to side. Sofia pulled on Stella's arms, but she wouldn't let go.

'Give Rubia to me! You're hurting her,' Sofia shouted.

Stella tried to twist her upper body away, but the movement made her stagger in her wheelchair. She held on to Rubia a little less tightly for a moment. Sofia quickly grabbed Rubia from her arms and walked away from the dinner table. She comforted the crying baby as if it were her own.

'Whore!' Stella yelled.

'You hurt your own baby. I understand that you are afraid of this war, but you are saying things that are not true.'

'I'm not afraid, I'm angry,' Stella said. 'You took Danilo away from me, he's my man.'

'He left you that night to come to me.'

Stella slapped her thin legs in the wheelchair with both hands. 'The car accident was your fault. You put me in this chair.'

Sofia was amazed. 'Do you remember anything about the accident?'

'Everything,' Stella replied. 'I know you were on the road that caused us to skid and to smash my head on the road. You are guilty of everything.'

'Your car door was open. That caused the skid.'

'You are lying.'

Sofia tried to guess if Stella really didn't remember this. Just like she thought they were her babies. She tried to stay calm.

'I'm sorry I was on the road,' she said. 'It should never have happened.'

Stella seemed to calm down and looked out the window. There was silence for a moment, the sounds from outside came in again. Birds whistled.

'I'm staying,' Stella said.

Sofia breathed a sigh of relief. She'd rather be here with Stella than alone without the girls.

'And I thought mistresses had rules of conduct,' Stella said doubtfully. 'Having babies is not one of them, I'm sure of that.'

'So, you know Valentina is mine?' Sofia asked.

'She's mine. You gave her up the moment you knew you were pregnant and decided to come and live here in the attic.'

8

Max stands at our bedroom door in the mobile home, his blond hair tousled; he looks in, and then gently closes it again. His curls have been lifted by the salt of the sea; his skin has taken on the color of honey.

'What's wrong with Dad?' he asks. 'He's in bed.'

My neat summer dress has a small pink flower print. Pretty, but not too noticeable. 'He's shocked by the renovation plan. Or actually, no plan yet.'

'Haven't you made a plan?'

'Sometimes things don't turn out the way you think. Not everything can be planned.'

'Well, we can write off Dad for the rest of the vacation.'

I grab my notebook, sit down at the plastic table on the patio and write *renovation plan* on a blank page.

'Maybe it won't be that bad if I come up with a plan quickly,' I say.

'Probably won't work. That's just the way he is,' Max replies. He picks up his towel that was drying on a plastic chair.

'Are you going to the beach again?' I ask. 'You didn't like to go without friends, did you?'

'Now I do,' he says.

In the distance is a girl with a beach bag on her shoulder. He waves at her, walks away and says something to Margot who has just come back from the beach.

'Darling, I have good news,' Margot says happily as she stands next to the table and claps her hands. 'Guess.'

She pauses to increase the tension. I have no idea which direction to guess.

'You are no longer in love with Adamo?' I ask.

'No, it's not that, I wasn't in love with him anyway, I believe. That was more lust. Guess again. Well, okay, never mind, guessing was never your forte.'

She taps her fingers on the table and looks at me expectantly.

'Tell me,' I say impatiently.

'I'm going to work with Silvan and Frederico! How nice is that? Can you see me walking in such a cute short black dress with a white apron? Oh, that's really for me.'

'Why?' I ask. 'Don't you want to go back home and work as a flight attendant again?'

'No, are you kidding me? It's lovely here, and August is coming up and that's the busiest month of the year. They can't get through the season without any waitresses.'

'Where are you going to live?'

She shrugs. 'You are always so practical. Can't you be happy for me first?'

She is right. 'Congratulations on your new job.'

'Thank you, darling. Where is Roger? I want to tell him too; he will be so thrilled that I stay.'

Brian comes walking across the grass.

'You look pretty business-like,' he says. 'The house viewing is fifteen minutes from here, near Ripatransone.'

The road winds up to the town with rolling hills on both sides full of olive groves and vineyards. When we leave the road and enter the grounds of the abandoned house, the German couple is already standing next to their car.

Brian parks his car next to it, gets out and shakes their hands. He introduces me as a project manager for Italian house renovations. Now I am a project manager again.

'I don't know,' says the German woman in a pink suit, looking at the house. She's short, but her high heels give her at least ten centimeters of extra height.

'It looks like a ruin to me,' she says. 'I want a villa with a pool and sea view. Here is only grassland, and those hills of silver trees whose name I keep forgetting.'

'Olive trees,' Brian says. 'Just like the other houses I showed you.'

'So those aren't the palm trees I want. I miss that luxury. And sea is far away from here.'

Her husband nods at every word his wife says. His flamingo print T-shirt is taut around his stomach. The contrast between the two makes her hips look even narrower and her stomach even flatter. Long blond locks ripple down her back and her fingernail polish is purple.

'We have clearly indicated in advance what we are looking for, haven't we?' says the man.

Brian takes off his sunglasses, wants to put the temple in his mouth, but then hangs the glasses on his shirt. 'You're looking for something that would cost more than 1.5 million euros and your budget is five-hundred thousand. This house, at the asking price of 220,000 euros, offers possibilities. After a renovation, it will be a villa with a breathtaking view.'

The woman looks back at the house. It is an elongated farmhouse with a beautiful large balcony that runs the entire length. The railing is made with openwork bricks. That looks familiar to me. From what?

'You saw the house in the architectural drawing on the wall of my office,' Brian says as if he can read my mind.

'It's terribly small,' the woman says. 'Don't you think it's too small, gummy?'

Gummy. It has always amazed me that people give each other pet names. What's wrong with your own name, or maybe darling or sweetheart?

The woman looks expectantly at her husband, who nods so hard that his double chin moves as well.

Brian shakes his head. 'It's not small, it's 350 square meters. You can safely call that big. The design is by a well-known architect who used to design many houses in this neighborhood.'

Brian hands me the old floor plan of the house. Below are the stables, on the first floor many rooms and an attic with no facilities which was used for drying food. Similar to other farms in Le Marche, but this design is more beautiful. It has more unique details.

Inside it smells of mold on the ground floor and it's dark. The German couple says they have seen enough already. This house is again not the house they are looking for. I go up the stairs, turn down a long dark hallway and open a bedroom door. The view through the small windows from this floor is stunning. All around are the green hills and in the distance the azure sea shimmers in the sunlight. The sky changes color from light blue to light pink. Large windows can be placed here, so that they wake up in the morning with this view. A door to the large terrace with its beautiful railing, fresh coffee in the fresh morning air. I muse. This region is full of ruins that are all worth restoring. The German man walks over and stands next to me.

'This is a beautiful view,' I say to him.

Further on, the woman is walking around with Brian and she complains that all the spaces are small.

I walk to the other rooms and tap the walls. The man follows me. The walls don't seem to be load-bearing, so taking out a few of them would be easy. The external staircase along the wall of the lower floor leads to the terrace, so from the bedroom you walk straight out into the garden, to a swimming pool that can be built so that it seems to flow into the endless sea.

As Brian and the woman walk downstairs, I look for a pen in my bag. Why do I never find one when I need it? The man hands me his pen, which has a tropical print. Those palm trees definitely have to be planted, that's clear to me when I look at the pen, just like an inflatable flamingo in the pool.

I unfold the drawings against the wall and draw large sliding doors on the ground floor near the living room. A kitchen with a cooking island. On the first floor I scratch away walls, make a large bedroom and draw a double bed in it. In addition, a half-opened wall has created space for a free-standing bath with a sea view.

'Can you note there that the bathroom is going to be Hawaiian style?' the man asks.

'Hawaii like in the island of Hawaii?' I ask, slightly surprised. 'This is Italy.'

'Yes, I mean, for example, let's recreate those garlands of flowers they're hanging around your neck in a large mosaic tiling on the wall. Something like that?'

I'll add it. Why not?

I continue with the drawings. The next room can become a walk-in closet. There is no sea view there, so this room is less suitable as a bedroom. The view to the small village on the hilltop is beautiful, actually too beautiful for a walk-in closet, but this is probably the luxury they search for. In the garden I draw a large swimming pool, close to the house. In between, I design a terrace with pergola.

The drawing has gotten dirty from the wall, yet I hand it over to the man. 'This is a beautiful place and the house has a lot of potential,' I say.

With the map in his hand, the man runs to the garden. His stomach swings back and forth. 'This house is getting a Hawaiian bathroom,' he calls out to his wife.

She takes the drawing. 'Really?' she asks. 'Where does it come then?'

The man points to the written words near the bathroom.

'Oooh, this is a dream!' she shouts. 'Which window is it?'

The man points to the house. 'There, behind that first-floor window.'

Brian winks at me.

The man taps on the drawing and looks at me. 'And you can arrange this renovation for us?'

Brian takes over and says that everything, including the Hawaiian bathroom, can be arranged.

The couple honks as they drive away, the woman hangs out the window backwards and waves enthusiastically as their car disappears from view.

At the cafe under the arcade in Ripatransone we walk in and through a back exit we reach a terrace with a view over the valley. Brian orders a bottle of white wine. It is now almost half past four, and still pleasantly warm. The music is soft.

'Brilliant, that Hawaiian bathroom,' Brian says.

'The man himself asked for it.'

'The wishes of the buyers always come first; you have a good sense for that. The rest of your plan was well thought out too. And in such a short time. How do you do that?'

'I feel the house.'

He nods as if he understands. It's better to leave it that way, because how do I explain that when I walk through a house, I automatically wonder who used to live there, what they did and how they used the house? The possibilities of the house unfold, as if the house was whispering it to me. Aron had called that 'sounding mellow' the last time.

'Do you know who the architect who designed the house is?' I ask.

He shakes his head. 'I haven't spoken to anyone yet who has actually met the architect. Many houses in the area were designed by him and all were built in the fifties and sixties.'

'There's also a drawing of a house on the wall in your office with the same ornamentation in the window above the front door as in our house,' I say.

'You see that pattern often. Your house was designed by an unknown architect. There is no stamp or name under the drawing. This also applies to most old houses from the 1930s. When will your renovation start?'

I shrug. 'The renovation is going to be more expensive than we hoped. And I don't have a plan yet...'

It's getting late. Roger is probably worried about whether we can still stick to the evening schedule.

'I have to go back,' I say.

On the way back in the car I make a renovation plan in my notepad. If we only have the necessary construction work carried out by a contractor – such as replacing the rotten roof beams and reinforcing the walls – and do the rest ourselves, this saves money. I put the amounts estimated by me next to it, as well as a date on which the work will start and when it will be finished. Brian occasionally looks to the side and smiles.

Roger is sitting on the porch and nervously moves his head.

'I have a plan,' I say quickly, holding up my notepad as I run up. 'Look, a plan, you see? I've worked everything out, every step. With start and end date and the total costs. Nothing can go wrong anymore.'

Roger gets up, walks to the kitchen and comes back with a glass of wine. 'I'm assuming you already had a glass of wine with Brian?'

'What's that got to do with it? We've been trying to sell a house to a German couple who seem to think Hawaii is a place in Italy.'

He gets up again and comes back with a glass of wine for me. He kisses my cheek and looks at my renovation plan. 'That's too global,' he says. 'For a house this size.'

'I'll work it out in more detail. As I always do, and which you love so much.'

'I don't know,' he says hesitantly. His body tenses.

'We decided to buy it together, didn't we? Then we will solve it together. Trust me, we can do this.'

He runs his hand through his hair nervously. 'We're going bankrupt because of this house.' He sighs deeply. 'I thought long and hard about it this afternoon while you were gone. I'm sorry, but I think we should sell it.'

No. No, I don't want this. My eyes start to burn, my throat is dry. In my head my thoughts are a mess, chaos.

'I can do it, really. I'm a project manager, I know how to handle this. For real. We must not give up. You wanted to look for a new job here, remember? And Max can study here and…'

Roger looks past me.

'…and I, yes, I can look for a new job as a project manager here. Then I won't do house viewings with Brian anymore, I won't have to pursue a new career in home renovation projects. I'll go back to being an IT project manager again. Does that make you feel better? And if we hire that Slovak contractor, it's cheaper and then…'

'Sometimes you have to admit that we misjudged a situation,' he says. 'This situation is uncontrollable. I have made all possible calculations; nothing works out fine.'

'I don't want to sell the house,' I say. 'It's not over yet, this adventure. I still have to clean up and there is this secret I want to discover so that I can better understand the past. We can still…'

'You're losing it,' Roger says. 'It's just a house.'

'Don't say that,' I shout disappointed.

I storm into the mobile home and slam the bedroom door behind me. Crying, I push my face into the pillow. Roger doesn't come after me. He knows that doesn't work.

The next morning Margot wanders restlessly back and forth in the mobile home, fiddling with the glasses and plates in the kitchen. She stands in the doorway of the bedroom.

'Are you sure you really want this, darling? This is your dream, you know?'

'Yes, and always will be. But Roger can't handle it, and we don't have enough money.'

We load the car with our suitcases. Roger says little.

'Well Mom, you ruined it again,' Max says as he walks by with his bag of gaming equipment.

'How did I do that?' I ask.

'You didn't have a good plan and that's why Dad is upset.'

'And why is that always my responsibility?'

He doesn't answer, looks down the boulevard as if looking for something.

When I want to drive away, I ask Margot again through the car window if she really doesn't want to come along.

'No darling, I'm staying here,' she says. 'Adamo will rent the mobile home for me for a while and I'll move to his winery as soon as his wife leaves the house. Are you sure you're going?'

She looks past me at Roger.

'Yes, Margot, we know for sure,' he says dejectedly.

In my rear-view mirror, Margot shrinks, waving lavishly and throwing air kisses. Further down the boulevard is a girl with long black hair waving at the car.

'Max!' she yells as she runs after the car.

I hit the brakes, turn to Max in the backseat.

'Keep driving, Mom. I already told her I can't stay.'

I slowly press the accelerator again. The girl drops to her knees and sits, bent over on the street.

'Who is that?' I ask.

'Just a girl I met on the beach. Her name is Sofia.'

Domenica, 9 Agosto 1942

Sofia picked up Valentina from her crib. The sun was shining through the high window and lit up the girl from behind, making it look like she had a halo. She stroked the dark hair, smelled it. Somehow, she hoped to be able to smell Danilo's scent through her. Rubia's crib was already empty. The two girls' room on the first floor with the pink walls and white shutters was the nursery for her own child and another woman's child, something she never expected when she drew this house.

'Congratulations, little girl,' she said to Valentina and gave her a kiss. 'You're two years old.'

She took a white dress with light blue flowers and dressed her. 'We won't tell Aunt Stella that your birthday was actually three days ago.'

Stella sat with Rubia on her lap, the little girl was wearing a white dress with pale pink flowers. Stella had worked hard over the past few days to get both dresses finished in time for the girls' birthdays. The same green eyes, the same dresses. Only Rubia's hair was slightly lighter than Valentina's dark brown hair. Both girls' hair curled at the ends.

'Good morning,' Sofia said.

'Congratulations, little Valentina,' Stella said, reaching out to take her. Valentina crowed and flapped her small arms.

Sofia gave her to Stella. 'Gently please?'

She kept warning her every time, even though Stella now had better control of her own strength and she had slowly started to regain feeling in her upper legs.

'I have a present for you, Valentina,' Stella said with both girls on her lap.

She held up a colorful package. Together the girls tore open the package. A rag doll with a light-yellow dress. Valentina pressed the doll against her body. Rubia cried.

'I had fabric left over from the dresses I made a few weeks ago,' Stella said, picking up another package from the seat next to her. 'I made one for Rubia too.'

Rubia tore open the paper, grabbed her doll by the arm and swung it around. The doll fell and Rubia cried again. Sofia quickly picked up the doll from the floor and handed it back. Rubia swung it again.

'They're beautiful,' Sofia said.

'Don't you have a present?' Stella asked.

'Yes, it's just not a toy, so they probably don't like it.'

She went to the kitchen cupboard and picked up a large sheet of paper, which she unrolled and held up.

'Ah, a drawing of a house,' Stella said. 'Nice, but not really a good gift for two-year-old girls.'

Sofia looked at her drawing. This was her first time drawing again after a long time. The house in the drawing was their house, with all the details, but colored with pink walls, light blue windows and a mint green roof. Flowers hung to the floor on the balcony and flowers were also on all the windowsills. The windows were open and two girls were hanging out, they had long hair. In the garden she had drawn Stella holding her embroidery and sitting on a chair and herself standing and waving happily to the girls. The sky was pale pink, the sun pale yellow, the olive trees pale green.

'This is us,' Sofia explained.

'It's a fantasy world,' Stella said. She took a sip of the coffee.

'This could be us. If we want, I mean.'

'This is not how we will ever be. Once Danilo is back, everything will be different.'

Sofia walked to the small counter, poured a glass of water and took a sip. Stella's moods could change so quickly and she didn't want to ruin the party atmosphere.

'Girls, today we have visitors. My mother, my sisters, and Rafaella with her children are coming soon.'

'Why?' Stella said. 'Why are they coming?'

'So we can have a little birthday party.'

'But I invited my mother and Danilo's mother,' Stella said, irritated. 'My father has gone to the front, but my mother will have bought Rubia an expensive present.'

'Then it will be a little bigger party,' Sofia said.

Stella slammed the flat of her hand on the table. The coffee cups jingled. Rubia started to cry, Stella ignored her. 'It's not normal for a housekeeper to invite her family and friends to her employer's house.'

It was incredible. Whenever Sofia tried to see her as a woman her own age with the same fears and insecurities in this war, and brought her closer, Stella said or did something that hurt or frightened her.

'I'm not the housekeeper and you're not my employer,' Sofia replied. 'Danilo would never accept that.'

'He's not here, and my mother pays your mother a monthly fee for your services.' She stroked Rubia's head, which turned her crying into a light sob.

That wasn't true. Impossible. Her mother might be poor, but she had pride and would never allow it.

'Hold on, girls,' Stella said, turning the wheels of her wheelchair.

'It's not true what you say,' Sofia said. 'You always twist the truth.'

'My mother and Danilo's mother are coming at three this afternoon,' Stella said over her shoulder as she wheeled out of the kitchen. 'Will you make sure everything is ready in time and that we have enough time to get down the stairs?'

Sofia had just finished outside, hanging the garlands and cotton flags she had made herself and setting the garden table, when Rafaella's three sons ran screaming from the road into the garden. They shouted hello, flew past her, and the six-year-old was already hanging in an olive tree before Rafaella could warn him not to.

'They don't know how to act in a place like this, such a big garden,' Rafaella said. They kissed each other on the cheek. Rafaella playfully pinched Valentina and Rubia's cheeks and moved on to Stella, who was sitting in her wheelchair at the end of the table. It had taken almost fifteen minutes to get down the stairs, with Stella sliding down step by step with Sofia's help. In front of the wardrobe in the hall, they had exchanged her soiled skirt for a dark red party dress to match her cherry red lipstick.

Sofia walked in to retrieve the pitcher of lemonade she'd made with strawberries and raspberries. In the kitchen, she filled another pitcher with water, adding mint and lemon. She walked to the china cabinet, opened the top drawer. It had been almost two months now. Way too long. He should have written again already. She picked up Danilo's letter and read it over one more time.

20 Giugno 1942, 20:00

Dear Sofia and Stella,
This may be my last letter to you. We leave for Russia to fight with Germany in the battle of Stalingrad. I don't know what the situation is there, but from what I've heard and seen, it's not good. The thought of you and the children helps me. Please take care of each other and stay home as much as possible for your own safety. I love you.

With love, your Danilo

She kissed the letter, but her lips trembled, as did her hands. So many weeks had passed, and no new letter had come.

'Sofia,' Rafaella called out.

She quickly put the letter back and looked down from the window.

'Big sister!' Sienna and Angelina called to her almost at the same time.

They laughed and waved.

'We made a present for our niece,' Sienna called. She was holding a large package.

'Haven't you brought anything for Rubia?' Stella asked.

Quickly Sofia grabbed both jugs of lemonade and went downstairs. Her sisters walked up to her and congratulated her.

'I sat with the package on the back of Sienna's bike all the way,' Angelina said. 'It took us almost an hour.'

She had her black hair tied in a ponytail and was wearing an old brown skirt. Her shoes were threadbare.

'Mom didn't want to come. She is still not at peace with your choice.'

'You're here, that's what matters,' Sofia said. 'Let's sit down and eat cake.'

Sienna put the large present on the table just in front of the children's highchairs. 'Look, Valentina, a present for you.'

'That's not Valentina,' Sofia said. 'That's Rubia.'

Sienna looked from one toddler to the next. 'They look so much alike.'

'It's Rubia's birthday too,' Stella said. 'So, it's okay.'

From the road, Stella's mother and Danilo's mother came walking down the hill, into the garden. They both wore a festive dress and heels. Their jewelry reflected the sunlight.

Stella's mother kissed her daughter on the cheek, patted Rubia on her head, and looked around the table.

'You didn't say anything about other guests,' she told Stella. She sat down next to her and pulled an empty teacup towards her. Then she looked expectantly at Sofia.

'How beautiful both girls look,' said Danilo's mother. She smiled at Sofia.

'I made the dresses,' Stella said.

Rubia began to pull the paper from the present on the table in front of her.

'Of course, they can play with it together,' Angelina said quickly.

'Exciting,' said Danilo's mother, and sat down next to Sienna.

Sofia poured tea for Stella's mother, and then also for Danilo's mother when she indicated with a friendly nod that she would like some too.

Rubia tore open the paper. Stella leaned forward from her wheelchair and helped her. It was a three-story wooden dollhouse with a red-painted roof.

'Can you tell?' Sienna asked Sofia. 'It's this house. We made it ourselves from scrap wood that we found in the harbor.'

'It doesn't look very much like it,' Stella said. Sofia took Valentina out of her seat and let her touch the wooden house. Valentina touched the roof and reached into one of the open rooms where Sienna and Angelina had placed a wooden bed with a piece of cloth.

'It's beautiful,' Sofia said. 'Thank you.'

Rafaella's boys gathered around the table and together with the toddlers they blew out the two candles on the birthday cake. Rubia and Valentina dug into it with their hands and pieces of cake flew onto their new dresses.

It wasn't until the sun had set behind the hills, the girls were sleeping in their beds, Rafaella's sons lay exhausted on a rug on the grass, the two mothers had returned to town and Sofia had poured the wine, that Rafaella started talking about the war.

'Have you had another letter from Danilo yet?' she asked. 'I haven't heard from Jerome in three months.'

'Our letter is almost two months old,' Sofia said.

'In our neighborhood, more and more parents have heard that their sons have died,' Sienna said. 'In Greece or Yugoslavia. That's so close by, just across the sea, and that's where the fighting is.'

She stared into the distance. Sofia's sister was no longer a child.

'Or in Russia,' Angelina added. 'I heard that two brothers from one family died there.'

Stella took a sip of her wine. 'Luckily, we're winning. Read the papers and you will understand what I mean.'

'It's a war that should never have started,' Rafaella said. She shook her head sadly. 'Our men will probably never come back.'

'I don't understand why Mussolini sided with Germany,' Sofia said.

Both her sisters nodded in agreement.

Stella hissed. 'It's like I'm sitting at the table with a bunch of anti-fascists,' she said. 'And this is supposed to be a party?'

She pulled on the wheels of her wheelchair and pushed herself angrily to the front door. There she turned around. 'Better think of your children when you talk like that. Do not let them hear that you are traitors to our country.'

Novembre 1942

It was almost eleven o'clock in the evening when Sofia walked into the nursery and carefully lifted the mattress Valentina was sleeping on. She searched underneath with her hand. It wasn't there. She tried again, felt around to the sides, maybe it had shifted.

'I found your notebook,' Stella said from a corner of the dark room.

Sofia turned abruptly. Stella sat in her wheelchair with a blanket over her legs and was looking straight at her. Normally, she would be asleep. She held up the small brown-covered notebook.

Sofia tried to guess how much of her notes Stella had understood.

'It's nothing,' she said. 'It's just a note about a mountain here in the Apennines where I want to go someday.'

Every time she'd jotted down a message and memorized it, she'd ripped it out of the booklet and burned it. Only the note for tonight was still there.

'That's not true and it's insulting if you think I don't understand. That you still think I have brain damage. I know what it is and what you're doing.'

'We are against this war, against Nazi Germany.'

'Who's against it?'

'I can't tell you. It is a network, but the mutual contacts are minimal. That is safer for everyone.'

'Do you hear what you're saying? You put us in danger. Me and the girls.'

Stella looked at Valentina and Rubia. Their brown wavy hair spread over their shoulders and both of them were wearing yellow nightgowns that Stella had made.

'I love them too much to let this happen,' Stella said loudly.

'Shh, the girls, you'll wake them up.'

'If you're afraid they'll hear this, you should be really scared to put such a note under a child's mattress. If Danilo hears this when he comes back, he'll kick you out right away. He is fighting for our country.'

'Because he has to. That doesn't automatically mean he agrees to it.'

'You should never betray your own country. Danilo thinks so too, just look at the balcony. Isn't it clear to you he supports Mussolini?'

'His father modified the original balcony I designed. This railing is too harsh for the house. It wasn't Danilo who chose it.'

Stella opened the notepad and tore out the page. Defiantly, she tore it up into small pieces.

'No,' Sofia said loudly and ran over to her. Stella laughed, letting the scraps fall to the floor. She had lost her note for tonight.

A few hours later, Sofia tied her hair up tightly in the back and put on a dark coat. She closed the door to her attic room, crept down the stairs and past Stella's bedroom, which was dark.

The barn door creaked as she opened it. Sofia pulled out her motorcycle. Once out in the yard, she pushed it up the hill toward the road. Only when she was sure no one was approaching did she start the engine. In less than half an hour she delivered the message that she had tried to reread and memorize as best she could, after she had reconstructed the puzzle of torn paper on the floor.

In the empty square of Massignano, she parked her motorcycle and looked around to make sure no one was following her, before walking down a narrow street. Empty, no one was there. She walked quickly, turning right, into an even narrower alley. She looked back. No one. She knocked on a door; twice short, once long. A man with jet-black hair immediately opened it.

'What grows in the night?' he asked.

'Hope,' she replied.

The man opened the door wider and let her in.

'Monday afternoon, five o'clock, encirclement of an enemy unit. Gran Sasso,' Sofia said. She was sure that this was the information she had received from her contact in Fermo.

'Thank you for your heroism,' the man said, opening the door for her again.

'Good luck,' Sofia said, looking left and right. The street was empty. She raised the collar of her coat further. She might never know what was going to happen at Gran Sasso, but as a courier she had contributed to a fight against the fascists. At the end of the street, she walked through the narrow alley again and came to the square. Too late she heard the regular tapping of boots on the cobblestones. Two soldiers marched towards her. She quickly bent her head forward and tucked it further into her collar.

'Good evening,' they said.

She said nothing back. Held her breath. She heard the soldiers walking behind her, not holding back. Just as she got close to her motorcycle, the sound of the boots on the cobblestones stopped.

'Lady, wait a moment,' one of the soldiers said loudly. They came back. She quickly passed her motorcycle.

'Stop,' one soldier shouted.

She stopped and turned slowly.

'Do you live in this village?' asked the soldier with a small mustache.

'I don't recognize her,' said the other, taller soldier. His voice was high, and she guessed that he was only a few years older than she.

What could she say?

'I was in the cemetery to pray. My brother died in the battle for Stalingrad.'

'We're sorry for your loss,' said the young, tall soldier.

'Did he live in this village?' asked the other soldier. He smoothed his mustache.

She nodded.

'And you don't?'

'Yes, I do. I live in the valley between Massignano and Cupra Marittima.'

'That valley is big. Which house?'

'The house with the balcony with the arrows and circles.'

'I know that house,' said the young, tall soldier. 'That belongs to the son of Mr. Marinolli, the director of *Marinolli Pesci e Reti* in San Benedetto del Tronto. Is Mr. Marinolli still working in his fish business or has it been shut down by the war?'

'He is fighting at the front.'

'Long live Italy,' said the older soldier.

They clicked their boots, saluted and walked on.

A little over half an hour later she rolled down the hill to the garden with the motor turned off and parked the motorcycle in the shed. Stella's bedroom was dark. She turned the corner to the front door. There, in the dark, was the balcony that had saved her.

Febbraio 1943

At the kitchen table, Stella was using silver thread to embroider a monogram she had designed onto a napkin. Her precision work was astonishing, especially considering that she couldn't even move her hands two years ago. The feeling in her legs had returned, although she was still barely able to walk. Sofia sat down next to her.

'A letter has arrived from Danilo,' Stella said.

'What? What do you mean?'

Stella didn't look up from her embroidery. 'Two days ago.'

He's still alive, Danilo's still alive.

'Why are you only telling me now?' Sofia said in astonishment. 'What does it say?'

'He's coming home. Finally.'

'Where's the letter?'

'In the book on my nightstand. The postman delivered it while you were gone.'

Sofia ran to her bedroom, pulled the letter from the book, and sank onto the edge of the bed.

19 Gennaio 1943, 21:00

Dear Sofia and Stella,
Good news, I'm coming home. My duty is over, my battalion is being repatriated. The situation here in Russia is dire. Most of the men have been killed, and the majority of the survivors have permanent injuries to their hands and feet from the extreme cold we experienced in the field. My dragging leg meant that I had to stay in the command center and suffered no consequences.
How are the girls? My joy to be with you soon is unprecedented.

With love,
Your Danilo

He was coming home. She would see him again, hold him in her arms. Valentina would get to know her father.

'He'll be delighted to see how well I can move and talk,' Stella said loudly from the kitchen.

'I was afraid to hope any longer for this news,' Sofia said. She dropped the letter on the bed and covered her face with her hands.

'It won't be long before we get married. I want more children.'

Sofia picked up the letter and went to her attic. She counted the black lines she had drawn on the wall with charcoal. There were twenty-one. He had been gone for twenty-one months, now he was coming home. She placed the letter with his other letters that she kept in her own room, tied the red ribbon around it again, and put them away.

For the rest of the afternoon Sofia and Stella hardly spoke to each other. Stella was quickly trying to get all the handkerchiefs ready before Danilo returned, while Sofia tended the vegetables in the garden, washed the clothes, and cooked dinner. The girls played with the wooden dollhouse and the rag dolls.

The valley was quiet and dark. Stella was already in bed and reading a book when Sofia put out the fire in the kitchen, picked up the candle from the table, and walked past her bedroom door.

'Good night,' she said to Stella.

Stella said nothing back.

There were no more toddler noises from the girls' bedroom. They were sleeping. She kissed them both on the forehead. Up in the attic, she put on her nightgown and listened to an owl in the tree near the house. Hope grew in the dark night. She fell asleep.

A loud banging on the front door woke her and she immediately sat up in her bed. Creaking wood, as if something was being forced. Stomping in the hall downstairs. A chair slid across the floor, a door on the first floor opened. She jumped out of bed and ran to her bedroom door. Stella's voice, high and whispering. A man's voice. Danilo. He was home. She went down the stairs. The man's voice again, boots on the waxed floor. Boots. The click of boots. Another voice. The nursery door squeaked. Rubia cried.

'Mamma,' Valentina called.

Sofia wanted to run to her. Stella's voice, soothing. Rubia stopped crying. Boots on the stairs up. Sofia ran back to her room, opened the large door of the linen closet. Too predictable. The trunk. She opened the heavy lid, pushed aside linen, and quickly crawled in. Just as she was about to close the lid, she heard her bedroom door open. She stopped breathing. Soldiers entered, looked around, and immediately headed for the trunk. They grabbed her, pulled her out, through the room and hallway, down the stairs.

'Why?' she cried. 'Why are you arresting me?'

They didn't answer, and they pulled her past the children's bedroom where Stella was sitting in her wheelchair with her back towards her. She had taken the girls on her lap and was singing a soft lullaby.

'Stella, please,' Sofia called.

Valentina peered over Stella's shoulder and looked at her.

'Mommy,' she called, stretching out her little arms to be lifted.

'I love you,' Sofia said. Her voice trembled. 'Never forget that. Wherever I am, I love you. And also Rubia. You are special girls.'

She disappeared into the night.

9

We drive through the valley with the wheat fields and small nurseries. There are old houses along the narrow country road that stood here long before we were born. Where lives had already been lived before we came. Where people were happy, or sad. Where there has been laughter and tears, and where wars have been fought and peace has been made. The balcony of Palazzo Puro in the distance, high above everything. What happened here and who left her?

The farmer on the tractor in front of us waves gesturing that we can pass him and shouts loudly: *'Buongiorno vicini'* as we drive by.

'*Vicini*,' I say to Roger. 'He's already calling us neighbors.'

'We also have neighbors at home,' Roger says. He turns to Max. 'And pretty girls.'

'That's a stupid thing to say,' I say. 'Max, are you okay?'

'Yes, Mom, never mind,' he says, staring out the window.

'Why don't you watch a movie on your phone?' I say.

'He can do that for another 16 hours on the return journey,' Roger says. 'Maybe he should pay attention to his homework first. You have a French test after the holidays, right, Max? You now have plenty of time for that. Did you follow the schedule Mom made for you?'

'Can't you just stop with all your schedules for once?' Max asks, irritated.

Palazzo Puro. Her shutters are closed. It's as if she's waiting and only wakes up when someone opens her shutters. I stop, set the parking brake and get out. The scent of wild mint wafts past me as I walk down the hill, stepping on the young leaves. The bird in the tall pine next to the house sings as it does every morning.

'Do you want to say goodbye?' Roger asks when he has caught up with me. He puts an arm around my shoulder. 'I'm sorry, sweetheart,' he says. 'I know this was your dream.'

The sun hides behind the clouds.

'Is. Not was.'

'We'll try again in a few years, I promise.'

My phone rings. An Italian number.

'Mirella?' a woman asks. 'This is Valentina.'

'Hello,' I say surprised.

Roger looks at me questioningly and I put my hand in front of the speaker. 'It's Valentina, one of the sister's we bought the house from.'

He nods understandingly.

'I'm calling to ask if you found out anything about the drawing Rubia and I gave you?' Valentina says.

'Unfortunately little,' I say. 'There is a lot of old furniture, as you know, and there are also clothes, crockery, newspapers and books. And we found magazines, where fragments of a letter fell out.'

'Mirella?'

'Yes?'

Perhaps she could not understand my Italian, or the connection was bad.

'Mirella, this is Rubia,' Rubia says. 'What was written on the paper?'

Roger gestures for me to come along so that I can continue the story as we sit in the car and drive off. I shake my head.

'It wasn't quite clear, to be honest,' I reply. 'The letter was from Danilo and...'

'*È nostro padre,*' they say almost simultaneously.

Their father?

'And two women's names were mentioned in the letter; Stella and Sofia.'

'Mom, are you coming?' Max calls through the open window of the car. 'We still have sixteen hours to drive home, and it won't help if you stay here.'

I put my finger over my mouth to tell him to be quiet. Bored, he picks up his phone. Roger smells the mint he picked.

The sisters confer in Italian. I can't follow what they're saying.

'No, we don't understand why both names are in the letter,' Valentina says.

'What year was the letter written?' Rubia asks.

'In the 1930s, the exact year was eaten by a rat.'

Consultation again.

'No, we don't understand. Will you call us when you find out more?'

'That is not possible. We are going to sell the house.'

Roger hears it and comes to me.

'Let's both work for another ten years or so, then we have a bigger budget,' he whispers. 'And if we have a good plan, we look for a smaller house in better condition, so that we run less risk.'

'I don't want another house,' I answer.

'Mirella?'

'Yes?'

'Why are you selling the house so soon?' Valentina asks. 'I loved the house so much.'

'I didn't,' Rubia says.

The wooden front door, the ornate window above, the small alcove next to the door through which the grapes were brought in. I also love the house. I gently stroke the wood of the door at the back of the niche. I push it.

'Shall we leave, sweetheart?' Roger asks.

The hatch springs open and in the dark space the outline of the wine vats is vaguely visible. I stand on tiptoe. Just around the corner is a blue glass vase on an old shelf.

'Mirella, don't do it,' Valentina says. '*La casa è bella*! You don't find anything like that anymore.'

'Of course she has to sell it,' Rubia says. 'It's an old house with an ugly balcony.'

I pull out the vase and wipe it clean.

'It's not good that the hatch is open now,' Roger says. 'Animals will be crawling in. Now we have to go back into the house and close it from the inside.'

He puts his arm on my shoulder, and turns us around, signaling that we should sort it out now and then head back to the car. The sun comes out from behind the cloud and gives the bricks their golden glow. A gecko crawls over the wall and looks for the crack in the broken window frame.

'Mirella?'

The grasshoppers are quiet. The birds too.

'Mirella?'

'I'm staying,' I say.

'*Che ne dici?*' Valentina and Rubia ask. They don't understand what I'm saying.

'I don't understand what you mean,' Roger says, taking his arm off my shoulder.

'This is our place, not another house,' I say to him. 'I want to be here now and not in ten years.'

Roger sighs. 'Why do you always want the impossible?'

'Impossible in your eyes. But I know I can make it happen. Without a big budget, the renovation may take longer, but in the end, we live where we want to be.'

The phone in my hand has gone silent. The sisters have hung up.

'Max has to go back to school next Monday. And I have to work. Let's go.'

He walks back to the car.

'Are we finally going?' Max calls through the open window.

'Yes sweetheart. Mom is coming,' Roger says as he gets in.

The car up on the road, parked on the shoulder, with everything I love. The house below, waiting in the valley, with everything I dream about.

'Mom, let's go,' Max says.

'I'm sorry,' I say.

He looks at me uncomprehendingly.

'I'm staying here, sweetheart.'

I want to run after the car, tell them to stop. That I still want to come with them. I'm standing in the middle of the road, with my red suitcase next to me. Max sticks his head out the window, looks at me and waves.

I wave back desperate.

Come back.

This is not worth it. Boy, sweetheart, I don't want to leave you.

Soon they will drive out of the village, past the campsites by the sea, towards the ugly Po Valley.

Stop, they have to stop.

Stay here, Roger, turn around. You love me like I love you. We are in this together, we wanted this house. He can't take our son, and leave me alone.

I sob, rubbing my eyes with my hands. In the distance, the car turns the corner and is no longer visible.

'What's wrong with me?' I say to Margot when I call her. 'I'm supposed to go with them.'

'Darling, calm down. Take a deep breath. Where are you?'

'I'm sitting here on my suitcase, in the middle of the road.'

'That's not helpful, darling. Why would you do that?'

'I got out and they're gone.'

'Where are you?'

'At Palazzo Puro.'

Half an hour later Margot and Aron arrive in his little white car. Margot jumps out and hugs me.

'Darling, darling,' she says. 'What a difficult choice.'

'I don't understand why I did it. And now they are a long way from here.'

'Palazzo Puro has changed you. That's why you did it.'

'This is exactly what I predicted,' Aron says, when standing close by. 'Marriages are under pressure from this kind of...'

'Not now,' Margot hisses at him. He gets back his tidy car with his neat white polo shirt and dark blue linen pants.

'Come on, let's go back to the mobile home,' Margot says. 'I'll make you a cup of coffee there and you can unpack your suitcase again.'

'I'm going to stay here. I'll clean the rest of the first floor and move in here.'

'Then I'll help you,' she says. 'Aron, darling, I'm staying here. Thank you for the ride up here, darling.'

On the first floor, both the bedroom and Max's room have been emptied. We clean up the kitchen. There is an antique wooden table and four wooden chairs with fabric upholstery. Along the wall is an old china cabinet. The doors are crooked, a drawer has been pulled out and lies upside down on the floor.

'There are all sorts of things, aren't there, darling?' Margot says, looking into the china cabinet full of old plates, cups, glasses, pans, and plastic cups. She takes out some of the plates and makes piles on the dining table.

'I make one pile to throw away and one to keep,' she says. 'How nice, these kind of old plates with those roses painted on them for your bed and breakfast. Just too beautiful.'

I leave her.

Above the small black and white terrazzo countertop is a drainer in the same style as the china cabinet. I yank it, until it comes off. It falls to the ground with a bang.

'Are you okay, darling?' Margot asks, looking at the broken wall cabinet.

'They're probably already driving up the Po Valley. That's nearly four hundred kilometers from here.'

'Don't think about it, you'll feel better tomorrow if you sleep here.'

She opens the small white oven and studies it.

'I suspect this one still works,' she says after a few minutes. She opens a drawer. 'You put coal or wood in here, which heats this steel top plate. It's just slow cooking. Totally the trend.'

The spring water flows into the bucket. A splash of green soap immediately makes the kitchen smell fresh. It's the smell of hope, a clean house where we can stay. I start washing the small countertop; it remains gray. I scrub with the brush, at least half an hour. Slowly what happened to the terrazzo staircase in the hallway happens again here; it catches the light. It shimmers, as if to say it's ready for a fresh start. I remove cobwebs from the corners under the counter top. I scrub the table and chairs, and the stove. We work for hours on end. Finally, I mop the floor five times until it's really clean.

Margot walks over with the blue vase filled with different colored oleanders that she has picked in the garden.

'Beautiful, isn't it?' she says. 'Do you want to do more this afternoon?'

'Just the bathroom,' I say.

The bathroom that is less than a meter wide. There is an old sink from the 1930s and a toilet in the corner. When I pull the handle on the tank, the flapper moves and there's a lot of noise. Water begins to flow. Margot turns on the shower next to it. The water slowly drips out. After more than an hour of scrubbing, the bathroom is clean enough to use.

We have two bedrooms, a bathroom and a kitchen. Temporary.

I wipe the sweat from my forehead. When I step outside, the sun has already set behind the hills. It's been a strange day. Roger and Max must have already left Italy. The golden field next to the river, the olive trees on the hill on the other side of the valley. The smell of the sweet figs in the tree next to the house. The waving palm leaves. I want to be here.

Agosto 1944

Through the crack in the tailgate of the truck, part of the highway was visible. They were crammed in like animals in a cattle truck.

It was the third time she had been transferred from a police cell to a prison. The interrogations had been rough, yet the numbing pain was not caused by that, but by how much she missed Valentina.

And Rubia, both girls. Did they understand why Sofia wasn't at home anymore?

'Why were you arrested?' the boy of about fourteen asked her. They sat involuntarily close to each other.

'I am against this war, a partisan,' she said. 'They call me a traitor.'

'When were you arrested?'

'More than a year and a half ago. I was in the prison camp near Servigliano in Fermo.'

She closed her eyes. Valentina and Rubia, the house. The sea. Danilo, who had come home in the meantime and must be looking for her. Stella raising the two girls and hugging Danilo. She had written them. Short letters on small sheets of paper that she was sometimes given in prison. A few sentences. She had never received an answer.

It was muggy in the cattle truck. There was little fresh air coming in and the urine smell was penetrating.

'Did someone betray you?' the boy asked.

'Perhaps. I will never know for sure.'

The nightmares that kept her awake lingered every morning until they were taken over by the screaming of the guards or other inmates. Stella's voice whispering to the soldiers, the two toddlers on her lap as she sat with her back to her in the nursery.

The truck exited the highway and continued along a bumpy road. Everyone shook. A few people wailed, others were silent and stood with their eyes closed.

'I was betrayed by a friend who went to school with me,' the boy said. 'He had discovered that we are Jewish.'

'I'm sorry for you. He was no friend.'

'He was a very good friend. The war does strange things to people, my mother says.'

The truck lurched and slowed down.

Stella. Had the car accident and the war changed her, or had she always been like this? The thought that Valentina was now being raised by her made Sofia want to bury her nightmares deep down.

The boy waved at a woman standing in the front of the truck.

'Is that your mother?' Sofia asked.

'Yes, and next to her is my sister. She's twelve.'

The girl in a simple green dress with mud stains on it looked up at the small flickering lamp on the ceiling of the car.

'We were taken from our house last night,' the boy said. 'Only my brother is still hiding. I hope he can open the closet door himself. He's only five.'

They drove onto an unpaved area. High walls with barbed wire were just visible through the crack.

The car stopped and the tailgate was opened. Men with guns were waiting for them.

'Get out. This is Camp Bolzano,' one man said loudly. 'It's better not to get used to it here, this is just the last stopover in Italy, before you travel on to Auschwitz.'

10

The pleasant temperatures of July days turn into a sweltering hot August. They heat the earth even more and dry out the grass in the garden, leaving only a yellow carpet. Early in the morning, when the sun is still low, I get up and open the windows to breathe in the still fresh morning air. My new mattress is covered with a thin olive-green cotton blanket that pairs well with the headboard and its bunches of painted grapes. It is striking how cool it still is inside, while during the day the temperature rises to almost 35 degrees Celsius.

It is still quiet; they won't come until eight o'clock. Under my dress I put on sturdy construction shoes, I put on the yellow hardhat and take out my writing pad. In the hallway there is now a wooden wall along the stairs with an improvised door to the ground floor and a door to the attic. The terrazzo staircase was clean, now it is full of construction debris again. I have to ask the men to cover it.

In the attic, daylight enters through the roof. All of the roof tiles are outside in large piles next to the house. The first new beams have been installed between the old wooden beams. These are anchored in the walls on the sides. I still think the beams are thin for such a high, heavy roof, but it's according to building codes, Gustav said. As soon as the first layer of terracotta tiles is back on top, a thin layer of insulation is applied and then the old roof tiles will be put back. Just to be sure, I asked Gustav if this isn't half a solution, and whether an extra layer of cement should be applied between the two layers of tiles, as Lorenzo once explained to me. Gustav consulted with his colleagues in Slovak and said it was absolutely unnecessary.

When I call Roger, he doesn't answer. I take a picture and send it to him and Max. *The new roof beams are in*, I write below. I probably won't get a response, or only much later. Roger occasionally sends me a new overview of the expenses I've incurred, explaining that our savings balance is rapidly decreasing. *The value of our house is increasing*, I keep writing back. Next summer we can live here. Roger doubts whether he still wants to after the moment when I chose the house and not them.

Outside, the rumble of the approaching van breaks the silence. They park along the road. The four men talk loudly, their voices echoing down the stairwell as they make their way to the top floor. They greet me and go to the espresso machine in the corner on an old wooden table.

'In two weeks, the roof will be closed and we will be reinforcing the walls,' says Gustav.

He takes a sip of his coffee, which is passed to him by the little man with the round glasses – whose name I still don't know. I open my notebook. Great, they're a few weeks ahead of my schedule.

'Are you still putting those special reinforcement nets over the old brick wall here along the stairwell?' I ask. 'I mean, for earthquake protection?'

Gustav consults with his colleagues in Slovak.

The walls here are more than five meters high. Totally unsafe, Lorenzo had explained to me. The wall has a few stones with charcoal lines drawn on them and the years 1941, 1942 and 1943 written above them. I follow the lines with my finger. I count twenty-one. What was counted here?

'No, those reinforcement nets are not necessary,' says Gustav. 'We're going to plaster the walls. That saves you money and time.'

'Do you know what this was for?' I ask, pointing to the lines. 'You'd almost think someone was trapped here...'

The little man with the glasses comes to stand next to me and looks at it.

'What's your name again?' I ask him.

'This is a child's drawing,' he concludes.

He walks to the other men who have already climbed up to the roof via the high scaffolding they've assembled along the wall.

I touch the lines one more time. When the wall is plastered, this message from the past will disappear under the stucco forever. I close my eyes; the cribs, the shredded letters and these lines. How are they all related?

A man shouts down through the open roof that I need to leave, because it's dangerous to be on a construction site. I reply that I am wearing a hardhat and try again to recall the image of the past. A saw roars loudly.

'I think sausages were dried in the attic, made from the meat of the cows they slaughter themselves,' Gustav shouts through the hole in the roof. 'They kept track of the number of months. Get out of there now.'

Downstairs in the kitchen, Margot in a plain gray T-shirt and panties is singing as she makes her coffee.

'You realize that the men are already here?' I say to her.

'Darling, you can't miss that circular saw. Really, it's worse than that freight train that rumbled by when we were in our seaside chalet.'

She has tied her hair in a simple ponytail. There is a dark outgrowth in her hair that contrasts with the light blond hair.

'Is your hair actually brown?' I ask.

'No, it's not. It is dark blond. Do you like it? I wash my hair with ice cold water from the well, so pure.'

Strange that I've known her for so long and yet didn't know her real hair color.

She puts a cup of coffee in front of me on the dining table.

'And I hardly wear any makeup anymore, darling, did you notice? So easy in the morning, I can be ready in no time. It was quite a thick layer of foundation that I was using.'

Her face is more natural, more real.

'Aron thinks I'm even more beautiful this way, he says. Oh, he's such a charmer, really, you wouldn't say it, but he is.'

'Aron?'

Someone shouts something on the roof, and the freight elevator on the outside of the house is activated. The platform comes past the kitchen window with a pile of roof tiles on it.

'They're going fast, aren't they?' I say. 'The first tiles are already on one side of the roof. If only Roger had believed in my planning. I mean, how long have I been a project manager? I really know what I'm doing.'

Margot nods. 'Yes, these kinds of jobs are easy for you. I can't do it, you know, but you organize everything very efficiently.' She takes a sip of her coffee. 'I've thought about it again. Maybe I just didn't want to admit it...'

I'm trying to understand what she means.

'I think I love him, yes really, I can't believe it myself, but if I think about it...'

Adamo again.

She ponders and looks at the elevator platform that is now going down, empty again. 'It's not lust, that's for sure. It's like love. Is that possible, do you think? That I feel that, I mean?'

Aron, she's talking about Aron. We hear the roof tiles slide across the roof, making a lot of noise.

'When I'm with him, I feel a kind of peace, darling. I don't have to do anything, and I don't have to pretend to be someone else. He accepts me as I am, and thinks I'm beautiful every moment, whether I'm in an old sweater or in a tight skirt. He asks what I'm feeling, what I'm thinking about and...'

'Aron?'

'Did you see his longer hair? And his real hair color is darker too, he bleached it like I always did. We are similar in that regard.'

That will be the only similarity.

'I feel that I just want to be with him for who he is.'

'There must be attraction,' I say. 'You're not having sex with him, are you?'

'Darling, don't be silly. Of course I have.'

How could I have doubted this?

'And do you still want to be with Aron when Adamo comes over at night?'

He regularly drives his big jeep into the garden late at night and parks next to the house, out of sight of the road. The headlights that illuminate the house are quickly extinguished, only to come back on a few hours later when he drives away.

'Then I want to be with Adamo. He has told his wife that he wants to divorce her and move in with me.'

'And what about Aron?'

'What do you mean, darling?'

'You just said you might be in love with Aron.'

'Oh, it's all so confusing, really.'

'Well, I think there is one big plus about Aron. He's not like Tom who cheated on you all these years. Adamo, on the other hand, we know for sure that he is cheating on you.'

She thinks about it. 'No, that is not true. Adamo does not deceive me.'

'What about the fact that he's married?'

'Yes, okay, that's what you mean. That's different.'

She walks to Max's room, which she's using as her bedroom for the time being. We took the bed frame with the white and blue upholstery from the attic and put a new mattress on it. Half an hour later she leaves for Silvan and Frederico's restaurant in her black waitress' uniform and white apron.

I open my laptop to search the want ads for project manager job openings. I read one job description, move my cursor to the button to apply, and I have a moment of doubt. Fluent in Italian and English are the skills they seek. I'm not there yet. Nevertheless, I press the button to send my profile with my work experience, and the screen shows the confirmation that my application has been submitted. I open the next ad, and after an hour I've sent out ten application letters.

The first rejection comes in just as I'm about to close my laptop. This is not a good sign, but I am relieved, and that's strange. For years I have lead projects, given presentations and managed teams. I worked through nights. Roger has often called me a workaholic, and got upset when I didn't come home in time to fit in with the evening schedule: cooking at six thirty, dinner at seven, watching the news at seven thirty and then free time from eight o'clock until ten thirty when it was time to go to bed. This house in Italy was a break with everything for me, and I almost lost it the day Roger and Max drove away.

After lunch I climb a high ladder in the kitchen in an old T-shirt and shorts. Brian transferred twelve hundred euros into our bank account as a commission for the sale of the house to the German couple, and I bought beautiful white lime paint for all the rooms on the first floor. The paint roller is attached to a long pole, but I can barely reach the three-and-a-half meter high ceiling. It covers well over the anti-fungal treatment I put on it yesterday, and the ceiling looks fresh against the walls with their old coat of paint. It's still astonishing how well the plaster layer has been preserved here after so many years of being abandoned. A blob of paint falls from the brush onto my cheek and I rub it away. I've pulled Margot's bright yellow jersey dress over my hair so that it doesn't get full of paint. In the front, the dress is wrapped under my chin, like I'm wearing a big balaclava. 'It's too tight for me anyway,' Margot told me when she handed over the dress. She found it strange that I was surprised at her statement.

Brian calls and asks if I can come tomorrow to a viewing of a house near the town of Offida. Then we can have lunch together, he suggests. I send a message to Roger to say that I am trying to sell another house and earn money for paint for the attic.

Just as I'm getting back up on the ladder, Gustav comes in.

'We can do that for you,' he says. 'Then you can take off that winter sports hat.'

'What do you want to say?' I ask.

'We're going quickly with the roof; it almost looks if those tiles are flying up on their own.'

'That's good.'

Really, I couldn't have wished for a better team. Except that I don't understand them when they talk to each other, they do a good job at a low price.

Gustav looks around. 'If you don't want us to do anything else here on the first floor, it might be a good idea for us to knock off that half-collapsed extension at the back of the house? That's not even a day's work.'

'Really? Would it go that fast?'

The extension was probably built in the 1970s and is the most unreliable part of the house. In my drawings I have removed it, so that the house regains its original shape. A square house, as often found in the villages and towns on the hills.

'Yes, we're coming with a bulldozer and we'll have it gone in no time.'

'Isn't that a bit rough?'

He shakes his head. 'That's only rough if you don't do it right. I ask Tironeski to arrange the bulldozer for next week.'

So that's the name of his assistant, the man with the round glasses.

'And the stucco on the attic walls, when are you doing that? If I know that, I can update my schedule. I want to send it to Roger tonight.'

'We'll start on that tomorrow. I have two new men from Slovakia who stucco perfectly.'

My phone rings. It's an unknown number.

'Sorry, I have to take this one,' I say to Gustav.

An unknown woman asks when I am available for the position. I have no idea what position she is talking about exactly, because of the many applications I sent out at the same time. She explains that their company's IT department in Ancona is not functioning well and they need a temporary project manager to improve the structure and processes of the department.

'Can you come by for an interview this afternoon?' she asks.

'This afternoon?' I ask.

'Yes, if it doesn't suit your schedule, I'll call the next candidate on my list and schedule that appointment first. I can schedule you later in the week, if we haven't found a suitable candidate by then.'

If I have a new job, it means Roger can quit his and look for a new one here.

'I checked my calendar,' I say quickly. 'And I can move my appointments around a bit so that I can come this afternoon.'

'Fine, I'll schedule your interview for three o'clock and send you the information later.'

I pull the bright yellow dress off my head. The ceiling has only had a few strokes of new paint; I push the painting stuff aside and head for the bathroom. It takes a long time for the shower water to become lukewarm. On the roof, the men are shouting at each other.

I run the brush through my hair, fasten it tightly in a ponytail and put on make-up. My neat dress and the dark blue blazer, which I brought for cold evenings, are warm. The woman I have been for years reappears in the mirror. She was far away.

From the shed I take the old, light-green bicycle with a basket. The tires are soft, the saddle is too low. When I cycle down the winding road to the station, I break out in a sweat. I stop at the side of the road, take off my blazer and hang it over the bicycle handlebars.

I arrive at the station in Cupra Marittima just in time for the train to Ancona. As the train slowly leaves the station, it passes the mobile home we stayed in and Silvan and Frederico's restaurant. I'd rather get out again.

The office is located in the middle of the old town in a tall, light-gray stucco building on an immense square with lawns, gravel walkways, oleanders pruned into trees, and a bronze statue in the middle.

A shiny nameplate with the company name hangs next to the sliding glass doors of the entrance. The woman behind the counter asks who I'm coming to see, and when she's done the necessary checks, she hands me a visitor's pass that I have to attach to my blazer.

I take a seat at the large oval table near the wall of real hanging plants in the hall. While I wait, a few people walk in and out, neatly dressed, sometimes shaking hands as they pass. There is white lime paint under my nails, I try to clean them. The elevator door opens and a woman in a well-tailored black suit introduces herself. We take the elevator to the fourth floor.

'Have you read the extended profile?' she asks as we stand in the elevator. Profile?

'The profile of this position, which I attached to the invitation?' she says.

Her mail came at the same time Gustav knocked on the bathroom door. I had just put on my dress and blazer, and Gustav asked me for a first-aid kit. Tironeski had stepped on a long, rusty nail sticking out of an old beam and it had pierced the sole of his shoe. He held his shoe and sock in his hand, and wrapped around his foot was a piece of paper that was already red with blood. In the kitchen, Gustav tended Tironeski's wound. I hadn't read the profile.

'Did you see it? That profile contains essential information about this position.'

She opens the door of a conference room and two men in suits stand up.

'Yes, I read it,' I say.

I walk to the table and the man in the white shirt introduces himself as the company's HR advisor before introducing the older man in a gray pinstripe suit as the IT director I may be working for. I smile kindly.

I only half follow the general explanation of the HR advisor about their company, which develops software programs for shipping companies. Although I have become accustomed to people speaking rapid Italian, the business terms used by the HR advisor are new to me. I nod and shake my head at the same time. The IT director takes over the conversation. He says that there are eighty specialists working in the IT department, but that a number of things are not going well. The concepts about computers, networks and security issues are easier to follow since he's using the English instead of Italian names for them. The problem sounds like any other company I've worked for in recent years. With similar problems: a dysfunctional department, a team leader who is not suitable for the position, costs that are too high, and project lead times that are too long.

My phone rings. I forgot to put it on silent mode. I quickly take it out of my bag, turn Margot's call down and put the phone next to me on the table.

'My apologies,' I say. 'It won't happen again.'

'What do you think of the profile you received with the extra information?' asks the director.

It's too hot with my blazer on.

'Good,' I say. 'Very good.'

A trickle of sweat forms at my hairline and I wipe it away as inconspicuously as possible.

'So, you also think that half of the company's IT specialists could be fired given the current circumstances. Would you be able to do this dispassionately?'

The screen of my phone lights up and out of the corner of my eye I read Margot's message: Adamo doesn't want to leave his wife.

Bad news. It happens to her over and over again.

A second message comes in with a big icon of a crying face.

'Would you like to answer that message first?' asks the HR advisor, looking at my phone.

'No, definitely not,' I say. 'It is not unexpected that this is happening.'

'What do you mean?' asks the director.

'A married man does not leave his wife. Uh, my apologies. That's an entirely different topic. Your question, yes, your question about firing employees, uh, I can answer that. It is true that I have often done these kinds of projects. Of course, it remains an unpleasant situation for employees, but with a good explanation and the correct lump sum payment, this can be easily arranged.'

The men listen and nod, while my phone continues to light up.

Once outside I immediately take off my blazer, walk back to the station and in the meantime call Margot.

'I'm so sad, darling. Why didn't you answer?'

'I was in a job interview.'

'Oh. But I really needed to talk to you, you know,' she sobs. 'Now I'm already with Silvan and Frederico. I just keep on crying. Everything of Tom comes back again. Like he cheated on me all these years.'

The train is overcrowded when I board for the journey back to Cupra Marittima.

'And now Adamo is doing the same thing,' she says. 'This is why I don't want a relationship. Empty promises and deceit.'

'Adamo is married,' I say. 'You shouldn't want to have a relationship with him.'

'You're looking at it so black and white again. Can't you just be sad for me for once?'

'I do feel sorry for you. We'll talk about it when I get home, okay?'

'Ah thank goodness, there he is. Frederico, darling, I really need to talk to you.'

'Sweetheart, how do you like my new pants with the legs just above the ankles? Totally in style, right? Hey sweetie, what's the matter with you? Come here with your sorrow, in my arms, come. What happens? Tell me.'

The old bicycle pedals move stiffly because of all the rust, and because of the wind coming from the sea, the ride along the coast takes longer. I ride out of the village, past some hotels and apartments, and arrive at the beginning of the valley. Behind an old iron gate there are parked cars with handwritten sheets of paper behind the windows with sales prices. Most of the cars still look quite new, but there are older cars in the back. I push open the gate and look at the first row. The prices are around ten thousand euros, which is too much if we still have to demolish the extension.

When I get to the last row, a man with a cigarette hanging from the corner of his mouth approaches me. He greets me and asks if he can help. I explain to him that I am looking for a car to drive to my job in Ancona.

The older cars have dents and some rust. At the very end of the row, an ice-blue hood rises above the other cars. I walk towards it and the man follows me.

'What kind of work do you do, ma'am?' he asks.

'I am a project manager and will be working at a company in Ancona where I have to lay off IT staff.'

'Then this isn't the car for you, ma'am. At the front are the cars that match your status. This car is for farmers who live in the valley beyond.'

On the body it says *Fiat Fiorino pick-up*. The bumpers are metal, mostly rusted, as are the hubcaps. The square headlights betray that it is from the 1970s. There is a small cab with two seats and behind it a large cargo bed. With this I can transport furniture and home accessories when the house is ready to be decorated. I can carry plants in it that I buy from nurseries in the valley. Maybe I should create a landscaping plan tonight.

'You look chic,' the man says, looking at my blue blazer and stylish dress. 'Again, you'd better pick a front row car.'

The sheet of paper behind the windshield says that the pickup truck comes with fresh engine oil and a full tank of gas. And that for only two thousand euros.

'I'll buy it.'

The man looks at me in surprise. 'Are you sure, ma'am? This car has been here for at least fifteen years.'

'It's still drivable, isn't it?'

'Yes, that's true. It just has no airbags, no headrests, and the passenger seat leather is torn.'

'Can I pay with my bank card inside your office?'

At the gate I put my bike in the bed of the truck. The gear shift creaks when I change gears. I open the windows and my hair blows in the wind as I drive home through the valley.

Gustav and his men have gone home, Margot is working an evening shift with Silvan and Frederico. She'll be able to talk about Adamo with Frederico.

I put a garden chair outside in the last of the afternoon sun and close my eyes. If Roger and Max were here now, everything would be perfect.

My phone beeps. There's a message from the woman from the interview this afternoon. They have decided to hire someone else for the job. A project manager who can downsize with an iron fist and is not distracted by friendships. She ends with a sad emoticon, which I find unprofessional.

Settembre 1945

The wheat field and the hills were as beautiful as Sofia remembered. The balcony railing with the circles and arrows that jutted out just above the oleanders was now softened by the grape vine making its way through the holes. The palm next to the front door had grown and the oleanders were bearing their last blooms of the season.

She stroked her short hair, which was slowly growing back. Children's voices in the garden. She walked down the hill. Laughter and splashing in water. Two girls played in a galvanized steel tub and poured cans filled with water over each other's heads.

'No, Rubia. Not so much water,' Valentina shouted. 'That's not nice.'

Her daughter, how she had grown. The toddler who had called to her the night she was arrested, spreading her arms to be lifted away from Stella's lap, was now a five-year-old. Lost years. Unnecessary and unfair.

'I do it anyway,' Rubia said teasingly.

The long brown hair of the two girls fell in waves down their backs. Valentina looked in Sofia's direction and smiled. Her green eyes matched with her mint green bathing suit with its white ruffles.

'Hello ma'am,' Valentina said.

'Mamma,' Rubia yelled. 'There's a strange lady in our garden.'

Sofia hid behind the oleander bush. Around the corner from the house Stella rolled up in her wheelchair. She wore a wide skirt of blue satin fabric and a white blouse. On her lap sat a baby in a white sun hat.

Sofia stooped further behind the bush. Rubia pointed in her direction. Stella stroked Rubia's hair and said something to her. She wore red lipstick. With one hand she grabbed the back of her wheelchair and pushed herself up. She stood, faltered for a moment, and then stood up. Stiff, Sofia squatted on her haunches.

'Stella, we'll be late getting into town if we don't get the girls out of the pool now.'

Danilo's voice.

Sofia gasped for breath. There he stood. After all those years. In a light blue shirt. Healthy. Strong.

'The girls heard something in the bushes,' Stella said, as Danilo walked over to her. 'I think a porcupine or a feral dog.'

'I'm sure that's what it is. Is Adamo ready to go yet?' Danilo said, taking the baby from Stella. 'My mother is waiting for us.'

Stella sank back into the wheelchair and looked once more in Sofia's direction. She called the girls and wheeled into the hall. Rubia and Valentina got up, held hands, and followed her inside. Danilo looked again at the oleander bush and closed the front door.

Sofia kept walking, faster, further. Away, she had to go away.

She had almost died, like most of the others around her. Due to cold, lack of food, abuse or illness. By a bullet, flying without notice, without cause or justice. Women in her barracks had died, crying for their children. She had clung to the hope that Danilo and Valentina were safe and waiting for her.

They were, safe. But they hadn't waited for her.

Their lives had continued while hers had stopped on that night. She tried to see everything clearly. Her feet hurt. The sun burned as she walked down the coastal road toward San Benedetto del Tronto. Were Danilo and Stella married? A painful sting. Danilo had chosen, he had been holding the evidence in his arms.

Valentina, her girl. Did she know that Stella was not her mother and Rubia was not her sister? Was she supposed to know? She now had a rich life with all the possibilities Sofia could never give her. As a working-class mother, unmarried, they would be considered scum.

Cars drove by, dust whirling up.

Sofia had to let her go.

The narrow street lined with tiny houses on either side hadn't changed, as if nothing had happened over the years. Her childhood home actually seemed smaller than she'd remembered. The same curtain hung in front of the kitchen window. A neighbor passed by and recognized Sofia.

'What a tragedy for your family,' he said. 'Sorry.'

He walked on.

She didn't understand him. She knocked on the wooden front door and waited. Nothing. Once again. Stumbling in the hallway. An unknown woman with a messy bun in her hair and an apron with a spot of tomato paste on it opened the door and looked at her questioningly.

'What can I do for you?' she asked.

The mirror in the hallway was still there, and the wooden coat rack with copper hooks hadn't changed either.

'I've come for my mother and sisters.'

'They don't live here.'

The woman wanted to close the door again, Sofia took a quick step forward and stopped her.

'Do you know where my mother and sisters went?' she asked.

'No, we moved here after a bomb devastated our previous street. This house was empty. We rented it through a broker.'

'Wasn't there anything left?'

'The house was fully furnished. There were even some dishes left on the counter. And all the clothes were still in the closet.'

'And where are our possessions now?'

'We mostly use the furniture ourselves; the clothing was old and we burned it in a hole in the garden.'

Her knees went weak, and she gripped the doorframe to prop herself up.

'We did keep a box of personal items,' the woman said. 'No one has come to pick it up yet. Just wait here.'

The woman closed the door only to open it a few minutes later and place a box on the ground in front of her.

'You can take this with you if you want,' she said.

She was transfixed to the ground. This box was all that was left?

'Don't you want it?' the woman asked impatiently.

She opened the box. Her sisters' notebooks. Diagonally below were a few reading books. She picked up the top notebook and took a pencil from the holder that stood upright next to the notebooks and books in the box. She had to write a message for them to leave behind with this woman.

'My lasagna is burning. Can you check the box elsewhere?'

She opened the notebook. There were scribbles in the middle of the paper. Large irregular letters, written quickly and carelessly.

Sofia, run.

We have been betrayed by

She turned the page; the rest of the notebook was blank.

'Are you Sofia?' the woman asked, looking at the note.

She nodded. The smell of the hundreds of women locked together in barracks, without water and heating, returned. Where they got so cold at night in their thin blouses and pants that they cuddled together in bed. Lice that itch and burn. Hardly any food after forced labor. It had almost, if not completely, broken her, just as it had broken women around her every day. Sick and emaciated, without love, without family, without hope, they had died.

'You've come back,' the woman said, seeming to think she had a riddle to solve. 'I don't know if your mother and sisters are coming back. We burned the pamphlets with partisan slogans.'

Mr. Armacci. It had taken three weeks before she found him waiting for her as usual at the entrance of his bookstore on a Sunday afternoon. He'd asked her to join him at the wooden table and picked up the drawing sheets without saying anything about where he'd been.

Her house designs with the symmetrical lines; they had soon given way to the block letters of slogans, and drawings of soldiers and prisoners of war.

At night, when the city slept, he closed the shutters of the low space above his shop and by the dim light of candles, he printed the pamphlets. Her sisters and Rafaella cycled through the dark city and pasted them to the walls, while Sofia, working as a courier on her motorcycle, delivered messages to partisans in the villages around the city.

Only once had Sofia made a sketch in her notebook at home, the image was of a house with men fighting in the foreground and the text *O Partigiano, siamo la resistenza* above it, she meant to work this out on a large sheet in the afternoon with Mr. Armacci. Just as she had finished her sketch and was about to close her notebook, Stella had come into the kitchen and stared at the drawing. She had only asked 'Are you going back to visit your mother and sisters later today?'

Sofia scribbled something on a blank sheet in her sister's notebook. 'Would you please give this note to my family?'

She folded the note in half and handed it to the woman.

'Every Sunday morning at nine o'clock I'll be waiting in the harbor for their return.'

She would wait for them. As long as it took.

'Estate agent Brennesi,' the woman said. 'They rented out the house to us. Perhaps they know more about what happened to your family?'

The nets were woven, the fish filleted. Nothing seemed to have changed, and yet everything was different. Through the open windows at the top of the wall, she heard Marta's voice urging the girls to work faster. She stepped through the swinging doors, recognized a few girls, but Rafaella wasn't there. Marta walked over to her.

'You were never the fastest,' said Marta. 'I won't hire you anymore.' She put her hands on her wide hips and looked at Sofia again. 'You're way too skinny.'

'Please, I need the work,' she said.

'You can report to Mr. Danilo Marinolli for other work, as long as it's not in my fishmonger's.'

'Danilo?'

'Yes, he's at his office in the weaving mill,' said Marta. She crossed herself. 'He took over the business from his father and uncle who died in the war.'

Danilo. In the office above the weaving mill. The place where his father assaulted young girls. It seemed a long time ago when she was still young and naive. When she still dreamed about possibilities that turned out to be impossible, like marrying a rich man she loved. The dreams of designing houses had been blotted out by what she had seen in the camp.

'And Rafaella?' Sofia asked.

Martha shook her head. 'I've heard rumors that she was arrested while distributing pamphlets with other girls at night.'

That night that changed everything forever.

Half an hour later, Sofia was standing in front of the window of the real estate brokers' office, the one who had rented out her family's house. She looked in through the window. There was a man behind a wooden desk. He was wearing a three-piece suit, his hair was combed tightly and waxed. He looked up from his work and quickly came to the door.

'Sofia, is that you?' he asked.

That voice. She recognized that voice.

'You're not saying you don't recognize me, are you? I have never forgotten you.'

Stefano, the boy next door from the street behind her. The man her mother thought she should marry. The man her mother had suggested she trick into thinking she was expecting his baby, when the child wasn't his.

'Stefano,' she said.

He took a step back and let her in.

'You're as beautiful as I remember,' he said. 'Do you still live in the valley?'

She shook her head.

'Your hair is different, it's short,' he said. 'Are you married?'

'Do you work here?' she asked.

'As a clerk. After the war, new opportunities arose. I no longer work in the harbor; I keep the books here at the office and collect the rents.' He smiled. 'If you don't live in the valley anymore, are you looking to rent a house now?'

'No, I'm not married and I'm not looking for a house.'

He looked at her wonderingly.

'I'm looking for my mother and sisters,' she said. 'Their house has been rented out to another family.'

'I'm so sorry for them. I respected your mother.'

'What do you mean?'

'Don't you know?' He looked at her questioningly.

'No, nobody tells me anything.'

He pointed to a leather armchair in the corner of the small office and poured a glass of water, which he set on the coffee table next to her.

'I'm really sorry,' he said again. 'I don't really know how to tell you…'

He sank into the other armchair opposite her.

He remained silent.

'I want to…' Sofia said. 'I need to know what happened.'

'I was still at the front when it happened,' Stefano began.

The glass of water in Sofia's hand trembled slightly.

'I heard from my parents that your mother and sisters were arrested one night in 1943. The whole neighborhood talked about it. No one knows where they were taken and no one has seen them again.'

The glass shattered into hundreds of splinters on the floor. Water splashed against her legs.

He rushed over to her, put a hand on her shoulder. 'I'm so sorry,' he said again.

A customer came into the office, saw the situation, and then left.

Her sisters who had wanted to know everything about boys, about kissing. They should have experienced crushes instead of perilous bike rides with bags full of pamphlets. Their mother hadn't known, or maybe she had.

Stefano had walked away and now returned with a dustpan and a brush. He swept up the glass.

'How can I help you?' he asked. 'I'll take you home. Where do you live?'

'I don't have a house.'

'Where do you sleep then?'

She had no idea.

He looked at her for a long time.

'You know, why don't you come with me?' he said. 'I moved to Ripatransone after the war.'

'What about your wife and children?'

'I am not married.'

It wasn't a good idea, but she had no other option.

Domenica, 23 Giugno 1946

Sundays were the days Sofia most looked forward to, but also the days that hurt her the most. Early in the morning she left Ripatransone on her scooter and followed the road down the hills towards the coast. The harbor area was still quiet, most of the workmen had the day off.

She drove to the closed doors of the weaving mill. She slumped to the floor with her back against the wall. She sat there for at least half an hour, sometimes longer. Peering across the water, across the terrain, hoping that one Sunday her mother or sisters would come round the corner. That they could hold each other, comfort each other. That there was an end to her uncertainty about what had happened to them.

She had often stopped by the town hall and the police to inquire, but there was never any news.

When it was well past ten o'clock, she usually got up and rode her scooter to her childhood home. The same curtain was still there. However, the plastered facade was painted light pink. If she stood in front of the door too long, the woman who now lived there would come out and say no one had come by.

She drove through the streets of the residential area and asked people if they had heard anything about her family. At the grocer's, she asked for information from the young girl behind the counter and the customers in line. She got groceries and left the city, and headed back towards Ripatransone.

Through the valley.

She slowed down as she passed the balcony with arrows and circles. She drove by slowly each week, hoping to catch a glimpse of the girls. Sometimes they were playing in the garden, sometimes Stella opened the window of the children's bedroom or hung the laundry outside. Once in a while Danilo was standing behind a window. The moments were brief, seconds rather than a full minute, and they cut through her like a freshly sharpened knife.

Today it seemed quiet at the house. You could usually see from afar whether someone was moving behind the windows.

Near the driveway, the girls were walking up the road. Their yellow dresses had small white polka dots and white bows on the back. They looked at her and waved. Sofia waved back as she approached.

'Hello madam,' Valentina said to her. She laughed wholeheartedly.

Sofia slowed down and put her feet on the ground. Rubia and Valentina both wore bows in their wavy hair. Valentina was a few centimeters taller than Rubia and her hair was as dark brown as Sofia's. Rubia had slightly lighter brown hair. Their green eyes were almost identical.

'Hello Valentina and Rubia,' Sofia said.

'Daddy,' Rubia shouted loudly. 'This lady knows our names.'

She turned and ran down the slope into the garden.

Sofia tilted her head slightly and looked at Valentina. She took in everything, her eyes, her skin, her lips. Her scent was familiar.

'You've grown up,' Sofia said.

'You too. Because I remember you from when I was little.'

It was as if Sofia had been punched in the stomach. She wanted so badly to put down her scooter and take Valentina in her arms, hug her, and tell her she would never leave her again.

'Valentina, come in to the house,' Danilo called. 'The street is dangerous.'

He walked out of the back of the house into the front yard, put his hand over his eyes and stared at her.

'Valentina, you're a special girl,' Sofia said quickly. She briefly touched her hair. Soft and smooth. She squeezed the throttle and drove off. As she drove past the side of the house, she saw that Stella was standing behind the window in the laundry room.

Please, be the best mother you can be to my daughter.

For the next few weeks, Sofia skipped the drive to the house on Sundays out of pain and fear. The pain of seeing Valentina and not being allowed to be with her, and fear that Danilo or Stella had recognized her. After the visit to the harbor, she drove straight back to Ripatransone where she put the groceries on the dining table in the small house. She was getting ready to go to church, like every Sunday. There she lit a candle for her mother, her sisters and Rafaella. She prayed for them.

After church, she made lunch and then later, prepared dinner. Like she did every other day of the week. Then she swept the sidewalk in front of their door and scrubbed the house. Polishing wax on the wooden cupboards and tables. Bleach on the tiles. His shirts uncreased on wooden hangers in his closet. Her hands immersed in cleaning products, for hours, until they dried out, turned red and showed small cracks. Stefano saw her damaged hands and asked if she was happy. Maybe she would rather live in the city again? At the harbor?

He loved the simple dishes she made for him. Over dinner he talked about his work at the real estate agency, the neighbors, his parents and brother who lived on the ground floor of the house. About the weather and the hanging plants further down their narrow street. About the winegrower in the valley or the silversmith in the square. The opera, the restoration of the streets. The new technologies and the desire to buy his own car. And about his love for her that grew more and more. Sofia listened in silence, nodding now and then. All the stories seemed to take place outside of her. Like she wasn't there.

'What do you really think?' Stefano asked her over lunch. 'Do you think that we should start selling houses at our office instead of just renting them out? I think home sales are on the rise. Now that the war is forgotten, everyone wants to spend money on improving their living conditions.'

The war was not forgotten.

'I think it's a good idea,' Sofia said.

She was silent again.

'There's money to be made with that,' Stefano said. 'My boss doesn't believe it and thinks the risk is too high. He has to keep up his reputation as a landlord, he says, but I don't agree.'

'Why don't you start your own office?'

He looked at her in surprise. 'What do you mean?'

'Start your own office here in Ripatransone. There is no real estate agent in this city yet.'

'Is that possible?'

He pushed his empty plate over to her so she could take it away.

'The bank may want to lend you money,' Sofia said, reaching for the plate. The soapy water in the sink made the kitchen smell like a freshly mowed lawn.

'I can help you,' she said without looking back. 'I can work in the office.'

He came and stood next to her. 'Women don't work in an office. Wouldn't you rather work somewhere as a maid?'

'I can help make the advertisement texts for the houses. I see the beauty of houses. We can become partners.'

'Love partners, you mean.' He put his hand on her hips and kissed her neck. No, she didn't mean that. But she was silent.

11

It's early in the morning as I sit at my laptop and read the nine rejections of the applications which I sent yesterday. Again, I am looking for available jobs.

When I call Roger at exactly five past seven – he's in the ten-minute slot that fits between his breakfast and leaving for the office – I say I've never been turned down for a position before and I don't understand the reason.

'Me neither,' he says. 'Usually you think your work is more important than friendships.'

'Indeed, that's exactly what I mean.'

'Why don't you come home to us?' he asks. 'Everything is still the same, you can pick up your old life where you left it.'

'Gustav and his men are making good progress. If I stay now, we can live here in a few months.'

'You've seen my cost summary, haven't you? Our savings are running out.'

'I'll have Gustav demolish the extension at the back of the house, that's the last thing. I am painting all the rooms myself.'

'What about the new kitchen and bathroom?'

'We can fix it next summer. For the time being, we can use the current kitchen and bathroom.'

'I don't even know if I still want to move. Especially not now that you're being rejected for jobs, while I know that you always make a great impression during an interview.'

'This time I was less authoritative and also distracted. That won't happen to you if you apply here. You always prepare well. And there are plenty of open positions for financial specialists.'

He sighs. 'Well, I don't know. Has Margot gone yet?'

'She's still working at Silvan and Frederico's and sleeping in Max's future room for now. She was planning to live with Adamo at the winery, but now he's not divorcing his wife.'

'That was to be expected. This keeps happening to her.'

'Yes, I tried to warn her about it. I feel so bad for her. Is Max around?'

'Yes, wait a minute.' He calls to him in the background.

'Hi Mom, where are you?' Max asks when he picks up the phone from Roger.

'Still in the house,' I reply.

'When are you coming home?'

My stomach tightens. 'The house will be beautiful.'

'If you don't come, I'll come to you,' he says. 'Sofia says there is a good high school in San Benedetto del Tronto.'

'I would love it if you came. Are you still in touch with that Italian girl?'

'Yes, we chat every day. Is there already Wi-Fi in the house?'

'No, not yet. However, I did paint your bedroom. Fresh white, that looks cool with the concrete floor which I'll leave as is.'

'Ok. Dad misses you; did you know that?'

'I miss you too.'

'He's sometimes so confused that the evening schedule doesn't go according to plan. Now we sometimes eat together at half past seven and watch a movie afterwards.'

'Is that very annoying for you?'

'No, it's actually nice. You probably like it better too. And he's finally considering letting me have a dog.'

'Oh no, not one with the kind of fur that creates such a mess that you have to add another cleaning time to an already full schedule?' I say with a laugh.

Years ago, I brought home a puppy, which I had to return the next day.

Max laughs too. 'I told him that I want two. One as a bonus for all those years of waiting.'

We laugh together. I miss them.

A flock of birds flies over the wheat field towards the hills with olive trees. Roger without a schedule and with a dog, that only happens in a parallel universe, doesn't it?

Just as I'm about to send my application to the next company, the farmer who works our land drives into our garden with his tractor.

I wave from the window and walk downstairs. He hands me a paper bag. '*Per la torta della nonna*,' he says.

A sweet-sour scent of full, ripe lemons rises. They're to make a 'grandmother's cake' which is a kind of lemon tart. The fruits and vegetables grow so abundantly here that everyone shares everything. I thank him. He smiles. His teeth are brown and almost stubs. His white hair is tangled.

'This house used to belong to a wealthy family from the city. The man even had two wives for a while, my great-uncle told me,' he lisps.

Sofia and Stella? From the letter shreds.

'Did you know them?' I ask.

'I didn't, but my great-uncle did. He thought one of them was a naive girl; she kept passing by on her scooter, against her better judgment.'

'Which girl?'

'Oh, I've long forgotten those names. It's been so long. My great-uncle always said *C'è la vita, ma non è dolce per sempre*. Do you have the recipe for the lemon tart?'

I nod. Life isn't always sweet. When life gives you lemons, make lemonade, or *torta della nonna*. But is that always possible?

I send six new job applications before closing my laptop. It's almost eight a.m. and I'm expecting Gustav and his men any moment.

I put on my old T-shirt from yesterday and put the bright yellow dress over my hair. Today I want to finish the kitchen. The farmer is still driving around in the garden, but now a roar comes from the back of the house. Just as I've climbed up on the ladder there's a loud thump and the whole house shakes. The ladder vibrates, threatens to fall. The light bulb on the ceiling swings hard back and forth. Just in time I put my foot on the ground so as not to fall over together with the ladder.

Another thump. Stones fall to the ground.

I run to the bedroom and open the window to the back of the house. There is a big gaping hole in the extension. The farmer is gone, but a bulldozer is lifting the front blade back up and it crashes onto the roof of the extension. The house shakes again. Windows vibrate in their frames.

Gustav stands next to the machine and watches. The blade goes up, and after it comes down again, the back wall breaks and chunks of masonry wall fall to the ground.

'Gustav!' I yell. He doesn't hear me.

I grab my yellow construction helmet, put it over Margot's bright yellow dress and storm down the stairs. Panting, I arrive at the backyard where the bulldozer has created an even bigger hole. Gustav looks at me enthusiastically and raises his thumb.

'The whole house is shaking,' I shout over the bulldozer noise.

He puts his hand to his ear and gestures that he doesn't understand me. I walk over to him and scream it again in his ear.

'That's no problem,' he says. 'The house will still stand; those walls are thick. And the roof has been repaired. No worries.'

With the next thump, the glass jumps out of a window. I point at it.

'Things like that are collateral damage during a renovation,' Gustav shouts. 'Nothing we can do about it; we'll solve that later.'

The part of the extension that has already been demolished is turning into a large pile of rubble. Bricks, roofing felt, windows, beams, everything mixed together. Behind it is part of the original wall of the house, which appears undamaged despite the violence of the bulldozer. I have to write down in my notebook that we are four weeks ahead of schedule.

I get in the pickup truck and drive up the hill. Just as I turn onto the road, I see Lorenzo standing on the side of the road, next to his car. He looks at the bulldozer.

'We had to do something,' I tell him as I stand next to him. His shirt smells like a meadow full of flowers.

'This is not allowed at all,' he says. 'I just came to tell you that your building permit has been rejected. What you're doing here can result in a fine of up to ten thousand euros.'

'Has the building permit been rejected?' I ask in surprise.

'The municipality wants to see the house back in its original state, without major changes.'

'That extension is not original, is it? That doesn't then seem like a problem to me.'

'Besides the rejected permit, there is also the fact that we agreed that I would carry out this renovation.'

'I left you a message with your colleague in the blue overalls. Didn't you get that? Your projects look great, but we can't afford it.'

'Now you've got yourself in bigger trouble. I know these men, every contractor in this area knows these men. They deliver shoddy work.'

'It's going really well. The roof and interior walls are already finished.'

'I'd like to see it for myself.'

Lorenzo steps down the hill and waits for me to open the front door for him.

When we get up to the first floor, he looks into the bedroom and kitchen. The house shakes again from the bulldozer and the noise of falling debris makes talking impossible.

There is a moment of silence until the next thump.

'You're not living here during this renovation, are you?' Lorenzo asks in disbelief.

'Yes, together with Margot.'

'Totally irresponsible,' he says, shaking his head as he steps through the makeshift wooden door and up the stairs to the attic. There he peers up at the ceiling.

'That's not good,' he says, climbing up the scaffolding along the wall. He gestures to follow me.

Halfway through, the scaffolding's tubes vibrate from the next thump.

'See those new beams?' he asks, pointing to them. 'They are not made of hardwood. That is dark-stained pinewood. If any type of wood is too weak for this roof construction, it's pinewood. And do you see that support?'

I follow his finger to the iron L shape at the end of the beam.

'A connection like this can never keep the beam in place for long. The beams must interlock and you cannot achieve that by attaching them to each other with iron profiles. You will have to notch the beams on both sides, so that they fit together seamlessly and cannot move in any direction.'

The house vibrates and so does the scaffolding.

'It's not noticeable from the ground,' I say, climbing down.

'It's shoddy work,' Lorenzo says, standing next to me again. 'They are cheap materials and wrong construction methods.'

I sigh deeply. Every morning I go through everything with Gustav and we didn't talk about this.

'This will cost you dearly in the end,' Lorenzo says. 'It was an irresponsible choice.'

We are in the backyard and the extension has completely disappeared. A large cloud of dust hangs over the pile of rubble.

'Did they reinforce the inner wall before demolishing this?' Lorenzo asks.

'Wait, I'll ask Gustav,' I say and walk over to him. Lorenzo follows me.

'Gustav, that went fast, but the whole house was shaking. Have you temporarily reinforced the interior walls to absorb the blows?'

Gustav looks at Lorenzo.

'What is he doing here?' Gustav asks.

'I'm here to fix your work later if things start to go wrong,' Lorenzo says, irritated.

Gustav yells something to Tironeski, who yells something back. Without saying anything, Gustav walks away.

'Call me if you need me,' Lorenzo says as he turns and heads back to his car.

Wearing the same neat dress and the same blue blazer as last time, I drive to Fermo. After taking the long straight road inland, the city lies in front of me, spread across the valley and the hillsides. Not as big as Ancona, but still big enough for a number of international companies to be headquartered here.

In total I have received twenty-seven rejections in the last few days and only Brullesco, a company which exports typical Italian cheeses, invited me for an online job interview. This time I was well prepared and was hired as the team leader of a group of IT specialists.

I open my new laptop that I got at the reception on the desk that was assigned to me. The IT specialists from my team are also in the open-plan office. Some greet me, others have earphones in and don't look up. Not knowing what to do yet, I install my own photos from my phone on the laptop as a screensaver.

Brian calls and asks if I can go with him for a house viewing with a couple from America. When I tell him I have a job again and work full-time, he sounds disappointed.

'Maybe it pays better, but you're wasting your talent,' he says.

'We need the money for the renovation and it's going fast. The extension has even already been demolished.'

'Yes, Lorenzo is a good contractor.'

'I haven't told you yet; I found another contractor who is doing the renovation for less.'

'In Italy, prices are largely regulated by the government, so that's impossible. Who's doing the work?'

'Gustav.'

'Oh no, really? You have to stop that right away, today. He's very poorly regarded. I recommended Lorenzo to you for a reason. This is a very unfortunate choice.'

'I can come along on the house viewing if you can reschedule it for the weekend?' I say, changing the subject.

An employee is standing next to my desk with his headset around his neck.

'I have to hang up,' I tell Brian.

'I'll try to reschedule the appointment for Saturday,' he replies. 'I'll be in touch.'

'You're new here,' says the man with the headset and messy hair. He wears a polo shirt with the company logo. 'I'm Marco and we've made a bet on how long you'll stay.' He points to a group of young men of about twenty-five, sitting together at a work island composed of six desks.

'Why should I leave?' I ask.

'No one survives Paul.'

'Who is Paul?'

He points to a man sitting alone in the corner of the open-plan office, hunched over at his computer screen. I guess that he's about fifty years old. The only elderly employee here and also the only one wearing a shirt and tie. His hair is neatly parted in the center.

'Paul has been working here for thirty years and has seen many managers. He drives them all crazy.'

'Well, it can't be that bad, can it?' I say.

'He's out of date, if you know what I mean. He does not understand the latest programming languages and does all kinds of coding that makes the IT systems start to function less well.'

My laptop jumps to the screensaver with a picture of Max.

'What school is he at?' Marco asks. 'I went to school here too.'

'He doesn't live in Italy.'

The photo of Max changes for a photo of the house.

'Did you come here alone after your divorce? You don't live in that dilapidated house, do you?' He points at the screen and waves to his colleagues to come and have a look. The boys slide their chairs back.

I close my laptop. 'I have a meeting soon and I have to be in the conference room early to prepare it,' I say, getting up.

Marco walks back to his colleagues and loudly tells them that I am a lonely woman who left her son behind. If I am able to do that, then Marco thinks Paul should be careful about what he does. Paul hunches down further. The stake of the bet is increased.

The meeting is long and I yawn behind my hand. The new department plan is due next week, and the IT director emphasizes that the numbers should be positive.

The next morning, I drink a cup of vending-machine coffee at my desk. Marco and his colleagues are talking to each other. Paul stands a little further away and is now coming towards me.

'You didn't say there would be a new department plan,' he says. He's wearing the same shirt and tie as yesterday.

'Yes, it's true that I'm making a new plan,' I say.

'Why don't you cut yourself back right away?'

'It's not about cuts or layoffs. The plan is about making better processes so that we can work together more efficiently.'

'It already sounds like a crappy plan,' he concludes and walks away.

Later in the afternoon Marco comes and stands next to me. 'Paul has done it again,' he says. 'He gave a command that bypasses the system's test environment and is coding directly in the live environment. You know what this means.'

I nod. 'One wrong programming line and the entire IT system is down.'

'Precisely. And no employee in the company can work when that happens.'

'I'll discuss it with him.'

Paul's desk is tidy and clean. No empty coffee cup, no paper. He doesn't look at me.

'How long are you going to stand there?' he asks.

'Why don't you program in the test environment first?' I ask. I pull an office chair from behind another desk and sit next to him.

'I've been doing this job for thirty years, so I don't think it's a relevant question.'

'Then you also know that programming in the live environment can cause major problems. And you, as a senior IT specialist, have to show the young men here in the department how it should be done.'

He looks at me for a moment, wants to say something, but changes his mind. He leans further toward his screen.

'Would you please make sure to program in the test environment first?' I say. I get up, slide the chair back.

When I walk past the desks of the other employees, they all look at me questioningly.

'And?' Marco asks.

'It's solved,' I say.

Hours later I'm outside. The sun is setting just behind the hills, and Fermo's square fills with tourists, locals and business people who are all drinking aperitivos on one of the many terraces.

'Let's ask her, she's alone,' Marco says, just too loudly for me to hear.

'Is that necessary?' one of the colleagues asks. 'She's our team leader, not our drinking buddy.'

There is a tap on my shoulder and Marco asks if I would like to come with them for a glass of wine. I pretend to be surprised and say no. When he returns to the group, they are clearly relieved.

Behind them Paul is walking with a shoulder bag diagonally across his upper body. He looks at the ground and takes big steps. Across the square, he enters a narrow house wedged between two cafes.

The hall at home smells of fish and paint. Aron is standing on the ladder and painting the hallway ceiling of the first floor, while at the small stove Margot takes the fish out of the oven and pricks it with a fork.

'Hey darling, right-on time. You just have time to change before we eat,' she says when I reach the kitchen door. 'How was your day?'

'Pretty good,' I say. 'Aron, you really don't have to do that for us.'

'I understood from Margot that Roger won't be back until the house is finished,' he says. 'I feel sorry for you.'

He smiles gently. His spiky hair has grown long and now falls around his face.

I raise my eyebrows.

'Let him go,' Margot says. 'He likes to do it.' She looks at him and smiles.

We cover the dining table with a lace-trimmed white cotton tablecloth. The floral antique plates match it nicely.

'So, it's really over with Adamo?' I whisper.

'He's busy with the grape harvest,' she says. 'I only see him now and then for a night, now that he's decided to stay with his wife.'

Aron whistles to the tune of *'O sole mio* as he walks up and down the ladder to put new paint on his roller.

Venerdì, 9 Agosto 1946

There must be a party in the garden. Balloons and a long set table with dozens of children and family members around it. Valentina and Rubia would each blow out six candles on a cake baked by Stella, to the encouragement and applause of the guests. Danilo would cut the cake, while Stella received congratulations.

Sofia didn't want to go there, but something forced her to lock their real estate office at noon and ride the scooter down to the valley. To catch a glimpse of her daughter.

There were no bicycles, scooters or cars on the roadside. Maybe they were celebrating the birthday in a different location?

She slowed down. The shutters were closed, as she had often kept them closed during the war. The garden was overgrown. A blackberry grew with its long tentacles weaving through the palm tree and oleanders.

She stopped. There was nothing to indicate that anyone was home, or could be coming home any moment. She got off and parked her scooter on the roadside.

She carefully walked into the garden. The front door and stable doors were closed. In the corner of the stoop in front of the house lay a metal child's shovel. She ran her hand over the door. Her house.

She put her ear to the front door and listened.

Nothing.

No voices, no sounds of sliding furniture or rumbling in the kitchen.

The sweet smell of the oleanders planted farther away. Close by, closer than the bushes along the edge of the garden. In the small alcove next to the door was the blue glass vase Danilo had once bought her, with two oleander branches in it.

Fresh oleander branches in water. There had to be someone.

She walked around the house. No one.

Back at the vase, she bent over, just above the flowers. The smell she loved so much. She pushed against the wooden hatch at the back of the alcove and to her surprise it sprang open. On tiptoe she could see inside. It was dark in the barn. Rays of sunlight poured in through the open hatch, illuminating the space next to it. On the shelf next to the slanting gutter where the grapes would be brought in to fall into the container below was something white. She touched it and pulled it out. A stack of damp envelopes, held together by a red ribbon, just as she had done with her letters in the attic.

Sofia mia. My Sofia. She lowered herself to the threshold of the front door. Her hands trembled as she took the letter from the top envelope.

6 Agosto 1946, 06:00

Dear Sofia,
Today our daughter turned six. I wish we could celebrate together. I see more of you in her. The other day I thought you were standing on the road at our house, because my hopes turned an unknown woman into you. I look for you in all women.
Valentina also spoke about this woman who said she was a special girl. She kept repeating it, and Stella told her to stop. Shortly afterwards we moved. Stella no longer wanted to live here in the valley, so we returned to San Benedetto del Tronto. We're living in my family home in the harbor.
I've been writing to you over the years to talk to you, to hear your voice in my head, even though I couldn't send my letters to you. When Stella slept, I was with you. Sweetheart, the war has taken everything from us, but in my mind, I remain yours forever.

With love, your Danilo

Sofia's throat was dry, her breathing chafed. The envelopes slipped from her hand, fell to the grass. It was as if Danilo was whispering the words in her ear. His voice, close. He hadn't forgotten her. A letter on their daughter's actual birthday, three days earlier than Rubia's, while Stella always celebrated as if the girls were twins.

She picked up another envelope from the grass. A letter from a year earlier.

6 Agosto 1945, 06:00

Dear Sofia,
I secretly and without words gave our daughter an extra kiss for her birthday. Yours, because you can't do it yourself. I thought about telling her about you, but I don't know where you are.
Stella says I've changed, become quieter and more serious. She tells me to leave the car accident and the war in the past and let them go.
A lot of things have happened that I don't understand. You don't have to return to Valentina and me, I'm sure you have good reasons not to, but if you're still alive, please, let me know you're okay.

Forever Yours,
Danilo

What had Stella told Danilo about the night she was taken away by the soldiers from the house? And had he decided to stay with her after all? The chaos in the war, the uncertainty afterwards. Thousands of people had disappeared, and what had happened to them was slowly becoming known.

There were at least ten letters in the grass. A long line of ants began to make their way across them. She saw an envelope with the address of the camp in Bolzano on it. Fear gripped her, she closed her eyes, it brought her memories back to the day in the truck. A woman in the barracks had told her that first night that she'd arrived at the portal of hell, and nothing could have been more true.

Trembling, she pulled the letter out of the envelope. Danilo wrote that he knew she was in camp Bolzano and that he wanted to come and get her.

He had received the information from the police in San Benedetto del Tronto where she had been imprisoned in the station as a traitor in the period before.

The next letter was from a few months later. A teardrop on the S of her name had blurred the ink. Danilo wrote that he had stood at the gate of the camp, but had not been let in. The guards had told him that she had probably been deported to Auschwitz.

She sat with her eyes closed for a few minutes before she was ready for the next letter. 1944. The letters had gotten mixed up on the grass, she had to put them in order to understand. Valentina believed that Stella was her mother and Rubia her sister, he wrote. He didn't know what to do, because the situation was not negotiable with Stella. She called the two children her daughters. She was a sweet mother and Valentina was happy. Maybe he shouldn't dwell in the past any longer?

She shook the ants off another envelope and opened it. He had decided to marry Stella, but part of Sofia was close to him through Valentina.

In a letter from January 1945, he wrote that his son Adamo had been born. In March 1946, he was still searching for her name in the papers, all of which he kept for fear that he would later worry that he had accidently overlooked her name. He checked them regularly. In May 1946 he said that he kept dreaming of a winery with hills full of grapevines, but without her the dream seemed unrealistic. No one believed in his dream like she had. He had taken over the business from his father and uncle and his life was good, but not complete.

His words, they could heal her. He hadn't forgotten her, had looked for her, and in the end – just as she had herself – had gone on living. He had chosen Stella as the mother of his children.

Stella now had everything Sofia didn't have, which she craved so much. Just like the first time Sofia had seen Stella and Danilo in the harbor under the streetlamp, standing close together. She had finally gotten what she wanted and Sofia wondered again how far she'd gone to get it.

On the right-hand side of the yellow house with the dark red shutters, where a bomb had fallen during the war, new warehouses had been built with large white signs with the words *Marinolli Pesci e Reti* in blue letters. A little further on, on the left, was the warehouse where she had woven fishing nets, with Marta's workshop beyond.

She put her hand on the door handle of the new iron gate with an ornate pattern that was clearly an attempt to break the harshness of the rest of the house. Once she passed through this gate, everything would change. A butler would open the door and give her a questioning look. She would say that she was Valentina's mother and that she came to pick up her daughter to take her to her house in Ripatransone.

The upstairs window opened. Valentina smiled happily and waved. She was wearing a festive green dress and her hair was tied in a ponytail with a large bow. She was slammed into the window frame as Rubia pushed her aside and came to stand beside her. She was wearing the same dress, but red. As if being dressed the same was supposed to make everyone believe they had the same mother.

Rubia screamed loudly for her mother. Carefully, Sofia raised her hand and waved back to Valentina.

'Hello ma'am,' Valentina called. 'Are you coming for my mother?' She looked back.

A stab of pain through her body. Blood drained from her face.

'I... uh... I am...' she said.

The girls were pushed away from the window. Stella appeared and pulled herself up on the windowsill. Festive dress in ocher satin and a pearl necklace. She stared down, as if she were seeing a ghost.

Did she have to wave?

'Stella...' she said. 'I've come...'

Stella closed the window with a loud bang.

Sofia ran to the door and rang the bell.

No one answered.

Loudly she called for Valentina, but got no answer. Through the garden, across the trimmed lawn, to the back door. Past a small pool lined with blue mosaic tiles with a black rubber band floating in it. There were streamers and balloons. In the corner was a trashcan with colored wrapping paper sticking out. A waitress was busy collecting the empty cake plates from a long table covered with white linen.

'Can I help you, ma'am?' she asked politely. 'The party has just ended and the birthday girls are inside. Their mother needs a rest.'

A white cat rubbed against her leg. Two bathing suits hung on a line to dry in the sun. A freight train rumbled by, but her daughter wouldn't hear a thing through the thick walls of the villa. Here she would grow up in more opulence than Sofia had ever known.

Nothing, she would know nothing of her ancestry, because no one in this house was going to tell her. Stella wouldn't, and clearly Danilo wouldn't either. She had written to him from the prison camp at Servigliano in Fermo, not far from the valley, but he had said nothing about it in his letters. He had chosen Stella.

Maggio 1948

The large sheet of paper took up the entire work table in the space behind the office. She bent over it and squeezed her eyes half shut. Everything seemed to be right. This house was to be built just outside the city wall, in the hills. Surrounded by many hectares of land planted with olive trees. Three weeks ago, she had made a small sketch of a house for this land that she and Stefano were selling through their real estate agency and hung it in the office window. Passers-by had stopped, pointed at it and consulted with each other.

On the third morning a man had come in who wanted more information from the architect about this house. He requested a meeting and wanted to see the drawing in a larger format.

For several evenings, Sofia had been drawing after workhours, to the surprise of Stefano, who thought she was a true artist. She wandered through the rooms of this house she had created. Her dreams had returned and all she had to do was transfer the images in her head to the paper. Once that was done, she checked everything for symmetry and proportion, as Mr. Armacci had taught her. She had visited his shop after the war, but the bookstore now housed a small grocery. No one knew where Mr. Armacci had gone.

The doorbell rang and she quickly walked into the office to greet the customer. The man stepped in, took off his hat and coat, and handed it to her. After hanging up his hat and coat, she pressed the silver bell on the wooden desk to let Stefano know the potential buyer was there.

Stefano came in with the large rolls of paper under his arm and shook the man's hand. 'Welcome, we'd be happy to show you the drawings.' He gestured toward the conference table.

'You made an excellent design,' the client said.

'It's not my design. My name is Stefano and I own this real estate agency together with my wife.'

'Ah, and what time is the architect coming?'

'Sophus is unfortunately unable to attend,' Stefano said. 'He has asked us to explain the plans.'

'You mean Mr. Sophus won't make time for me?'

Sofia unrolled the drawings on the large wooden table. 'This house is on the prettiest side of the hill. It is an elongated farmhouse, built with local bricks that are a golden yellow color. Below you will find the stables for livestock and agricultural machinery, upstairs you will find the living areas. The balcony runs the entire length of the house and the open masonry structure is made of the same bricks as the walls, making it a beautiful whole.'

The man looked intently at it and nodded in satisfaction. He looked up at her. 'Can you get me a coffee? Then I can discuss it further with your husband.'

Sofia took a deep breath. 'Sure, I'll brew a fresh cup for you.'

She walked away and heard the man ask Stefano what he thought of the balcony railing. The ideas of this new architect were brilliant, Stefano replied.

As the coffee machine heated up, she gently opened the door to her workspace. It was quiet, he was still asleep. 'You've got a big sister,' she'd whispered the first time she'd kissed her son Alessandro's forehead. He was born less than ten months after her visit to the yellow house on Valentina's sixth birthday. Stefano was thrilled to find out she was pregnant with his child and a few weeks later they were married in the big church on the town square.

She brought the client his coffee, and he bought the plot of land with her house design.

12

The air is fresh after the huge rain shower of the past few hours. The water forms puddles between the olive trees and reflects the sunlight that breaks through again.

It won't be long before the bright colors in the garden will fade into autumn tones. The pink and white of the oleanders and the purple of the lavender will disappear and wait until next spring to bloom again. What remains are the gray-green hues of the olive trees and the yellows and browns of dried grasses.

Rainwater has remained in the bed of the pick-up truck. It rocks back and forth as I drive to the beach.

Silvan and Frederico's beach club is quiet for a Saturday morning. Frederico is on the boulevard cleaning the sunbeds and storing them in the shed next to the restaurant. He waves. Silvan walks around on the beach and pulls the umbrellas out of their stands. He puts them on a large cart with inflatable wheels. Inside, Margot is clearing the tables.

'Weird that the season here ends on September 15, isn't it, darling?' she says as I enter. 'It seems so smack bang. I told Silvan that it is strange to set a fixed date, because we had rain last night, but there could still be warm days, right?'

Through the large windows, the sea comes in again as blue and clear as any other day last summer, and although nothing seems different, it is.

'No, I didn't know either,' I say. 'The whole atmosphere is different.'

Margot puts all the salt and pepper mills together on a tray.

'Very different, darling. As of Monday I will be out of work until May next year, Silvan just told me. How unfortunate is that. Would you like a coffee?'

I sit down at a table by the window and wrap my scarf more snugly. Even inside it's cold. Whitecaps are visible on the waves, the wind blows hard over the beach and moves the sand until small hills form along the boulevard. Soon I'll be cycling here like at home in the fall; with driving rain in my face. On the autumn days that then turn into dark winter days, the lights in the house have to be switched on earlier and we curl up by the wood stove. The dancing candlelight, Roger's smile. Max sitting on the couch next to me, talking about the game he won.

I make a video call to Roger. When he picks up, he still looks a bit sleepy. His hair is messed up.

'Did you just wake up?' I ask. 'Isn't it a quarter past eight?'

'On the weekends I sometimes let go of the schedule,' he says and yawns. 'I'm still in bed.'

I tell him about the rain showers, the empty beaches and the closed restaurants.

'Did you expect anything else?' he asks.

Yes, no, I don't know what I expected. The summer rhythm of the past few months has seduced me, and now I am roughly shaken awake as if the rain has cleared everything up.

'I thought everything would be different here,' I say. 'Once I had renovated the house and we lived here together. I miss you.'

'We miss you too.'

We remain silent.

'How's your work going?' he asks. 'I've already incorporated the salary that you will earn in the financial overview.'

'I don't find the work exciting, but there is good news. The bedrooms are ready, the kitchen and bathroom are usable and the attic is safe. When are you coming?'

Suddenly the phone screen fills with a blurry, brown mass.

'What's that?' I shout.

Laughter from Max. Soft beeping.

'Mom, this is Rover,' he yells enthusiastically. He steps away from the camera on the phone and stands there with a puppy in his arms. Long brown hair, huge floppy ears and those cute eyes that only young animals can have.

'You have a dog!' I shout.

Margot comes up behind me and bends over my shoulder to watch. 'Oh my gosh, what a cutie,' she cooed. 'A soft ball of fluff, really too sweet.'

'It gets even better, wait,' Max says, putting Rover down on the bed. He picks up something from the ground.

'And this is Benz,' he says. 'We couldn't leave him alone without siblings. He was the last in the litter.'

Max pulls the puppy against him and hugs him. The other puppy wriggles in.

'Two dogs?' I ask in surprise.

'Oh, too sweet,' Margot says. 'Frederico, darling, come and see what Max has!'

Frederico stops spraying the sunbeds and turns off the tap. He walks slowly, the cuffs of his wet pants are just above his ankles.

'They are named after car brands,' Roger says. 'Did you notice that?'

Max romps with the dogs on the bed.

'They're cute,' I say. 'What breed is it? Will they become big?'

'Sweetie, too cute. Everyone should have this kind of fluffy stuff,' says Frederico.

'They're cocker spaniels,' Roger says. 'I don't think they get that big, about to your knees, I guess?'

I would have figured this all out in advance. I would have tabulated everything for him. The breed, so we knew if we were dealing with a hunting dog, yard dog, or guard dog. The height at the withers. The maintenance of the coat, because it makes a difference whether it is a long- or short-haired breed. An estimate of the costs of the feed, the vet and the grooming salon on an annual basis. The necessary puppy-training classes we should be taking.

'Are they vaccinated for Italy?' I ask.

'No, Mom, they're not yet,' Max says. He tries to hold a puppy under each arm as they frolic in all directions. 'I'm going to walk them. Bye mom.'

'Max is so happy with them,' Roger says.

'Great that you did it,' I tell him.

We hang up.

'Palazzo Puro changes people,' Margot concludes, removing the liquor bottles from the shelves behind the bar.

'Roger is sixteen hours away from here,' I say. 'He hardly spent any time in the house.'

'He has been here and experienced life here. That works. Plus, you're not there to plan his life.'

Is that right? Did I reinforce his lust for control by making plans for him?

Monday morning it is raining hard again when I drive to Fermo. When the coffee machine fills my coffee cup, Marco rushes towards me.

'Have you heard?' he asks. 'We might as well go home.'

'It's Monday morning, we have yet to start the week,' I say.

'Paul did it. The whole system is down.'

Most of the workstations are empty, the employees are not yet in the office. Paul isn't behind his desk either.

'That's impossible, he's not even here,' I say.

'He was here yesterday. Look, his food is still there.'

On Paul's desk is a half-eaten panino and a bottle of wine.

'He never leaves his desk like this,' I say. 'It was clean and organized every day.'

I walk to Paul's desk and grab the almost-empty bottle of wine. Meanwhile, more IT people are coming in and trying to start up their computers. The screens remain black. Immediately Paul's name goes around. Along with statements like *he drinks too much, he never listens, he just does what he wants, he doesn't understand IT*. The group who made the bet come over to me.

'You're not going to make it,' one of them says. 'I had bet on two months, but you didn't last two weeks.'

'I had nothing to do with this,' I say.

'The director thinks otherwise,' says another guy. 'I can tell you that already.' He points to the open-plan office door and there is the IT director. He gestures for me to come over.

Half an hour later I'm out on the street. The director emphasized that my detailed planning and approach seemed so promising, but that they were totally unrealistic if I didn't manage the IT specialists in the right way.

Fired while on probation. I've never been fired. A window slides open upstairs. Marco and his colleagues are hanging out of it. 'You made me a rich man,' Marco shouts, waving a stack of bills.

I cross the square where the market stalls are. The market vendors wear gloves as if it were already freezing. Women search among the racks of winter coats. The terraces of the restaurants that are still open are covered with transparent plastic sheeting and there are heaters underneath.

The sky turns gray. Another rainstorm is on its way. I walk across the square to Paul's narrow house. The faded green shutters are closed, the plants hang withered in the containers. A market vendor in an orange apron shouts loudly that the Parmesan cheese is on sale. I ring Paul's doorbell and wait.

'He had already left this morning when I set up my stall here,' says the man in the apron. 'With two big suitcases.'

'But he was in the office last night...'

'He's really gone. Do you want cheese?'

I buy a piece of parmesan and some gorgonzola from him.

'Do you live here?' he asks.

'No. I used to work across the street at the Brullesco company,' I say. 'But not anymore.'

He hands me the bags of cheese and studies me.

'You're clearly disappointed about this, I see. Maybe it would help to see the sights of Fermo. Do you know them?'

'I don't want to go sightseeing.'

An old woman with a large, bright pink shopping bag comes, stands next to me and looks first at the cheeses, then at me.

'The inland area around Fermo is also beautiful,' says the merchant. 'I am there at the weekly markets of the villages of Falerone, Servigliano, Monte San Martiono. Ever been?'

I shake my head and hand him the money for the cheese. He searches his cash register for change.

'You'll be in the high mountains in an hour from here,' the old woman says in a sweet voice. 'Sometimes you have to broaden your view to gain new insight.'

Surprisingly. She smiles. Just when I want to ask why she is saying this, she orders mascarpone.

When I drive inland towards the Apennines, I see that the high peaks are already covered with snow. One bad day doesn't make a winter, my mother always said when I came home as a child with a bad test grade and felt like I wasn't good at anything. I just had to do my best next time, was her advice, and then everything would be all right.

Margot lights the fireplace in the evening and we drink a glass of wine at the dining table.

'You were always so good, darling,' she says. 'But I don't think you've been so sharp lately. You are distracted, I guess.'

We put a blanket over our legs. It's windy outside. The house has started to cool down. The thick walls that have soaked up the sun's heat for months are slowly releasing it. The concrete floor is cold when I walk over it with my socks on and a damp spot is developing under the new coat of paint in the corner of the kitchen. The wind finds its way in through the doorways that have been installed on the ground floor since the extension has been demolished. There are large gaps between the planks that Gustav's men put together for it. The debris from the extension is still in the yard, despite Gustav's promise to remove it. They have removed the wooden partition in the hallway, but in the attic, there is loose stucco powder scattered all over the floor, along with the empty plastic bags that contained the stucco and coffee grounds around the coffee machine that is still there.

'I don't think Gustav is coming back, do you?' Margot asks.

'In my schedule, I have set aside a week to clear the rubble and install the new doors in the openings in the back wall. In fact, I already paid him for it.'

'Oh, well, then it will be fine, darling.'

Aprile 1958

Three projects at the same time was a lot of work, but Sofia didn't want to turn down assignments. Along the walls were three large drawing tables whose worktops she could fold down or swivel up, so she could walk from one worktable to the next to adjust the drawings. In the lower right corner, she stamped *Sophus Architects, founded in 1948*, on each sheet.

The bell in her studio rang and, in the front office, the secretary was talking to someone. Stefano was away with a contractor with whom he had built a house designed by her. She put down her drawing pencil and walked towards the front office.

'Sophus isn't here,' the secretary said politely. Like every day, she had tied her hair up in a neat bun and painted her nails. 'We don't see the architect much. Honestly, I've never even met him.'

Two young women were standing in front of her desk. They were both wearing ponytails and mini dresses. One wore an orange dress printed with large circles, the other a yellow one with a graphic print.

'I already told you that,' said the woman in the orange dress. 'Nobody meets him.'

'His designs are sold from this real estate agency, so the owners probably know him,' said the other woman.

'May I help you?' Sofia asked.

The women turned and Sofia saw it immediately. Tall and slender, almost mature. Green eyes, wavy brown strands of hair that had escaped from their ponytails next to their faces.

'I'd like to speak to the architect, ma'am,' Valentina said politely.

'She wants to be an architect,' Rubia explained. 'I keep telling her it's impossible, yet she persists. You're acting really weird, Valentina.' She nudged her with her shoulders and Valentina tottered on her low heels.

'I like houses,' Valentina said.

Sofia's throat was dry, she wanted to say something. Her words did not come.

'Could you arrange an appointment for me with Mr. Sophus?' Valentina asked.

Sofia nodded, almost unobtrusively.

'See it can be done, Rubia. That's what I said, didn't I? Women can have careers too; we don't all have to stay at home with the kids if we don't want to.'

'Mamma will never approve.'

'Well, Daddy says I have to choose what I want to do.'

'Shall I put an appointment in the agenda?' the secretary asked, holding the pen between her fingers and her red-painted nails as if the polish had yet to dry.

Sofia cleared her throat. She wanted to say it was impossible, but said nothing.

There was some chatter between Valentina, Rubia and the secretary. She didn't hear it anymore. Alessandro came into the office on his way home from school and looked at Valentina and Rubia. 'Who are they, Mom?'

'Um, well...' Sofia stuttered.

Valentina and Rubia walked towards the door.

'That lady said nothing to us,' Rubia said to Valentina as they went out. 'We'd better not come back here.'

'Mrs. Sofia,' the secretary said, stroking her fingernails with her thumb. 'The appointment is for tomorrow morning, is that all right?'

For the rest of the day, Sofia was unable to focus on the house designs. A ruler was attached to each work table with which she normally drew straight lines in exactly the right place, now she made each line too long or too short, or in the wrong place.

The part of her life that she'd hidden from her husband and son slowly surfaced. For over ten years she'd kept everything away. She had told no one about her past. And no one knew that she was Sophus, who had already designed and built more than thirty houses in the area. Her designs were scattered across the surrounding hills like tiny dots. She had a good view of it from the terrace of the café in the square. Sometimes she drove past a house that had just been built to see if her ideas had turned out well in reality. Usually, she just caught a glimpse from the road she was standing on, and then she asked Stefano to go over and take a picture of it. All the photos were on a large bulletin board on the wall in her studio, and someone with a keen eye for detail could see that she left her signature on every house. Every house had something that reminded her of the house in the valley. Sometimes she had made the division of panes in the windows exactly the same, sometimes it was the color of the bricks, the ornaments above the windows or the front door.

'Ma'am, are you okay?' the secretary asked. 'Shall I call Sophus for tomorrow's appointment?'

'I'll take care of it myself,' she said to the secretary and went to her workspace. Tomorrow she was going to tell Valentina everything.

The next morning, she stood behind the window in the front office and waited. An elderly couple passed arm in arm in the square.

She fiddled with her little gold earrings. Her black dress with its wide, white, graphic stripe on the right side was reflected in the window. Between the advertisements for the houses, she stared at the square. The sound of the secretary's typing filled the room.

'Your appointment isn't for half an hour,' the secretary said. 'Can you tell me what time Mr. Sophus will be arriving? Then I can take that into account when I go to make coffee.'

Sofia shook her head. Even her secretary was not allowed to walk down the hall and enter her studio.

Valentina crossed the square. Her short skirt bounced along with every step she took and Sofia saw passersby looking at her and laughing. She rubbed her sweaty palms on her skirt. Images flashed through her mind. The beach, Danilo, the house, Valentina in her white baby dress, the girls along the road, the letters behind the hatch. She opened the front door.

Calm.

She had to remain calm.

'Good morning, Valentina,' she said as normally as she could.

'Good morning, Ma'am. Thank you for meeting me. I'm by myself, Rubia didn't want to come. She and my mother think I have unrealistic goals.'

'Would you like coffee or tea?' the secretary asked Valentina.

'A coffee, please, thank you. What time is Mr. Sophus coming?'

The espresso machine hissed in the corner of the office.

'Follow me,' Sofia said to her. She led the way down the narrow hallway towards the studio in the back.

'Ah, Mr. Sophus is here already?' said Valentina, taking the cup of coffee from the secretary and walking along.

Sofia stood in the doorway, took a deep breath, stepped aside and let Valentina in.

Valentina walked slowly from drawing to drawing, studying everything carefully. 'This is exactly how I imagined the studio of a famous architect. How inspiring.'

She looked at the picture board last. 'The details of each house are so excellent,' Valentina remarked. 'Look, here the balcony fits perfectly with the ornaments above the windows.'

She pointed to one of the photos of a house Sofia had designed a year ago. 'And here the house has a patio that looks out over the valley. It will be an honor to speak with Mr. Sophus later.'

Valentina turned to Sofia who was standing by the desk. She opened her shoulder bag, took out a double-folded drawing sheet and gave it to Sofia.

'Do you believe that only men can design houses?' she asked.

Sofia unfolded the drawing sheet. A house drawn with great precision, and beautiful symmetry.

'I've added the measurements,' Valentina said, pointing to the small numbers written along the walls and windows.

Sofia studied it. The symmetry was right. The sizes were in the right proportion, as Mr. Armacci from the bookshop had taught her in the past.

'Your design is very good,' Sofia finally said. 'And women can do what men can do, I have no doubt about that.'

'That's what I always say to my mother. She gets angry and doesn't want to hear anything more about it. My sister laughs at me, she thinks I'm pursuing a dream that can never come true.'

'You have talent, and you can learn the rest of the discipline.'

'This summer I will be eighteen and then I want to go to the University of Rome to study architecture.'

'That makes me very happy. You don't know how happy, because I eh…'

The conversation fell silent for a moment and they looked at each other.

'Valentina,' Sofia said.

She was silent again.

If she told her, there was no turning back.

'Mr. Sophus is not going to meet you.'

Valentina gave her a disappointed look, took her drawing back from the desk and put it back in her bag. 'I was so hoping for it.'

'Sophus doesn't exist.'

Sofia took the wooden stamp with which she stamped Sophus' name on each drawing.

'My name is Sofia and I am the architect.'

A smile appeared on Valentina's lips. 'I knew it! I already told my father that I felt like a woman was making these designs. Why I thought that, I have no idea, I felt it.'

Sofia put down the stamp. 'Go to Rome. Study and show you can do it. I have never dared to do that, but I am convinced that you can.'

Valentina walked over to her and hugged her. Sofia smelled her hair, her skin. Her daughter. Her throat swelled; her eyes burned. She never wanted to let go of her and held her tight. She closed her eyes. Then Valentina let her go again.

Mercoledì, 6 Agosto 1958

The for-sale sign was posted on the side of the road. It had to happen at some point, and yet Sofia was upset. The house had been empty for over ten years, and there was no indication that Danilo and Stella had ever returned from the city with the girls, not even for the weekends. On the balcony, the circles and arrows had taken on a green tarnish of moss. She walked into the garden, just like she did every year on Valentina's birthday. The palm tree had reached the height of the eaves. The tall grass tickled her legs.

The blue vase. Fresh oleanders. A letter? She stood on tiptoe, pushed open the hatch. There was an envelope. She opened it with a trembling hand.

6 Agosto 1958, 09:00

Dear Sofia,
She has grown up, our daughter. Eighteen years. You have missed her childhood, but in my mind, we were always together. Now it's time to let go of you, just like I have to let go of Valentina. I can tell you she looks a lot like you; she's going to Rome to study architecture. She's living your dream.
I should have taken better care of you and proposed to you right away. I still don't understand why then, in those few weeks we didn't see each other, I made the unforgivable mistake of starting an intimate relationship with Stella. However, I believed she had that with more men.
Stella's anger at me breaking off the engagement while claiming she was carrying my child caused the car accident. Stella saw you on the road, said you were unimportant, and threw open her door.
I am guilty of everything that happened to you and I deeply regret it. It wasn't until I held Rubia in my arms that I saw that she was my daughter. She has my green eyes, just like Valentina.
Our house has too many memories and I'm letting go of it, but I'll always love you.

You live on in my thoughts and through your daughter.

Forever Yours,
Danilo

The little girls danced in the garden again. The same green eyes, the dresses that looked alike. The teens in miniskirts in her real estate agency. They were half-sisters. Stella had told the truth; Danilo was the father of both of them. Long ago, yet it didn't make the pain any less. She lowered herself to the threshold in front of the door and put her hands over her eyes. It broke her. Again.

For years she had felt guilty about Stella's suffering in her wheelchair. Lame legs from the accident she herself had caused. If she had known then what she knew now, she would have made different choices. Then she'd have walked into the garden with her short hair to hug Danilo and Valentina.

She stuffed the letter into her bag, not knowing what to do with it. Everyone had gone on with their lives. Wasn't it better for the past to remain what it was: the past? She now had Stefano and Alessandro. She was Sophie. She had to let it go.

She walked around the house one last time. What would it look like inside? The door rattled in the lock as she pushed it, but it didn't budge. A dove flew past her, up and through an open window. The bedroom window where she'd first shared the bed with Danilo, and then where Stella had lain. Was there a ladder? She searched the barn, there was only an old rusty children's pool.

She knocked on the neighbor's front door. An inaudible answer came from the vegetable garden. An old man bent over the heads of lettuce and rose to his feet.

'Did you see how big my vegetables are?' he asked. 'We are here on a natural spring, but nobody knows that.'

'Good afternoon neighbor, do you have a long ladder I could borrow?'

The old man looked at her for a long time and pointed at her with his wrinkled finger. 'You probably don't believe in dreams anymore, do you?'

She shook her head.

'I told you then that rich man was not of your rank. He lived here during the war with a distinguished lady. Most of the time she was in a wheelchair. The house is up for sale again, have you seen that?'

He bent down to inspect the lettuce heads again.

'Do you have a ladder I can borrow?'

It wasn't easy dragging the long ladder through the berm back to the house, into the yard. The sun was burning and she was sweating. Once the ladder was under the window, she climbed up and pushed the interior shutters further open.

In the bedroom the double bed had been made up, as if someone was sleeping here again tonight, if the rats hadn't gnawed holes in it. The linen closet with mirror. Two old dresses and a lace nightgown on a hanger. Stella upright in bed, waiting for her tea. She shivered.

In the kitchen she opened the shutters and the light fell on the white enamel stove where she had cooked countless meals. Where she'd warmed up the milk for the girls' porridge. The coffee cups were still on the counter in the dish rack, an embroidered monogram lay unfinished on the dining table. Everything in the house was still, as if a pause had been inserted. Above the fireplace was a yellowed photo of Valentina and Rubia with braids and bows in their hair. The flowers in the vase next to it had dried.

The dark hall with terrazzo stairs, where only some light fell through the window at the top of the stairs. Soldiers dragged her down the stairs, past the nursery. Stella on a chair with her back to her, the two girls on her lap. Valentina calling to her.

She slowly opened the door to the nursery. Pink painted walls in a dim room. The wooden dollhouse Sofia's sisters had made stood in the corner of the room, above it hung her fantasy drawing of the house. Two cribs. She ran her hand over Valentina's white iron crib. The rag doll lay on the mattress. She picked it up, smelled it, and held it to her cheek. The rag doll was dirty and damp. The girls turned two, partying in the garden; long ago and far away, yet so close. She reached under Valentina's mattress to see if her notebook was still there. No booklet, but she did feel loose pieces of paper. She pulled the mattress aside, dust flew up. Her short letters, folded like an envelope and stamped from the Servigliano prison camp, were scattered across the mesh frame. Unopened.

She ran out of the room, climbed through the window and descended the ladder. The rag doll stuck out of her dress pocket. She ran across the yard, started her scooter and drove off. Memories, deep pain, it followed her all the way back to Ripatransone. In the narrow street in front of their house, Alessandro was playing with a friend.

'Hello Mom,' he said. 'Where were you? Daddy was looking for you.'

Sofia hugged him. 'I love you so much.'

'I love you too. Can we cycle to the beach ourselves?' Alessandro asked.

'I promised you next summer. When you are twelve years old, not before.'

Alessandro looked at his friend. 'I told you she wouldn't agree to it. She's afraid I'll have an accident. Mothers are weird.'

The living room and kitchen were empty, Stefano was probably in their office. She locked herself in the bathroom, slumped to the floor against the wall.

She had no idea how many hours she'd been sitting there when Stefano knocked on the door and called her. She opened it.

'What's wrong with you?' he asked concerned. 'Your eyes are all red. Have you been crying?'

He took her in his arms, comforted her. He rubbed her face gently with a washcloth.

'Are you okay?' he finally asked. 'Can you tell me? Whatever it is you've been hiding from me for years? I can help you better if I know.'

She swallowed, looked at him. Her throat was swollen, as was the skin under her eyes.

'I want to buy the house in the valley,' she said in a hoarse voice.

Stefano was surprised. 'Which house?'

'The house with that balcony with circles and arrows.'

13

The evening is ominously dark. It's a strange moment. It seems an eternity ago that Margot and I came here to clean up the house and explore the area, now we live together in an unfinished house, and we're both out of work. A window flies open and the wind blows out the candle. I quickly get up and close it. The olive trees and the palm are swaying back and forth.

'A storm is forecast for tonight,' Margot says with concern.

'Come on, let's have another glass of wine,' I say, lighting the candle again. 'It won't be too bad.' I want to reassure her as the rain beats against the windows. Storms make everything unpredictable; nature has a power that is sometimes unbearable. The wind howls through the chimney and blows the flames in the fireplace.

'I didn't know things could get so raging out here.' She looks out the window in fear.

'We'll sleep through it later on,' I say.

When I close the shutters an hour later, the wind is blowing even harder and there are large puddles in front of the house where the bulldozer has left deep ruts. The fire has been extinguished.

Margot checks the weather forecast on her phone. 'The storm won't pass until tomorrow morning.' She blows out the candle.

In my bedroom the wind is whistling through a crack in the window frame. At the end of the grain field, the tall reeds by the river bend in the wind. A large branch flies past the window just as I am closing the bedroom shutters. I keep my socks on when I go to bed. I pull the woolen blanket tightly around me against the draft.

A bolt of lightning lights up the hall where the shutters are still open, followed by a thunderclap that shakes the house. I turn in bed, close my eyes.

Another flash followed by a clap of thunder. The crystal prisms of the chandelier in the balcony room clink together as the ceiling vibrates.

My door is thrown open. 'It's not normal how hard that was,' Margot says, panicked. 'It's worse than that freight train that thundered past our chalet at night.'

'Yes, I...' My voice disappears in the violence of the next thunder clap. The thin window glass vibrates in the frame. Margot slides into bed next to me, just like Max used to. Then, we counted the seconds between the flashes of lightning and claps of thunder together to determine how far away the storm was. The storm lingers between the hills and has aimed its arrows right at the house. After another flash I count out loud, within two seconds the thunder rumbles. In the distance, the siren of a police car sounds. Wind blows across our faces and we pull the blanket higher.

Margot folds the pillow against her ears on either side to shut out the noise. 'We're like toddlers,' I say.

'Rain and wind are okay, but I don't like thunderstorms,' says Margot. 'It's like heaven...'

A bright flash. A long, loud thunderclap. A huge bang, something heavy falls on the floor above us, the ceiling shakes. The clink of the chandelier's prisms and then a bang as the chandelier crashes to the floor, crystal shattering. I sit up in bed, Margot hides under the blanket. Debris is falling in the attic, one after another, we hear the sound of something banging into the floor above.

'The roof,' I scream and fly out of bed.

Lightning illuminates the hallway, another clap of thunder. The chandelier lies broken on the floor. I run up the stairs and stand frozen. The rain is pouring in through a large hole in the roof, pattering in my face. The lightning overhead lights up the sky. Rainwater mixes with the loose plaster powder and forms a white slurry. It flows slowly towards the stairs. Roof tiles sail down and break into pieces on the floor.

'Margot!' I scream. My face is soaking wet from the rain. 'Margot, we have to get out of here. Now!'

I storm down the stairs into the bedroom. I pull the blanket off her, she stares at me wide-eyed, stiff. In the attic the beams creak, the cracking sound of wood on steel.

I pull on her arm. 'Come out, it's not safe.'

Margot doesn't move. I open the linen closet, pull out a thick sweater, throw it on the bed.

'Quick, put on,' I say. 'We're going outside now.'

I pull another sweater over my head.

'Margot, put it on,' I yell, shaking her shoulders.

She looks at me.

'Now!' I shout.

Slowly she takes the sweater. A beam falls to the floor, it thumps in our bedroom. I grab my phone on the nightstand next to the bed, run to the kitchen and grab my handbag, back to the bedroom. I pull Margot's arm, drag her along. Water is flowing down the stairs, white with the stucco. Margot slides down two steps, I hold her upright. The stairwell lights up, goes dark, lights up, goes dark. Water flows along the walls. A heavy thump in the attic, we're at the front door. I pull it open, driving rain pelts against us. We run into the garden, while everything around us lights up. Olive trees sway, the palm rattles. Roof tiles fall down and land around us. Margot shouts, grabs her arm. A roof tile has hit her. Water is flowing down the hill, it passes in front of the house, splashes against the walls, flows into the hallway. I quickly go back to the front door and pull it shut against the running water. We run to the pickup truck. I get in, click the other door open for Margot, and start the engine. A branch from the fig tree lands with a bang in the bed of the truck. The headlights on, windshield wipers on the highest setting, we speed up the hill. The car skids back. Full throttle again, screeching tires, splashing mud. We are on the road and in the light of the street lamp I stop. Our hair clings to our faces, the sweaters already soaked. A bolt of lightning makes its way towards the huge hole in the roof, and strikes the fig tree a few meters from the house.

I put my hand on Margot's shoulder. 'It's okay, we're safe.'

She puts her hand on top of mine.

When we drive off, my cheeks don't dry. Rain mingles with tears.

The bell of the church tower strikes twice as the thunderstorm passes and the driving rain turns into a drizzle. The moon is behind the dark clouds and the wet square gleams in the orange glow of the street lamps.

Aron opens his front door and wraps his arms around Margot.

'Sorry, we had nowhere else to go,' I say. 'All hotels were closed.'

'It's okay,' he says. He is wearing short blue pajama pants and a matching shirt. His hair is all over the place.

'Her whole house collapsed,' Margot says as Aron closes the front door and leads us into the living room. 'And I didn't do anything when it happened, oh, darling, I…'

The living room has a white fabric sofa, a white painted coffee table and a few plants in the windowsill.

'We couldn't do anything,' I say to Margot.

Aron approaches with a sheet, pillow and woolen blanket and makes up the couch. He hands me a white T-shirt.

'It may be too big, but at least it's dry,' he says. 'Just take your wet clothes to the kitchen, I'll put them in the dryer.'

When I'm on the couch, I send a message to Roger and tell him that Margot and I are all right, but the house is not.

With the hum of the dryer in the background, I eventually fall asleep restlessly, only to sit up again after a few hours. The sun finds its way between the slats of the shutters. I put on my dry clothes and leave the otherwise still quiet house.

There is a huge crater in the roof. A shiver runs through my body and I get a tight feeling in my chest, as if I can't breathe anymore. The old fig next to the house is split and broken, the center shows a black scorch mark from the lightning strike. Broken roof tiles are scattered in the garden. Beneath the oleanders, the ground is strewn with faded flowers, torn by the wind and laid out like a carpet. The window in the kitchen is wide open, the glass is broken.

Everything I just thought I knew, the rhythm I had just found, has been dissolved by last night's rain, sucked into the thunderclouds and destroyed by lightning.

I take pictures, send them to Roger, write that it is a disaster and that I will call him as soon as I have checked the damage inside.

I'm calling Gustav. He doesn't answer.

When I open the front door, I immediately step into a thick layer of wet stucco that dripped down the stairs last night. I have to clean it before it hardens, otherwise the red and white terrazzo will be gone under the layer for good. The chandelier is in pieces on the floor in the hallway upstairs, and the floor is also here soaking wet and dirty from the stucco. I close the window in the kitchen, the broken glass is on the floor. The sun shines down the stairs from the attic where it wouldn't normally reach. Heavy beams have come down, one beam is still dangling next to the hole in the roof. The insulation is torn. Roof tiles are broken on the floor. I bend down to look at a fallen beam, the iron L-shape is bent. Thick bolts that were supposed to hold the construction together have vibrated out and are some distance away.

My hands are shaking. The dirty coffee machine in the corner, with the coffee grounds and empty plastic cups. Furious, I knock the device off the rickety table. It lands on the ground with a bang, the plastic water tank pops off and flies away. Shouting loudly, I take another shot, the glass sugar bowl smashes on the floor, the plastic cups fly through the air. I knock over the empty table so that it bangs against the floor. I scream long, loud. Everyone told me that the construction wasn't strong enough, but I didn't see it. My plan, my grip. All worthless. I kick a roof tile and it slides towards the stairs and clatters down. That low cost was too good to be true. It was the only way to have Roger and Max with me. A fast way, a shortcut, which has just led to a dead end.

I pace through space as I try to call Gustav again. I let the phone ring endlessly, he doesn't answer. A fallen beam has hit part of the wall. The stucco has burst, the charcoal lines are visible again.

A brick is sticking out from the wall, and diagonally above are three more loose bricks. There is no mortar. Strange.

My phone is ringing, it's Gustav.

'Half the roof collapsed,' I say immediately as I pick up the phone. 'You must come now.'

'Collapsed? That's impossible,' he says.

'It only took one storm. If you fix it, I want you to use hardwood and make solid wood joints. What time can you be here?'

'We are in Slovakia. The season is over for us.'

'What? No, that's really impossible. You must come here now to restore your work.'

'We'll be back in the spring. However, please know that damage from natural disasters is not my responsibility.'

'You've done shoddy work!' I say.

'It was fine when we left. You will have to pay the costs for the repair work yourself.'

Angrily I hang up the phone. The loose brick, I pull it away. Everything is already broken. It sticks, I pull harder. A point of white paper becomes visible in the gap. I grab the next brick and pull it away. Envelopes. A glimpse of graceful handwriting. I pull away another brick, a red ribbon. It's still stuck under the last loose brick I remove.

It's a pile of old letters, held together with a faded red ribbon that is tied with a bow. Carefully, I untie the bow. Graceful lettering on the yellowed envelope. I take out the letter. The paper has some brown spots from moisture, but is otherwise in good condition. An Italian postage stamp from 1942. *Sofia e Stella* is written on it in fountain pen. The same handwriting as on the shreds we found earlier.

20 Giugno 1942, 20:00

Dear Sofia and Stella,
This may be my last letter to you. We leave for Russia to fight with Germany in the battle of Stalingrad. I don't know what the situation is there, but from what I've heard and seen, it's not good. The thought of you and the children helps me. Please take care of each other and stay home as much as possible for your own safety. I love you.

With love, your Danilo

Stella, Sofia and Danilo. The same names. I browse through the stack of envelopes; most are white, some pink or blue.

'Woohoo, darling,' Margot calls from the hallway below.

Danilo's handwriting is on every envelope except the bottom one. It is addressed to Danilo. I want to take out the letter, but I'm not sure. I tie the bow around the stack of envelopes again.

'Ah, here you are. I called you already, darling,' Margot says, looking around. 'What a horrible mess, so sad. We've come so far, it was almost done, and now this. Oh, it's so terrible. What time is Gustav coming?'

'He's not coming,' I say.

Aron also enters the attic. 'Well, I was afraid of this,' he says. 'You see this more often, when they are trying...'

Margot gives him a poke in the side. He grabs his stomach, looks at her and, without another word, walks on to make an inventory of the damage.

'What have you got there?' Margot asks.

'Old letters. They were hidden between a few loose bricks.'

'You're kidding me! How beautiful. Are they love letters? Let me see.'

She takes the stack from my hand, unties the bow and takes the top letter out of the envelope.

'I don't know if we should read them,' I say hesitantly. 'It's so personal...'

'Don't be silly, of course we should read them!'

Aron is standing next to her again and is reading along.

'So, the big secret is in some old letters?' he asks. His eyes glide over the old writing paper. 'It is written in an old Italian dialect. That will be difficult to read. Shall I take them and translate them for you?'

'Yes, that's a good idea, isn't it, darling, that Aron helps you with this?' Margot puts the letter back in the envelope and ties the ribbon back on.

If she tries to give the stack to Aron, I'll take it away. 'It's not up to us to read this, it's up to the two sisters. I'll give the letters to them.'

'Ah, what a shame,' Margot says as she follows me down the stairs. 'The sisters asked you to find and reveal the secret.'

'It doesn't even seem important anymore, I guess' Aron says. 'It's been so long. The house has been empty for twenty-five years and the two sisters wanted to get rid of it. I would let it rest.'

'The sisters searched the house for something they wanted to know,' I say. 'Maybe it's in the letters.'

I pull my dresses off the hangers and throw them in my suitcase. My blue blazer, T-shirts, flip flops. Margot and Aron are discussing something in her bedroom, I can't hear. I put the letters in the zippered front pocket of my suitcase. I text Valentina for her exact address in San Benedetto del Tronto and wheel my suitcase into the hallway, where Margot is already standing with her suitcase with its Prada logo. In the garden I throw my luggage in the back and wait for Margot to do the same.

'Darling,' she says. 'I've decided to stay with Aron. I can live with him until I can find my own apartment.'

'Are you serious?' I ask in surprise.

She nods. Aron puts an arm around her shoulder.

'What an adventure it was, huh?' she says, looking at the house. She gives me a kiss and gets into Aron's car.

'Bye, darling,' she calls through the open window, waving until I can't see her anymore.

I lock the front door. The oleander flowers have already blown away from the garden. Only the broken roof tiles on the ground are witnesses of last night. When I get in the car, my phone pings. Roger thinks the damage is terrible and says we're back to square one.

As I drive up the hill and the house fades further and further into the background, the blood drains from my face. A pressing headache sets in. I am alternately hot and cold; my ears are ringing.

I pass under the small railway tunnel and park in the deserted area near the harbor by the sea. The small campsite with the mobile homes is closed. The sea ripples, nothing betrays that in the same bay yesterday the waves were capped with white. A fisherman walks past my car, but doesn't look up. No answer from Valentina yet, and I don't have Rubia's phone number. When I call her, I let it ring for a long time, but she doesn't answer. Brian, I can ask him for the address. He doesn't answer either. Really, does no one answer their phone in the winter? One more time I walk to the tide line. It was great here for weeks, but it's all over.

It is still quiet on the road along the coast. The campsites with swimming pools and water slides are empty. A train races past. When I reach Ancona, the highway bends inland. One last look at the sea. Oh, Palazzo Puro, I'm opening her shutters. The sun on my face. The wheat fields, fresh sea air that caresses my skin.

A truck honks. He's driving too close behind me. I press the accelerator, my suitcase vibrates in the bed of the truck. I can't go any faster than 95 kilometers per hour.

The truck honks again, and the impatient driver throws his car into the left lane to pass me.

The rolling hills give way to fields of bare fruit trees, occasionally interrupted by a fruit-juice factory. It's getting busier as I enter the Po Valley, full of cities and industrial estates. Cars fly up and down the entry and exit ramps, passing me left and right.

After almost five hours of driving, I get off the highway just before the Swiss border. A narrow road leads to Lake Como. A few tourists are walking down the gangway of a tour boat for a trip across the lake. The water ripples against the sloping quay where the smaller boats are bobbing up and down in the water. A modern restaurant is hidden under tall pine trees. I order a coffee. An elderly couple walks by hand in hand, they smile at me as if they are welcoming me to their city. The lake shimmers. High up on the mountains are houses that look out over this water. I google the prices and they're in the millions of euros.

The border with Switzerland is a five-minute drive from Lake Como. The blond customs officer looks at me as I slowly drive past. He gestures for me to stop. I hurriedly search for my passport, roll down the window and hand it to him.

'You are not Italian,' he concludes. 'But you do drive a very old Italian car.' He looks at the dashboard and the torn leather upholstery.

'We have a house here,' I explain. 'Palazzo Puro.'

He shakes his head. 'Never heard of it. Where are you going?'

His colleague is standing next to a dark blue van and opens the back doors. He takes an enthusiastically barking German shepherd out of a crate and puts him on a short leash. He taps on the window on the other side of my car. I lean over the passenger seat and roll it down.

'Amsterdam,' I say to the blond-haired man. 'I'm going to Amsterdam.'

'Hmmm,' says the man with the shepherd. 'Do you ever use marijuana or other drugs?'

'No, I don't.'

'Are you sure?' he asks, commanding the dog to jump into the bed of the truck and sniff my suitcase.

'Get out,' says the other. 'We're going to check for drugs.'

'But the dog hasn't barked, has it?' I say in surprise.

'Your suitcase has white powder on it.'

I get out. Other cars drive across the border without being stopped.

'It's stucco,' I say. 'Because of the water damage. It was all over the house.'

'Open your suitcase,' says the man with the drug-sniffing dog.

The dog sniffs at my crumpled dresses, but doesn't bark. The man gestures to the dog to sniff one more time. No barking again. He opens the zipper on the side pocket, looks inside and takes out the letters.

'I'm going to send them,' I explain. 'But I don't have an address yet.'

The man pulls the dog, who has stuck his nose into the side pocket, back and puts the letters back. He wets his fingertip in his mouth and runs it over the white spots on the suitcase. He checks if there is enough on it and puts his finger in his mouth again.

'And?' the blond-haired man asks him.

'It's stucco. Have a nice trip.'

'How do you know what stucco tastes like?' asks the other as they walk away.

'Experience.' He makes the German Shepherd jump back into the crate and rewards him.

When I'm back on the highway, I call Margot.

'Yes, I miss you too,' she shouts enthusiastically, as if she had to bridge the few hundred kilometers with her voice. 'How's it going, darling? Are you already well underway? Where are you now, already in Switzerland?'

'Yes, I was almost busted for using stucco,' I say.

The mountains are closing in on the valley. Small villages lie in the shadow of the high, snow-capped peaks. Locked up in a dark valley with only a river, a highway and a sun that doesn't reach here, but stops halfway up the mountainside.

Three and a half hours later I drive into Germany. Still at least eight hours to go before I get home. At night, when I'm too tired to keep driving, I stop in a parking lot. I take my blazer from my suitcase, lay it over me and tilt the seat back. I close my eyes for a moment. Palazzo Puro, her collapsed roof and closed shutters. Roger and Max, waiting for me. I am in between two worlds and fall asleep restlessly.

I wake up at the first light of the morning. I shiver, the car cooled down overnight. My plan wasn't to sleep that long either, because I don't want to be here. An elderly couple sits under the awning of their motor home and beckons me. They ask if I would like a cup of coffee.

The drive through Germany is eight hundred kilometers of uninterrupted highway, enclosed by forests, with the occasional view as I drive over a hill. Gray cities and gas stations where bratwurst are sold.

The border with the Netherlands. Only two hours more to drive.

'Mom,' Max calls out. His voice has changed; it's lower. With big strides he comes running, the two puppies sprint after him. He is now half a head taller than me. I bury my nose in his hair, my child.

'I love you, sweetheart,' I say, kissing his cheek.

'I love you too,' he replies. He takes my suitcase out of the bed of the truck.

'Honey, good to have you back,' Roger says, coming over. 'It was quiet without you.' We hug.

Roger has put pink roses in a vase. On the wall is an old weekly plan with all the appointment blocks and the menus, which I made before I left a few months ago.

I am home. Palazzo Puro is further away than ever.

Who cares about her now?

Venerdì, 6 Agosto 1965

Carrying the blue vase filled with water, she walked to the oleander bushes. She clipped short branches; bright pink, pale pink and white flowers. It promised to be a hot summer day. Through the tall grass she walked to the alcove next to the front door and put the vase in it. Valentina turned twenty-five today.

A red car with the top down drove by. It slowed as it neared the house. A man looked at the house, into the garden, but drove on again.

In the hall it was still cool because of the thick walls. This day was like any of Valentina's birthdays; Sofia lived it in silence. Then, in her mind, she held her in her arms again as a baby and kissed her. The little girls on the side of the road playing in the pool, the two teenagers in her office and that one special day when Valentina had spontaneously hugged her. Had she studied architecture in Rome? Was she in love or already married? Sofia hadn't seen her since that encounter, but the sweet memory of the embrace remained.

The girls' room. She and Stefano had bought the house six years ago, but she didn't want to change this room. She picked up the rag doll she'd washed and sat down on a chair. The doll against her face.

Footsteps in the hallway below. She was still ducking and trying to hide. Yet, like all neighbors in the valley, she left her front door open during the day. Did she recognize the footsteps?

It was Stefano. He was carrying a large can of white lime paint. Tiny beads of sweat formed on his forehead and his shirt hung halfway out of his pants.

'It's a hot day,' he puffed. 'I thought, what if we start working on that old nursery today?'

He set the paint can on the dining table. 'That's the only room on this floor that we haven't tackled yet.'

Indeed, the kitchen walls had already been given a fresh coat of paint, and she'd decided to paint a light blue stripe around the baseboard; more modern, less like the past. In the bedroom where she had painted the walls light terracotta, the bed had new mattresses and headboards decorated with painted bunches of grapes. The new carpet, the new linen cupboard and the soft armchair in the corner, together they brushed away the harshness of the war years. She hadn't looked in the attic with her old bedroom. Stefano had been upstairs once, and told her there was still an old bed, a trunk, and a linen closet. 'There are black charcoal marks on the wall,' he'd said.

'What do you think? Shall we paint?' he asked. 'We can turn that old nursery into a spare room for Alessandro for when he comes home from university on the weekends.'

'Tomorrow,' she said. 'Let's do it tomorrow.'

'Fine, then I'll take those cots to the dump today.'

'No!' she screamed.

Stefano looked at her inquiringly, his forehead creased. 'Are you all right? I feel like I'm losing you more and more since we bought this house, that I no longer understand you.'

Behind the window the palm tree whose leaves danced up and down. That palm tree had been small when she planted it and now it almost reached the kitchen window on the first floor.

Stefano sighed audibly.

She understood. This was her fault. 'I'm so sorry.'

'I've always known I loved you more than you loved me,' he said. 'I laid that down a long time ago, however...'

It crackled in her head. She wanted to be in this house, alone, living in the past. And she wanted to be with Stefano and Alessandro in their house in Ripatransone, with their real estate agency; her real life. It didn't seem to unite in this house, no matter how hard she tried to make it work.

For days he had asked her why she wanted to live here. There had been better houses that were in better condition and had better sea views because they were higher up the hill, and she said she couldn't imagine a more beautiful house. He wanted to keep her happy, as he showed her every day and she much less so, and in the end, he had agreed on the condition that they also keep their house and office in Ripatransone and add a small extension to the house in the valley for his parents, so that they could come to live here later if they needed to be cared for when they got too old. She'd wondered if the extension wouldn't detract from her original design, and now that it was empty tacked against it, she knew it was a design flaw.

More and more often Stefano slept in Ripatransone after a working day and she drove back to the valley alone.

'It feels like you're slipping further and further into a world where I don't belong,' he said.

He was right, of course he was right.

'It's not your fault,' she said. 'I'm really sorry.'

'Do you want me to leave you alone for a while?'

He was putting her first, as he always did.

'I will stay at our house in Ripatransone if you wish,' he said.

She nodded slowly. She didn't want to be without him and Alessandro, but the past continued to haunt her.

'Are you still coming to the office?' he asked nervously.

What did she want?

'Maybe I'll temporarily set up my design studio here in the attic,' she said hesitantly.

He shrugged, came close to her. 'I'm going to miss you, but I'm waiting for you.'

He hugged her, gave her a kiss and walked away with his back bent, looking at the ground.

The paint can stood on the dining table, showing how the day could have gone differently.

It was messy in the attic. Old chairs lay on their sides in a corner, and along the wall were old mosquito screens, a door, and shelves. The blue-and-white striped fabric on her old bed springs had faded. Her old nightstand had dozens of holes from woodworm. The big trunk was still there. She cracked open the lid. Baby clothes. She picked up the creamy-white crocheted cardigan. She used to tie the strings at the front with small bows for Valentina or Rubia. A summer hat, the yellow dress with white dots that Valentina had been wearing on the road that afternoon. Her hand ran over the clothes. She closed the lid and tidied the room.

She didn't stop until early evening; then she put a kitchen chair on the balcony and poured a glass of wine. Refreshing. The neighbor was walking through his vegetable garden with two dogs. The sun above the hills was just touching the roof of the house. She had spent hours tidying up, swept and mopped the floor. Tomorrow, she wanted to get her work tables and put them in the attic along the walls.

Silence.

Peace.

The tension of the afternoon slipped away from her. Tomorrow Valentina's birthday would be over and the past would slowly take its place in the background again.

A small silver-grey car parked along the road. A young woman dressed in a tight turquoise dress got out, looked at the house and walked down the hill. Her way of walking. Sofia almost dropped her wine glass.

'Good afternoon, Mrs. Sofia,' Valentina called up to the balcony.

'Um… uh… Valentina?'

Valentina examined the house inquiringly. Her eyes scanned the windows and the balcony. She looked around the yard, picked something up from the tall grass and held it up. The metal child's shovel. She studied it.

'You have a beautiful house,' Valentina said, finally looking up at the balcony again. 'I feel like I know it from somewhere.'

She put down the child's shovel. 'Although the balcony doesn't seem to match the rest of the architectural style. Can I come in?'

Before Sofia could answer, her footsteps sounded in the hall. Sofia got up, turned around.

There she stood, between the swinging doors with opal-green decorated glass.

More beautiful than ever before.

With wavy dark brown hair and green eyes that matched her turquoise dress.

'I heard from your husband that you are going to set up your design studio here?' Valentina asked. She looked out over the wheat field to the sea. 'It's a beautiful place, I understand it's inspiring.'

Sofia nodded.

'I graduated, Mrs. Sofia. And I am going to start my own architectural firm in San Benedetto del Tronto.'

Her daughter had succeeded.

'That's fantastic,' she said. 'Really. I cannot wish for more.'

'The architectural office will be located on the ground floor of our house in the port. Maybe you know it, it's that yellow house with red shutters?' said Valentina. 'By the way, I am going to have it repainted, those colors are way too harsh for the house. White shutters will look much better. And a lighter shade of paint for the stucco, like the color of scoop ice cream.'

The house in the harbor with the room on the top floor where Mr. Marinolli watched over his property through his binoculars. Where the birthday party next to the pool had just ended and she had been left standing in the garden, Valentina hanging out of the window and Stella not letting her in.

'I live in the house with my father, my sister and my brother, but my brother will be moving soon. He's going to start a winery in the hills just outside Ripatransone.'

'And your mother?' Sofia asked.

'My mother passed away.'

Sofia was shocked. 'Stella?'

It was too late. She had said it without thinking.

Valentina looked at her in surprise. 'Did you know my mother?'

There was silence, as if Valentina was trying to understand what had just happened.

'My condolences for your loss,' Sofia said almost inaudibly.

'Thank you. My mother spent much of her time in a wheelchair and that affected her. She was sweet and caring, but so different from me. She disapproved of my ambitions.'

Her daughter.

'I'm sorry for you. Your ambitions are admirable. You are a special girl.'

Valentina looked sad. 'That's the exact opposite of what my mother would say when she was mad at me. "You don't think you're special, do you?" she would shout.'

Her daughter; special, as any child to a mother.

'The doctors said she didn't remember who she was or where she was after her stroke,' Valentina said. 'She was in the hospital talking about the war and the people she had betrayed.'

Betrayal.

Stella had betrayed her. Somehow, she'd always known. She sank into the chair on the balcony and rubbed the railing. The circles and arrows had saved her when soldiers stopped her that night in Massignano where she was delivering a message, but she had never wanted to believe that the woman she cared for after the car accident would betray her. A partisan and fascist together in a house, both mothers of a daughter, and both only in their early twenties when the war slowly engulfed them and sucked them into its danger. Choices were made, while agony gripped them.

'I sat next to her bed that last night,' Valentina said sadly. 'I wanted so badly to talk to her about us, but she kept repeating names I didn't know, like she was far away. In another life.'

'Names?'

'Yes, she kept saying she was sorry. Also about the letters from the camp that she had hidden under a mattress.'

'What names?'

Valentina shrugged.

'Well, I don't remember exactly. At least I remember Sienna and Rafaella. There were a few more. Very strange. Sometimes you don't realize what happened in the war. She has...'

The blood drained from Sofia's face. She clamped her hand tighter around the concrete balcony railing to keep from falling off her chair. Her mother, sisters and Rafaella, she had been looking for them for months, for years, but Stella had erased them as if they had never existed.

'Mrs. Sofia, are you okay?' Valentina asked.

Her daughter's voice, far away. High breathing, dry throat. She picked up her wine glass and emptied it in a single swallow.

'I'm sorry to tell you this,' Valentina said. 'The war must have been an anxious time for her. Maybe for you too.'

Stella had sat with her back to her and allowed Sofia to be carried off in front of Valentina that night. She was the only one who had come back, broken by what she had been through and so lost that she had not been able to be strong and embrace her own daughter and the man she loved so dearly.

'I'm sorry, I shouldn't bother you with this,' Valentina said. She said a quick prayer for her mother, and opened her small white handbag and took out a rectangular card. 'I just came to invite you to the opening of my architectural office.'

Smiling, Valentina handed her the invitation. With trembling hand, she took it.

'Hello Mom,' Alessandro called up from the garden. 'I've come to bring some of your drawings.'

He came running up the stairs with heavy steps, and stood in the doorway with the large rolls of paper under his arm. He smiled broadly.

'And who is this beauty?' he asked without embarrassment.

He looked at Valentina, she looked at him.

'I'm Valentina,' she introduced herself. 'Your mother encouraged me to become an architect a few years ago.'

'Did you tell her you're Sophus, Mom?' Alessandro asked in surprise. 'You've really never told anyone that.'

He looked back at Valentina and smiled at her. She smiled at him.

They had the same smile.

'Do you live around here?' he asked. 'I thought I already knew all the girls, but apparently I missed the most beautiful one.'

Valentina blushed and dropped her eyes to the ground. 'I don't live far from here.'

In a blur, Sofia saw it happen. This was the moment she could no longer be silent.

14

When I enter the office, it's impossible not to notice. Streamers hang over my desk and two balloons are taped to my desk chair. Colleagues clap. I wave to them. When I turn on my computer, my screensaver has changed. The photo of Palazzo Puro with its collapsed roof has been replaced by a new photo that someone got from Instagram. My colleague Anne-Marie comes over with a large cake and puts it down in front of me. It has a photo of Palazzo Puro with the text *Congratulations on your move*. She hands me a knife.

'We're going to miss you,' she says. 'Even if it was only seven months that you worked here.'

'Thank you,' I say and cut the cake.

Less than two weeks after I got home, I was hired for this position. The days had passed the way they always did whenever I was working as a project manager – painfully slowly. The evenings at home had changed. Everything was looser, simpler. Roger and Max went for a walk with the dogs after dinner, while I put the dirty dishes in the dishwasher and cleaned the dining table. One day, Max came home from school, told him that he'd earned an 8.3 on his math test and that he wanted to study in Bologna or Rome. 'You see,' I had said to Roger, 'he also wants to go to Italy.'

When my friends asked if the house in Italy had already been sold and if I didn't regret the whole adventure, I told them that there was something about Palazzo Puro that always attracted me. It seemed as if I was not completely here, but partly still living there. It made the old trees in the park opposite our house turn into olive trees on rolling hills. The pond in the middle of the small lawn where ducks bobbed loudly croaking, turned into the azure sea that rippled calmly and where the fishing boats bobbed up and down. Sometimes I thought I was slowly going crazy because I saw things that weren't there. That's called desire, Margot said when I told her about these experiences during a video call. She was sitting on the terrace of the small apartment with the white sofa and white coffee table, then she called Aron to say hello too. His hair was dark blond and longer.

Valentina had called me back about the letters and told me that I could read them and didn't have to send them to her. And asked whether I could call her and Rubia if I knew more. My Italian was good enough to let the past slowly reveal itself through the letters.

In another conversation Margot asked me if I had already convinced Roger and Max to come back, because she missed me. Soon the summer season would start again, and Frederico had already asked if her plain-looking girlfriend was coming back.

The moment Roger told me over dinner that he could start as a financial specialist at a company in San Benedetto del Tronto, I cried. Max shouted that he was ready too and that Sofia was waiting for him there. Roger smiled. I shouldn't ask him too often why he was doing this, he said, because then he would start doubting again. But he wanted me to be who I was again before I came back from Italy and seemed so distant from them. We placed a for sale sign in the garden and with the profit from the sale of the house Lorenzo repaired the roof, installed a good bathroom and new kitchen and repaired the back wall where the extension had been demolished.

'Speech, speech,' a few colleagues shout. They cheer as if my farewell is a big celebration. Just when I'm about to say something, the director who has joined my colleagues in the circle clears his throat.

'Mirella. Today is your last day with us,' he says loudly as if performing in front of a large audience. 'It was seven special months and we all learned a lot from you, especially me. While I had always thought that sound project planning was the most important thing, you showed us that a personal approach and building a good team yield much better results. A big round of applause for you.'

Everyone claps, eats cake and wishes me a nice adventure. I can only hope for less adventure than last time.

After I hand in my laptop at the end of the afternoon, I answer the message

Brian had sent me earlier in the day. *Yes, I can come to the house viewing on Wednesday.*

'Are you ready?' I ask Roger when I get home.

He's wearing a simple dark blue sweater and jeans, and is busy loading the suitcases into the car.

'Hmmm,' he says. 'Ask me again in two months.'

'I'm convinced that you'll feel at home with your new job in no time. And it's only a fifteen-minute drive from the house. It will be nice to have so little travel time.'

Max plays with Rover and Benz on the floor of the empty living room. All of our furniture has been sold.

'Are you excited?' I ask.

'Yes, I texted Sofia that I'll be there in two days and won't leave again.'

'Nice that you already know someone there.'

'Yes, she's glad I'm coming. Besides, I'll be riding with you in the truck.'

'It rocks terribly. You'll be completely shaken up by the time we get there.'

'Doesn't matter. The truck is cool.'

Roger takes a last round through the house to make sure we haven't forgotten anything.

'Don't you regret leaving the house you designed yourself?' he asks when he's done.

I shake my head. 'This house is going to make another family happy, I'm sure.'

Max is already sitting in the front of the pickup truck with Rover and Benz on his lap. We drive down the street.

I sing *'O sole mio*.

'Is that necessary, Mom?' Max asks. He turns the knob on the old radio and tries to find a station. We only hear static.

The long German highway, the high Swiss mountains and the Po Valley; this time they won't break me.

The pickup truck growls loudly as we struggle up the hills, it doesn't matter. We're emigrating, that's what it's all about.

'Darlings, there you are!' Margot shouts. She jumps up from the folding chair she's set up in the shade of the palm in our yard. Aron stands up too. She hugs me and kisses me on the cheeks. 'Oh, how nice that you're here. I missed you so much.'

She hugs Roger.

'Hello Margot,' Max says. 'What do you think of Rover and Benz?'

'Oh, darling, you're so lucky, aren't you? Two dogs, a beautiful house and soon an Italian girl on every finger.'

Palazzo Puro.

For now and forever.

Roger and Aron shake hands. Lorenzo comes down the hill and joins them.

The grass is almost knee-deep and the crickets are chirping as if it hasn't been a year and nothing has happened in the meantime. A few bees are buzzing above the oleanders that are in full bloom. The roof tiles have been cleared from the garden. And, high above, where the bright sun shines, is a brand-new roof.

While filming with his phone, Max comes walking back. He types in something.

'I made a video for my friends,' he says. 'Then they'll know what it's like here when they come to stay with us in a few weeks.'

He runs off again with the dogs, which are jumping in the high grass that they barely rise above.

'It's still beautiful here,' Roger tells me as he walks back to me.

'Do you want me to plan for the next few days?' I ask.

We laugh about it together.

'Aron has offered to help me fix the shed,' he says. 'He's a nice guy.'

Aron and Lorenzo walk around the old barn together.

'Does Lorenzo think that's a good idea?' I ask concerned.

'Yes, he is now giving us tips on how to deal with it. We have to use hardwood beams to repair the roof.'

'And make wood joints,' I say.

It is wonderfully cool in the house, despite the blistering heat outside. The new kitchen has been installed in the old stable, which I have only seen in videos up until now. A concrete counter top with open compartments underneath. No upper cabinets, but a smoothly plastered wall. Simple, pure; just the way I wanted it. Built with craftsmanship by someone nearby, at his own pace and without strict planning from me.

The stairs to the top floors are clean, the dirty layer of stucco has disappeared. Roger and Aron walk by with the suitcases and put them in both bedrooms.

'Remember that horrible night?' Margot asks as she comes and stands next to me. 'I was so scared, darling.'

I nod. 'What happened was out of our control.'

'A lot of houses were damaged that night, I heard from Adamo later,' she says.

'Adamo?' I ask, bewildered.

She shrugs. 'Sometimes we still talk.'

'Why? You're still living with Aron, aren't you?'

'Yes, of course darling, don't be silly. We only call sometimes, nothing special. I don't have sex with him.'

'Are you sure?'

Lorenzo joins us.

'Do you think it turned out nice?' he asks. 'Have you looked at the beams in the attic yet? So, that's how it should be.'

'I'll take a long look at it later so that I never forget,' I tell him.

Margot smells his shirt. I pat her on the shoulder. She smiles.

'I know why the sisters got the children's drawing of the house,' I say. 'I've read the letters.'

10 Agosto 1965

In front of the yellow house with the dark red shutters was a white metal sign with the name of *V. Marinolli Architetti* in graceful gold letters. In the garden, two painters were preparing to paint the stucco. The iron gate with the ornate patterns was open.

Both windows on either side of the high front door displayed professional home designs. Sofia pressed her small handbag firmly against her stomach. Maybe she'd better turn around and leave. Going home, forgetting everything and tearing up the letter she had written. Instead of turning lives upside down just to prevent a possible disaster.

Could she pretend she hadn't seen what she saw last Friday when Valentina and Alessandro met? Over the weekend, she'd written the letter over and over until she found the right words. She hadn't wanted to bring him along on Monday, because that day was Rubia's birthday and the girls probably still celebrated their birthdays together in the garden, but now she couldn't postpone it any longer.

'Ma'am, apologies,' said a young man coming up on his bike. He got off and took the bike in the hand. 'Can I help you with anything?'

A voice from the past. The beach on Sunday, Danilo coming over as she came out of the sea and dried herself off. The tea, sweet temptations, the endless horizon and promising future.

The boy must be in his early twenties by now. He was almost a head taller than her and had luscious, light brown curls. The baby that had been in Danilo's arms the day she'd stood by the road.

'Excuse me, ma'am, I should have introduced myself,' he said politely. 'I'm Adamo Marinolli and I live here. Are you looking for an architect? My sister is very good, I can certainly recommend her.'

Sofia shook her head, opened her bag and took out the letter. She squeezed the envelope so hard that her knuckles turned white. 'This letter is for Danilo.'

Adamo grabbed the envelope, Sofia wouldn't let go.

'You can give it to me for my father. Or would you rather hand it over yourself? He is at his office in the harbor.'

The office in the harbor. Without realizing it, her grip slackened. Adamo took the letter and examined the envelope.

Go, she had to go.

'Where can my father reach you?' the boy called after her. 'I don't see an address on the back.'

She turned. 'In the house in the valley.'

Her heels clicked on the sidewalk.

'Ma'am, what house in the valley?' he cried.

Every morning she put fresh water in the blue vase with oleanders. She looked through the hatch to see if there was a letter. Nothing.

There had been no reply all week. Maybe Danilo hadn't got her letter, or he was angry with her and would curse her for not saying anything before. Or was he so disappointed that she never wrote back that he decided not to waste any more ink on her.

She packed her bag and drawings, and left for their real estate agency in Ripatransone to share her designs with the clients, together with Stefano.

At noon they had lunch under the arcade of the cafe near the opera.

'I miss you,' he said. 'Will you ever come and live with me again?'

She secretly hoped that he would fall in love with another woman, who would give him what she could not give.

'Maybe,' she said. 'I don't know.'

She came home late at night and checked the hatch. No letter. What else could she expect after all these years of silence?

She poured a glass of white wine and went to work in her studio in the attic. Versions of the letter lay everywhere on her desk. Carefully written with fountain pen, but unfinished. The right words had been hard to find. She read what she had written again.

Dear Danilo,
It's Valentina's birthday and she came by here. How beautiful she is, our daughter. There hasn't been a moment in my life that I didn't think about you ~~and our daughter~~ both. I don't know ~~how~~ what I can say ~~now~~

She crumpled up the paper and threw it in the trash. She picked up the next sheet.

Dear Danilo,
It's Valentina's birthday and she came by here. How beautiful she is, our daughter. There hasn't been a moment in my life that I didn't think about you both. I don't know what I can say to explain it to you. How can I find the right words to tell you why I didn't come back, while I've stayed so close by all these years?
Let me start by saying that ~~everything is different~~

She'd tried it again at least fifteen times, and then she'd transcribed the text at least three more times until it was flawless. She looked for her latest draft and read it.

6 Agosto 1965, 20:50

Dear Danilo,
It's Valentina's birthday and she came by here. How beautiful she is, our daughter. There hasn't been a moment in my life that I didn't think about you both. I don't know what I can say to explain it to you. How can I find the right words to tell you why I didn't come back, while I've stayed so close by all these years?
Let me start by saying I'm sorry ~~I made you think I never came back after the war~~*. I left you. The war has left deep wounds. I was in the Servigliano and Bolzano camps, then I was taken by train to Auschwitz.*
You saw me, that's right. Still, coming back was impossible, because you were better off without me. I had to let her and you – you chose Stella – go. From a distance I watched Valentina grow into the beautiful woman she is today.
I have always loved you, but I am now married and have a son, Alessandro, who is almost twenty years old. He and Valentina are the reason I can no longer be silent. They met last week, and the way they looked at each other scares me. It's the way we looked at each other. Do you remember that feeling? How do we tell them who they are to each other?

Love, your Sofia

He may have been so furious with her that he had torn up her letter. If he had read the letter, could he understand why she had done it?

She went to the kitchen and lit a candle. The flame moved gently back and forth. Danilo. Opposite her at the table. A smile. His trust in her. In the two of them together. So long ago, never forgotten. Headlights from the road illuminated the wall. The stucco went bright white, then darkened again when the headlights turned off. A car door. She quickly stood up, looked through the window. A man. She only saw his outline. He wore a trench coat that fluttered with every step he took. He held up something in his right hand. What was it? A machine gun? She quickly stepped away from the window. Someone was banging on the front door. She dove to the floor, sitting with her back against the wall. Head between her knees. She suddenly felt warm, and started sweating. They had come for her. More banging on the front door. There was a whooshing sound in her ears, she put her hands over them. Breathe calmly, stay calm. Hide, in the closet, no, in the chest in the attic. She crawled into the hallway on all fours. The hinges of the hatch next to the front door squeaked. To the stairs, quickly. Faster.

'Sofia!' the man shouted loudly through the hatch.

She sat very still, listening.

'Sofia, I know you're here.'

The pressure in her head eased, she wiped the sweat from her forehead. His voice. After all those years. Carefully she stood up, her knees buckled.

He came for her, after all the years she'd let him think she was dead.

She walked downstairs, slowly opening the front door a crack.

Danilo.

His green eyes glittered in the moonlight. In his hand he held up a bunch of red roses.

Her lower lip trembled.

'I'm so sorry,' she said. 'I can explain…'

Tears ran down her cheeks. She quickly wiped them away. 'I… what can I…'

He hugged her. His warmth came through the trench coat. His cheek against her cheek.

'Don't say anything,' he said. 'I understand why you did it and it's okay.'

15

Now that I know I can't keep it to myself any longer. The sisters asked me to find the secret and share it with them. Whether they ever expected this secret to turn out like this, I don't know, that's not my responsibility. I enter the phone number, the phone rings.

'Put it on speaker, darling,' Margot says. 'Then I can follow it.'

She sits opposite me at the dining table under the palm tree. Roger and Aron are talking down in the garden and Max has gone to the beach.

'*Pronto*,' a woman says.

'Valentina?' I ask. 'This is Mirella.'

'Mirella, so good to hear from you. Yes, this is Valentina, do you like the house?'

'Yes, it's beautiful. The roof and walls have been repaired.'

'Excellent, the house is worth it. The architecture is beautiful, although the balcony remains a bit strange. Are you going to change that?'

Margot makes impatient movements with her hand. 'Now tell her,' she hisses. She leans forward so far that she's just above the phone in my hand. Golden chains dance in her cleavage as she wiggles back and forth.

'I discovered in the letters the secret you asked for,' I tell Valentina.

'Are you serious?' she shouts enthusiastically. 'We searched the entire house more than twenty years ago when we inherited it and never found those letters. Wait, I'm calling Rubia.'

She says something in the background to someone.

'Are you sure you want to know?' I ask hesitantly.

This news could have a big effect on her.

Margot shakes her head furiously. 'Just say it.'

Voices talk over each other on the other end of the line.

'Sorry, what did you say?' Valentina asks. 'It's busy here in the house with all of the preparations. We're planning to have a big family celebration soon.'

'I asked if you really want to know.'

'Yes please. I just consulted with Rubia. She wants to hear it too, and asks if you're coming to the party with your family tonight? Then you can meet everyone and do the unveiling.'

Margot angrily points to herself.

'Thank you for the invitation,' I say to Valentina.

'Darling, tell them I'm coming too,' Margot says. 'I love parties so much.'

'Is it okay if I bring my friend?' I ask. 'She likes parties.'

'Of course. It's a big party in my brother's garden. I'll text you his address. It starts at eight. See you tonight.'

I hang up and look at Margot.

'Great, a party in the garden,' she exults. 'With a big Italian family. You usually only see that in movies, huh darling, do you realize that?'

'I don't know if a party is the right time to tell this secret.'

The address comes in on the app and I check it out. The house is in the hills just below Ripatransone and I feel like I've seen the street name before.

As I drive along the narrow roads, it is already getting dark. Roger and Max discuss whether climate change will have an impact on the location of our house in the valley, because if it does and the sea level rises, the grain field will be flooded and our house will be by the sea. Once the discussion is over, they start talking about a video Max saw on YouTube where people compete to see who can eat the most hotdogs in ten minutes.

'How many do you think there were, Mom?' Max asks from the back seat. 'And I don't just mean those sausages, eh, but with such a soggy bun on the side. Well, how many do you think?'

Aron's little white car is following right on my bumper. Margot is sitting next to him and has flipped the mirror down to touch up her makeup.

'I think seven,' Roger says enthusiastically.

'No, wrong. And you are actually not even allowed to participate, because you know these kinds of videos. Mom, what do you think?'

'Twenty?' I ask.

We drive out of the valley and follow the winding road to the high hilltop where Ripatransone is located. The navigator tells us to turn left instead of following the main road. I brake hard for a small white sign with gold letters and stop.

'What is it?' Roger asks.

'Well, guess again,' Max says.

'I know this intersection,' I say, clasping my hands around the steering wheel.

'How many do you think, Mom?'

'Max, stop now,' I say, irritated.

'So not nice.'

'Well, okay, fifty hot dogs then?'

'Woohoo,' Margot yells, appearing next to my window. 'Roll it down, darling.'

'It's in only ten minutes, eh?' Max says.

I roll down my window.

'I know,' I say to Margot. 'This is the same road as the one to Adamo's winery.'

'Do you want to go back, darling? I understand that, you know, with your fear of heights.'

'Hey Margot, how many hot dogs do you think someone can eat in ten minutes? In America, I mean.'

'Three I think, darling, is that right?' She looks at me again. 'Shall I ask if Aron is leading the way?'

'I can drive,' Roger says.

'No,' we say at the same time.

'Yes, let Aron lead the way,' I say to Margot.

'Well Mom, you were the closest. It was seventy-five.'

Aron passes me with his eyes fixed on the road and I follow him. We round the sharp bend along the cliff and there are cars parked in a long line diagonally on the shoulder. Aron parks behind one of them.

'This is at the winery itself,' I say. 'Shouldn't we go on?'

'Aron knows what he's doing, I guess,' Roger says.

'Can you please check your phone?'

Slowly I drive past the cars and we arrive at a crowded parking lot in front of the house.

'Yes,' Roger says. 'This is it for real. There are no other houses in this area, so you can park here.'

We drive around, but we can't find an empty space.

'I was afraid of that,' Roger says. 'There's a reason why other people were already parked along the road.'

'Those Italian families are always so big,' I say.

I park the car right behind two other cars.

'This is probably not allowed,' says Max.

We wait for Margot and Aron to come, arm-in-arm, up the steep hill. Her heels are too high for a garden party.

We walk to the white stucco winery with the olive-green shutters. Music is playing from the garden. Another family approaches and greets us. We follow them around the house and see dozens of people standing under a grape leaf pergola and countless strings of fairy lights. They talk, laugh and toast with each other. White streamers hang between the olive trees, supplemented with white balloons. At the end of the garden is a small stage where a DJ is playing lounge music. The doors of the wine room are open. We walk over. There is a bar with people standing by it, busily talking and gesturing.

'Let's get a glass of prosecco first,' Margot says loudly over the music.

Ahead I see Valentina. She is wearing a beautiful green evening dress made of satin.

'Our hostess is standing there,' I say. They're already gone. They make their way through the crowds to the bar and Roger raises his hand to order the wine.

'Welcome,' Valentina says. She stands next to me and smiles.

'Thank you for the invitation,' I reply. 'It all looks fantastic. Very magical.'

A waiter walks by with a tray full of glasses of prosecco, and Valentina takes two glasses and hands one to me.

'*Saluti*,' she says. 'We're celebrating my father's 100th birthday, can you believe it?'

She points to a corner of the patio where an old man with silver hair sits in a chair, watching the family members celebrating.

Her father?

Her father. It's Danilo.

'Come on, let me introduce you to him,' Valentina says. She takes my hand and leads me through the crowd. She regularly says hello to someone and kisses him or her on both cheeks.

Rubia, who is talking to a group of guests, breaks off her conversation and comes over to us. Her pink satin dress moves elegantly with every step she takes.

'You're going to tell us the secret later,' she says. It doesn't sound like a question, more like an inescapable fact.

'Yes,' I answer. 'We started renovating the house and after the roof collapsed I found...'

'No, wait,' Rubia says. 'Tell it later on. More people need to hear this. Nobody understands why Valentina and I inherited the house in the valley.'

'Come on, let's say hello to Father,' Valentina says, taking my hand again.

When I stand in front of Danilo and Valentina introduces me as the woman who bought the house in the valley, he looks at me earnestly. His skin is deeply wrinkled, and he's balding at the temples. His eyes are strikingly green. I shake his hand and congratulate him on his birthday. Rubia calls Valentina and she tells me she'll be right back.

'Do you like the house in the valley?' Danilo asks. His voice sounds like macramé.

I nod in agreement. He pats the chair next to him and I sit down. Where is Margot? She probably wants to meet Danilo too now that I've told her the secret from the letters. Her blond hair stands out among all the people with brown and black hair, she is talking to Adamo a little further along. They are close together, too close. Aron is standing next to them and is talking to Roger. And where is Max? Danilo leans toward me, his breathing close to my ear.

'I have a secret,' he says. 'Now I'm a hundred and I've never told anyone. The architect of your house was the most beautiful woman I have ever known.'

He puts his finger over his lips and leans back, as if he's already said too much.

'I know about you and Sofia,' I say. It's out before I can think of it. Tact would have been better.

He looks at me for a long time without saying anything.

'Valentina and Rubia gave me a drawing of the house at the handover and asked me to look for more information,' I say. 'I found the love letters in the wall. Look, they're in my handbag.'

I bend over to grab my bag from the floor, he pulls my arm back. I'm amazed at the amount of strength he still has at his age.

'This should never be told,' he says. 'You have to let it rest.'

'Valentina and Rubia asked me to share it right after I discovered it.'

'What you have read must stay where it belongs. In the dark depths, hidden under layers of sorrow, pain, lost time. I'll take it to my grave.'

It's his birthday and he's thinking about his death.

'I'm sorry,' I say. 'About everything that happened in the past.'

A man of about seventy-five approaches and wants to interrupt our conversation.

'Not now, Adamo,' Danilo says.

The man immediately turns and walks back into the crowd.

'Sorry, that's my son,' Danilo explains. 'This winery belongs to him. He started the company that I'd always wanted so much, and I helped him do it. His son Adamo junior is talking to that blond lady over there.'

He points past a group of people to Adamo and Margot.

Adamo junior.

'Margot is my friend,' I mumble.

'She's talking to the wrong man. My son and grandson are not good to their wives. Just like my father wasn't. And I also made wrong choices...'

He looks around. My empty wine glass is refilled by a waiter. The lounge music turns into dance music and some women start dancing. The DJ on the small stage waves both arms in the air. Men watch the dancing women.

'I didn't know she kept the letters,' Danilo says.

'Have you seen her since the last letter from August 1965?' I ask. Secretly I hope they had a flaming romance.

He looks at the grapevines in the distance on the dark hill. Silhouettes in long rows.

'What are you doing with my father?' says Rubia, standing in front of us. 'He seems so absent. He does that often.'

'We're talking about the house,' I say.

'I've never understood what's so interesting about that house. Valentina loved it and never wanted to sell it. Now we have waited twenty-five years and for what, I wonder.'

She turns and walks away. I watch her take a glass of red wine from the waiter's tray and join a group dancing in front of the stage.

'Typically like her mother, in the words she chooses,' Danilo says.

'Especially if she drinks too much.'

Max arrives.

'My Italian girlfriend is here!' he says excitedly. 'I just said *"ciao bella"* to her and she laughed.'

Danilo laughs. 'Good boy.'

'Can I have a glass of prosecco?' Max asks. 'The other kids are drinking too.'

'No, you can't,' I say.

'Yeah, go ahead, kid,' Danilo says.

Max thanks him and walks away.

'I'll leave you alone so you can talk to your other guests,' I say at last.

'Sofia and I saw each other every night in the house for about thirty years,' he says.

I sit down again.

'She was married, but the evenings were ours. We talked together. Crying and laughing. Danced. Toasted. Celebrated love. We wanted to make up for the lost years.'

I shiver on a sultry summer evening. His eyes seem to sparkle more, his voice is getting stronger. He sits up straighter.

'She was a very strong woman who made a heartbreaking choice. After the war, so much was unclear and everything had changed. I understand why she did it and her letter was the happiest moment of my life after the birth of both my daughters and my son.'

He beams.

'And Valentina?' I ask. 'Does she know Sofia is her mother?'

'No, we never told her. Fortunately, they spent a lot of time together, even designing some houses together. Sofia was also present at Valentina's wedding, can you imagine? Our daughter married...'

He looks again at the grapevines.

'Uh, Sofia, is she...?'

'She was terminally ill. She was way too young; I would have loved to have had so many more years with her. I pressed my cheek to hers that last night at our house and told her she was the love of my life. She said she could finally put everything to rest.'

He stares at the partying people. A tear rolls down his cheek. The letters in my handbag, maybe I should give them to him? I hesitate and bite my lower lip.

'Do you want the letters?' I ask.

'No, it would have been better if there were no letters. I promised Sofia never to tell. There was one moment when we considered telling it, but by then it was too late.'

I look at him surprised. 'What was it too late for?'

He searches the crowd as if looking for someone. He points to a girl of about sixteen in a white dress and white All Stars sneakers with her back to us.

'She shouldn't have been here,' he says.

The girl gently rocks to the music.

'But they were young and brash, just as we once were.'

'What do you mean?' I ask.

'What else could we have done? It had already happened.'

Someone blows into the microphone and taps it twice. The speakers are squealing with feedback, people are squeezing their hands over their ears. Danilo tries to stand and I jump up to help him.

'I'm sure they'll sing for me,' he says.

I hold his arm. A woman grabs his other arm. She smiles at me. I don't know her, but she seems like family to me.

Again, someone blows into the microphone. I'm standing on tiptoe. Valentina is on the podium.

'Father, will you come forward?' she says loudly into the microphone. 'Can it be turned down a little?' she asks the DJ.

Danilo walks and I move along. He clamps his arm in my arm and I dare not let go. We walk past Margot and Aron, and right next to Margot is Adamo. Adamo junior. He has his arm around the shoulders of a beautiful woman. The woman who was in the pool when we tasted wines here.

'Way to go, darling,' Margot says as we pass. 'You really fit into this Italian life already.'

Roger looks at me surprised when I pass by. I shrug.

'Father, there you are. Are you coming on stage?' Valentina says. She taps the chair she has set up and smiles at me. Next to her are Rubia and Adamo senior on the small stage. Dozens of people under the strings of lights follow us as I help Danilo to his seat. Once he's seated, I quickly walk to the side of the stage.

'Wait a minute, Mirella,' Rubia says. She leans in front of Valentina towards the microphone and gestures for me to come back. 'You have something to tell us.'

The buzz is getting less and everyone seems to be waiting for something to come now. Nervously, I run one hand through my hair and clamp my handbag tighter with the other.

'Mirella bought the house in the valley that Valentina and I inherited,' Rubia says. 'And now she's going to tell us why we it was left to us.'

The DJ puts on music with a drum roll. Danilo looks around startled, and when he sees me, he gestures that Rubia has had too much to drink. Valentina sees it.

'Shall we sing to father first?' Valentina asks into the microphone.

'No,' Rubia says. 'Reveal first!' She claps her hands. 'Disclosure, disclosure.'

Some people start clapping. A man raises his wine glass and cheers me on loudly. No, impossible, this cannot be true. You don't tell a secret about a family's hidden past on a stage, do you? My throat is dry, my hands are clammy.

Margot stands with her hands over her mouth and shakes her head.

My handbag hangs heavily from my arm. These letters will forever change all the relationships between the people here.

'I suggest we sing *Tanti Auguri*. This is a birthday party,' Valentina says. 'I count to three. One... two...' She waves her hands in the air as if she were a conductor.

'... three!' She starts to sing, and the DJ quickly finds the right music. A few people sing along, but fall silent again.

'Mirella,' Rubia says. She pulls the microphone from the stand and hands it to me. 'Go ahead.'

Drum roll. The DJ makes a show of it. Dozens of people watching in anticipation.

Blood rushes to my cheeks; I break out in a cold sweat. What should I say? Where does the story begin?

The DJ focuses a spotlight on me and turns on tension building background music.

'Um... we bought the house in valley...' I say and try to think about a careful choice of words, '...because I fell in love with the house instantly.

And speaking of crushes…'

It sounds more like a business speech I'd give to a team as a project manager, and not even my best.

'No, it's enough,' Danilo says loudly. The DJ stops the music. I breathe a sigh of relief.

'It's about time, Father,' Rubia says, irritated. 'Something happened that we don't know about, otherwise Alessandro would have inherited the house, and not Valentina and I.'

Alessandro.

How do I tell Alessandro that the woman who inherited the house is his older half-sister?

'Wait, we're bringing him on stage,' Rubia says. 'Alessandro, where are you?'

Everyone looks around, searching.

How is this going to fit on the small stage? Are Italian parties always this chaotic? Roger pulls at his hair with both hands to indicate that it is madness. Adamo junior gives Margot a quick kiss on the cheek as he whispers something in her ear. She steps aside, away from him, and hugs Aron. Max, where is he? Many faces in the crowd, but not his.

Someone is hissing next to me. Danilo. He shakes his head. Valentina sees it.

'We can also sing,' she tries again.

'… yet Alessandro didn't inherit his mother's house,' Rubia says loudly into the microphone.

She's not going to let it go until she knows the secret. Even if she has to get everyone on the podium for this.

A man walks on stage and he waves as if he were a performer. He even makes a small bow. The people clap and the DJ plays with the colored lights above the stage.

'Alessandro, I'm sure you want clarity about your mother's legacy too,' Rubia says. Meanwhile, she's now holding another full glass of wine.

'Rubia,' Alessandro says. 'I've said before that we never cared if I or Valentina inherited that house.'

He gives Valentina a kiss on the lips and presses her tightly against him. They smile at each other. The same smile.

'In the end, everything will go to our daughter,' Alessandro says.

I drop my handbag in shock. It thumps heavily on the wooden planks of the stage. Danilo has stood up and shuffles off the stage at the back, Valentina takes his arm to help him. Margot comes on stage.

'Darling, I'm here to save you,' she says. 'You don't want this.'

It had been too late to tell, Danilo had said. Did he mean that Valentina had gotten pregnant without her knowing Alessandro was her half-brother? Margot tugs gently on my arm as Rubia pushes the microphone closer to my mouth.

'Tell me, what's such a big secret that no one ever reveals anything about it?' Rubia asks.

It's dead quiet. The DJ decides it's time for tension-building music again.

I search for words. Who am I to reveal this secret and shake everything to its foundations? Suppose I had never found the letters, then everything would remain the same. Everyone, except the drunk Rubia, seems to be happy with the way things are now. I'm looking for Danilo. He is standing on the grass behind the podium and is holding a large black power plug together with Valentina. The same type of plug as Gustav used to operate the lift for the roof tiles. A lot of wattage was all it took for a good renovation, he'd said. Which wasn't true.

A girl laughs loudly.

'Sofia, I hear it's you, shut up,' Rubia says. 'Your granddaughter is always so present,' she says to Alessandro, looking around. 'And where is Valentina now?'

Granddaughter?

The DJ moves the searchlight over the people's heads to where the laughter came from. In the bright white light, the girl in the white dress and All Stars sneakers appears. She quickly pushes a boy away from her and, looking down at the floor, she rubs her lips. Then she looks up again. Green eyes. The boy steps back into spotlight, puts an arm around her.

So, that's where Max was.

People laugh, applaud. Sofia's name is called and there is cheering. Roger rushes through the guests towards Max. Margot shakes her head and says something to Aron. Rubia says 'shhh' out loud into the microphone. Behind the stage, Danilo and Valentina both pull the plug; Danilo nearly loses his balance.

Dark.

Everything is dark. The dozens of lights in the olive trees and the colored spotlights have gone out. The music has stopped abruptly. Guests begin to talk loudly to each other, their faces fade into the night. The only light is coming from the wine tasting room.

'It's a power outage,' Alessandro yells next to me on stage.

I jump off the back of the stage where Danilo is sitting in the grass with Valentina crouching next to him.

'The letters... shall I give them...' I say.

'Please let them rest where they belong,' he says. Valentina nods and puts her arms around him.

We squeeze through the crowd of chatting people. They need no light to continue the party. The waitresses come out with trays of candles and place them on the high standing tables.

At the car we say goodbye to Margot and Aron.

'What a party, huh, darling?' Margot says delighted. 'Italians know how to increase the tension so well.'

She hugs me, then Roger. 'Beautiful girl, Max, but you have to talk to your parents about her.' She takes the arm of Aron who also says goodbye to us and they walk to their car.

'Why, Mom?' says Max. 'What did Margot mean this time?'

'I'll tell you later, sweetheart,' I say. Maybe this is what Sofia and Danilo also thought when they saw it, and were they too late?

'Tomorrow,' I say right after as I get into the car.

Roger sits down next to me and kisses my cheek. 'It's a pretty chaotic start to our lives here,' he says and smiles.

The house is dark, Max and Roger are sleeping. I sneak up to the attic with the small bucket full of mortar. The walls are plastered, but where the charcoal lines are on the wall, I left it bare and plastered around it. I didn't want to gloss over this message from the past. I also left the bricks loose, and they are stacked on top of each other without mortar. On the old wooden trunk next to it is the blue vase with oleanders, every now and then I change out the flowers if I think of it in time. Maybe I should replace them with some silk flowers, that would be easier. On the wall I've hung a large collage with the covers of the *Il tempo* magazines from the 1960s. And next to it hangs the framed children's drawing of the house.

I'm pulling away the bricks. The hole in the wall reappears. One last time I unfold the letter that I wrote in the kitchen by candlelight and read it over.

Dear Sofia,

We don't know each other, but I feel a connection with you and this house. It's like the walls are telling me your story. No one will understand this, or will think it sounds vague, but if we had met, we would have understood each other. I am allowed to live in your house, it's like she's been waiting for me. Her walls are fresh again, the wind is allowed to move freely inside. Your secret remains yours and may rest where it belongs.

With Love, Mirella

I put it on top of the letters from Danilo and Sofia, tie the red bow around it and put them in the hole in the wall. In the bucket next to me, the cement I made in the shed is already starting to harden. I quickly spread it with the spatula on a brick and press it into place in the wall, straighten it and rub off the excess mortar. The next. Less than ten minutes later the hole is closed. The color of the mortar is slightly darker than the original, but when it dries in the morning it will have lightened and the difference will no longer be visible.

Palazzo Puro will keep the secret of the past forever.

ACKNOWLEDGMENTS AND ACCOUNTABILITY

This is a novel, inspired by the things we found in the house, such as the old love letters, and my feelings about this house and its surroundings. I wanted to do justice to the historical events by basing them as much as possible on real life at that time, while the characters and scenes are fictional. The fictional characters in the present are inspired by people I know, while any resemblance to real persons or events is purely coincidental.

I want to thank Roger and Max for sharing this adventure in Italy with me. I am also grateful for the time I spent there with my parents. I would like to thank my friend Marije for our special friendship and for her help in cleaning up Palazzo Puro - what a wonderful adventure we've had together. I would like to thank Dana van Leeuwen for my portrait photo. I am grateful to my proofreaders for carefully reading my manuscript and giving me their comments on the story.
Bianca Nederlof edited this novel and I would like to thank her for not missing a single detail. I am also grateful for the beautiful book cover created by Richard Turylo.

Finally, I would like to thank you, the reader, for reading this book. With all my heart, I hope you experience this book as an adventure where you were immersed in the Italian good life.

WHAT'S HAPPENING NOW?

Would you like to know how things are going at Palazzo Puro now? You can follow Roger and me on Instagram, TikTok or YouTube - our account name is @renovationpalazzopuro.

If you're already following us, thank you for being with us on this journey. Your support keeps us to motivated to hold on to the dream and take the next step.

Do you want to contact me? You can reach me via direct message on Instagram.

I'd love to hear from you.

Ciao,
Mirella

Printed in Dunstable, United Kingdom